It's very hard ... . ,
on it when I know about it, but Theresa Sneed has accomplished time travel so well, I find myself in awe of how she did it. Twists and turns at every point in this tome. I love how she wove in the true history, which includes her own many greats-grandmother, Susannah Martin, who was one of the "witches" hung for no more reason than the rants of young women. I loved how I was transported back in time to 1692 to the Boston area. Sneed described it perfectly and now I want to go there. I love how the main character, Bess Martin (also a fictional descendant of Susannah Martin in the book), is transported back in time. I really did enjoy SALEM WITCH HAUNT and couldn't put it down. I spent many nights reading into all hours of the early morning, then struggling to get up to go to work. But that's not a complaint; just the hazards of a reader with a good book. – S. Knight

Salem Witch Haunt held me spell-bound from the beginning and then kept getting better and better. At the end, I found myself wishing there were more pages to read. Sneed is an excellent writer with a wonderful, engrossing story to tell. It has a clever, satisfying twist at the end. That she is a descendant of the people she writes about enriches the story. You can feel her love of the topic and personal involvement in these lives even though the story is fictional. Excellent read! – Saguaro Blossom

I absolutely loved *Salem Witch Haunt*. I couldn't put this book down once I started reading it. The author does such a great job telling this story and the twist at the end was great. I really hope there will be a sequel. – Nathalia Goodwin

Salem Witch Haunt is amazing! It has an element of history that is often explored, but not really in depth. Theresa Sneed takes us into the world of Puritan Salem with a 21st century viewpoint, and it made me feel all the emotion of actually living in Salem at the time of travesty. This will keep you on your heels excellently, and it has amazing twists to it that you would never expect! I can't wait for there to be a sequel, and I would love to see it as a movie! – Amazon Customer

I loved *Salem Witch Haunt!* Well-researched, it kept my historical-fiction interest from beginning to end. I delighted in the author's family connection. Her reminders of 2015 (I'd like to see her with a tablet) amused me. Who should read it? Anyone interested in historic fiction. Way to go, Theresa Sneed! – Sheila Summerhays

Okay, so the first part of the time traveling to Salem was pretty scary. Though I would imagine that our time would be even scarier to them. After that *Salem witch Haunt* was a sweet romance with some surprises that I appreciated! I wasn't expecting the end! A great read! – T. Westhoff

A true adventure that takes twists and detours I never in a million years would have aligned with the Salem Witch Hunts but Theresa Sneed has woven the events into such a rich tapestry, one is left to question, how much of this story might be real. Fiction? Fact? Fantasy? Who cares, *Salem Witch Haunt* was FABULOUS! – Maliceon Books

Enjoyed this history, mixed with the romance and magic. Definitely recommend *Salem Witch Haunt!* - PEaton

Salem

Witch

Haunt

Dear Reader,

I hope you enjoy reading *Salem Witch Haunt* as much as I enjoyed writing it! If you loved this book, please consider leaving a good review on Amazon, Goodreads, Barnes & Noble, and other social media forums. Your kind words might be the reason that someone else decides to read my books, and for that, I thank you in advance. ☺

- Author, Theresa Sneed

Salem Witch Haunt

Book One

Theresa Sneed

Other Titles by Theresa Sneed

No Angel series

No Angel
Earthbound Angel
Destiny's Angel
Earth Angel

SONS OF ELDERBERRY SERIES

Elias of Elderberry
The Wood Fairies of Estraelia

Salem Witch Haunt series

Salem Witch Haunt, book one
Return to Salem, book two
Salem Bewitched, book three

ESCAPE SERIES
Escape

FACING MORTALITY
Dreams & Other Significant Things

So You Want to Write series
A Guide to Writing Your First Book
Fantastic Covers and How to Make Them

Dedication

This series is dedicated to my 9th great grandmother, Susannah North Martin, unjustly hanged as a witch on July 19, 1692 and later exonerated by the state of Massachusetts on Halloween, October 31, 2001, 309 years after her hanging.

CreateSpace Independent
www.theresasneed.com
Cover art copyright © Shutterstock.com
Cover Design Copyright © 2015 by Theresa Sneed
Interior Design Copyright © 2015 by Theresa Sneed
Text Copyright © 2015 by Theresa Sneed

ISBN-13: 978-1499792621
ISBN-10: 149979262X

Acknowledgments

Many thanks to authors Betsy Love and Deirdra Eden for picking through this project with a keen eye for content and grammar.

A special thanks to my editor, Linda Prince who always takes what I write and makes it better.

One

Bess Martin

The abandoned road dead-ended into a dense thicket. They would have to hike the rest of the way. Bess Martin took a quick glance at Trent Hanson. Since the first year of high school they'd been best friends, and she trusted him like a brother. This was their senior year. She felt excited and miserable at the same time, knowing that soon, many of her friends would move to different parts of the country to attend college.

Seth stirred on the back seat, then sat up and peered out the window. He scrambled out of the car and grabbed Bess's hand. "Come on!" She couldn't help but smile as she climbed out of the vehicle. He was six, almost seven, and for five of those years, he'd been mostly in her care while their mother worked to support them.

Trent pushed the branches aside as he led the way through the thick trees. Bess steered Seth forward, keeping him between them. She was deep in thought when she heard a twig snap off to the side. She jumped and looked toward the sound.

"It's just a deer or some other animal," Trent said, turning around. He waited for Bess to catch up. "So, my cousin's play really got to you, huh?"

She grimaced. "No way." Samantha's newest take on the Salem debacle was a disappointment, but no surprise. Bess was tired of all the hype in her hometown of Danvers, Massachusetts, formerly known as the old Salem Village. As the eleventh-great-granddaughter of a woman hanged as a witch, Bess had had her fill of absurd stories and loud tourists. Every summer they invaded her town in droves, disrupting her sanity—there was never a dull moment, and she longed for that.

"What did you think about her play?"

Bess smiled weakly. "It was, well, um . . . just as I expected."

Trent grinned. "A lot better than last year's, don't you think?"

"Definitely." That was an understatement. Last year, Samantha's play was like watching a poor attempt at horror with a touch of comedy, except the comedy part wasn't intended, and Samantha hadn't appreciated Bess bursting out laughing during a "really intense scene," as she had put it. At least Samantha had the names and dates right, if nothing else. She sought Bess out for that—Bess, with her near-perfect memory and uncanny ability to spew information off the top of her head.

The trees broke into a clearing where the river made a turn, creating a small pool of water before heading deeper into the woods. Trent set their gear down and gestured for Seth to sit beside him while he threaded a worm onto his hook. Bess got her fishing pole ready and cast out the line. She reeled it in then cast it out farther. In no time, they had settled down with their poles perched against their knees. Trent spoke softly to Seth, patiently answering all the boy's questions about fishing.

After a while, Seth grew tired of fishing and set his pole down. He wandered along the side of the river, then bent over to investigate something. Before Bess could get to her feet, he snatched it up and let out a gleeful "Whoop!"

"Shh!" She put her finger to her lips and rushed toward her brother. He held a green tree frog in his hand that squirmed to get away. *Well, that should keep him busy.* "Take it over there away from the water, Seth," she whispered. She returned to Trent's side and checked her pole, wondering if the fish had scattered.

He seemed to read Bess's mind. "Yep, that'll keep them away for a few minutes." He put his hands behind his head and leaned back, then turned to her. "So, what did you really think of Sam's play?"

Bess took her brother's Swiss Army knife from her pocket and began poking it into the earth. Their uncle had given it to Seth, and she had confiscated it until he was old enough to safely use it. She glanced over at Trent. His green eyes locked onto hers as he waited for an answer. "Do we have to talk about this?" she said.

"Not good for the blade." He gestured to where she had left it stuck in the dirt. "The play was pretty bad, wasn't it?"

Bess pulled the knife out and cleaned it, then closed it and put it in her pocket. "Well, let's just say that it lacked originality."

"Originality," Trent repeated. "How could anyone create an original play about Salem?"

"Exactly." Bess twisted a loose strand of hair around her finger. "It's all been done—same old same old. I can't believe there are people who still believe in witches. It's so archaic."

He grinned wide. "You don't believe in them?"

"Of course not. Do you?" She expected him to answer without hesitation and when he didn't, she rolled over and stared at him. "You do not!"

Trent shrugged. "I don't know, Bess. Samantha read some of the personal accounts to me a few months ago. They're pretty weird."

"The year 1692 was weird, Trent—the whole pious Puritan thing."

"Yes, but I think there was more than that going on."

She didn't like the sound of his voice. "Like what?"

"Weird stuff. For instance" —he brought his hands up in the air and wiggled his fingers— "OooOooo!"

She reached over and slapped him on the shoulder. "I don't want to hear it, Trent Hanson, and don't you buy into that mumbo jumbo either!"

His countenance sobered. "Seriously, though, some people believe differently than you do, and you need to stay quiet about it. Don't offend them."

"What?" She huffed. "I'm not like that. I'm okay with what other people believe."

He lowered his eyes. "Really."

She sighed. He was right. Her mother often warned her to hold her tongue. "Yeah, okay. I will work on it."

A low rumbling in the distance brought their attention to the darkening sky. "Whoa! Where'd that come from?" Trent stood and pulled Bess up beside him. "Do you see that?" He pointed to a strange haze rolling across the sky. "We'd better get going."

Bess took Seth's hand and they hurried toward the trees. A light rain fell as they rushed down the narrow trail, and before long, the heavens unleashed their burden and heavy rain came down in stinging sheets.

Trent removed his jacket. "Put this over Seth."

"It wasn't supposed to rain today!" Bess called out through the rain, taking the jacket from his hands.

"Yeah, well, this is Massachusetts—it rains whenever it wants." Trent pushed through the thick undergrowth. A loud crack tore through the air above them. "There's a small cave not far from here." He turned off the trail. "Something's not right. We should've run into it by now." He looked back the way they'd come, and Bess followed his gaze, but in the near-torrential rain, it was hard to see much of anything. Trent started back, but stopped again. He looked to his right and then to his left. "None of this looks familiar."

Great. If Trent couldn't find the way out, no one could. He had a reputation for knowing these woods better than anyone. They'd been in his family for generations.

"I don't think we should go any farther." He glanced around, pushed through the boughs, and then slumped down against a large tree. Seth snuggled on one side of

Trent, who reached for Bess's hand and pulled her down near them.

Trent's jet-black hair hung wet across his face, and his eyes held a soft intensity. Something squirrely wrestled in Bess's stomach. She pulled Seth between them. Cold rain trickled down her back, making her shiver. Trent pressed closer to Seth, reached behind him, and wrapped his arm around Bess's trembling shoulder.

Bess's mother would be getting home about now. She worked at the mansion—Trent's grandfather's estate. That was how Bess had met Samantha, and then Trent. He was like a protective brother to Bess, though right now his warm arm around her shaking shoulder felt a little more than protective.

She ventured a quick glance in his direction. His head leaned back against the tree and his eyes were shut, but a grin played about his lips as if he knew she was staring at him. Bess pushed his arm off and scooted away a bit. She shook her head—the things she had to do in the name of friendship.

When the rain let up, a thick fog settled in. "Okay, let's go," Trent said. He squinted and pointed to the setting sun muted behind the hazy fog. "I could've sworn that direction is east, but it must be west—so weird." He stepped forward, then screamed, stumbling headfirst into the gathering mist.

"Trent! What happened?" Bess clutched Seth's hand.

"My leg! My leg! Get it off!"

"What? Where?" She reached through the fog toward the sound of Trent's voice.

He groaned. "Bear trap! Help me, Bess!"

Her heart leaped to her throat. She'd heard stories of old, rusted-out bear traps—illegal now, but set long ago. A bear trap could rip a man's leg right off. She dropped Seth's hand and felt her way through the thick mist to Trent. He lay crumpled over the trap, pulling at its iron jaws.

"AAAHHH! Help me, please!"

Bess grabbed one side of the metal teeth while Trent pulled at the other. He lifted his bloody leg out, and they let the trap snap shut. Trent gritted his teeth and held his mutilated leg above the torn flesh. He grunted, ripping his wet shirt off his back. "Your knife, Bess. Give me your knife." She fumbled to get it out of her pocket and hand it to him. He flipped the blade open and cut into his shirt, then tore it into long strips. "Wrap these around it."

Trying to be gentle, she wrapped the strips around the wound, then tied another strip over the top to keep everything secure. She helped Trent to his feet and braced him against her shoulder. Patches of the dense fog had lifted. Her eyes darted around. "Seth?" She turned to Trent and helped him lean against a tree. "Seth? Where are you?" she called. "Come here, please!"

Trent pushed her forward. He groaned and fell back against the tree, but motioned for her to hurry. "I'm okay— go find him."

After Bess marked the spot where she had left Trent, she moved through the darkening woods, calling her brother's name. High above her, lights in the night sky streaked and twisted in random patterns. "Seth! Answer me, now!"

A pitiful whimper pierced the still woods. "Seth?" She spun around. The fog prevented her from seeing clearly, but someone was standing there—someone *taller* than Seth.

Bess stood perfectly still. She peered through the wispy mist and made out the slight form of a young girl. She looked Bess's way. "Come play with us . . ." she said, her voice empty and thin. Then the girl turned and disappeared into the fog.

Shivers ran up Bess's back. "Hello?" She hurried toward where the girl had been. "Wait! I need your help!"

Bess stopped in front of the fog and dropped her hands to her sides. "Who's there? Who are you?" She clenched her fingers into fists and called out a panicked hello.

"Bess." Seth's voice wafted through the chilly air.

She whirled around. The sound came from behind a large boulder surrounded by tall pine trees. "Seth?" She stumbled through the trees and let out a long sigh. Her brother sat on a small rock on the other side of the boulder. Her heart beat hard in her chest. "Oh, Seth, you had me so worried!"

She hurried toward him, but her foot caught in a bramble of roots and she fell against the boulder. Sharp pain shot across her forehead. When she gently touched the spot, a trickle of warm blood met her fingers.

Seth clutched the moss-covered rock and sobbed. "I want my Bess!"

"I'm here." She knelt in front of him, wincing from the pain, and gazed into his teary eyes. "Why did you wander off?" He looked past her and wiped his nose. "Come on, we've got to help Trent." She reached for her brother, but he ignored her. "Come on, Seth. It's getting dark."

A loud wail left his throat. She jumped back, a little irritated. "Come on. Now!" She grabbed for his hand, but her fingers slipped past his. "Come on!" Again she tried, but her hand passed through his. "What's going on?" She placed a hand on his shoulder, but it passed straight through him. She fell back, aghast. "Seth?" Her voice broke. *He is dead!* Her knees buckled beneath her, and she slipped to the ground and wept.

A noise to her right startled her. Two hunters broke through the clearing. They seemed shocked to see anyone there and moved quickly to the rock.

"I've seen him in town before. He's Marvin's kid, I think."

"Marvin Martin—the widow Martin's late husband?"

"Yep."

One of the hunters knelt down and said to Seth, "What's your name, kid? How'd you get way out here?"

"We're lost!" Seth replied between sobs. "Me and my sister and Trent!"

The hunter looked over at his friend. "We'd better get you back to your mama, then gather some townsfolk together to look for the others."

Bess jumped to her feet. "Here I am!" She rushed toward them. "Look at me! Why won't you look at me?" She swung at the closest man, but her hand passed swiftly through his arm. Her hands flew to her face and a scream erupted from her throat. A twisted wisp of fog rose from the ground, wreathing and wrapping around Seth and the hunters, who faded into the hazy mist.

Two

Vanished

My heart slammed against my chest as Seth and the hunters faded before me, like the end of a black-and-white movie. A scream ripped through my throat. I raced from tree to tree, but found nothing, no sign of them. *Where is my brother? What's going on?* Suddenly, it hit me. *Maybe they didn't fade at all. Maybe it's me.*

Maybe I'm dead.

I wrapped my arms around myself. "No!" It felt like a nightmare, yet I wasn't asleep. Salty tears trickled down my lips. I fell against a tree, and its bark pressed into my shoulders. Suddenly a calming thought came. *A dead person couldn't taste salty tears or feel rough bark, so I must be alive.* Yet my hand had passed through Seth and the hunters. Maybe the sensory feelings were just strong memories that hadn't left me yet. I groaned. *Maybe this is what death is like. Alone. Hopeless. Afraid.* Violent tremors swept up my body and my teeth chattered, but not from the cold. *No, I can't think like that!* With shaking hands, I pulled my cell phone from my pocket. Though I knew there was no coverage this far into the woods, I checked anyway. Then I stuffed the phone back into my pocket and glanced around. Which was the way back to Trent? I needed him more than ever now.

A few minutes later, I pushed my way through a bramble of bushes, then stopped and looked around. *This is it. This is where I left Trent.* The bloody bear trap lay beneath the tree, its jagged teeth clamped tight, but there was no sign of my friend. My heart sank. The hunters must have found him. Of course, I was relieved to think he was on his way to safety, but what about me? I fought back a sudden rush of tears.

All at once through the trees, a small light passed by and then another. My heart skipped a beat. Were the search-and-rescue people already out looking for me? *Oh, please let it be true!* I hurried toward the lights but then halted. These were no ordinary lights, but candles on small dishes held by young girls. I peered around a tree at the girl I had seen earlier. She weaved her way through the trees with quick, determined steps.

I ought to have been grateful to find other human beings this deep in the woods, but this was seriously weird. Not only were the girls carrying candles, but they were dressed strange, like something from out of the past. I stayed hidden behind the tree and watched. Appearing to be in a hurry, they did not speak to one another as girls often do. I counted eleven girls, mostly my age but a few younger, as they walked down a narrow trail through the trees.

I let them get a little ahead, then followed the light from their candles. Suddenly, all of their lights went out. It was pitch dark and I didn't have a flashlight. I groaned. *Wait—my cell phone.* I kept its small light aimed toward the ground and turned it off when the path broke through to a meadow. A few houses were nestled in a valley beneath me, silhouetted against the dark sky.

A sudden wind whipped across my face, making me shiver. The weather had been unusually warm for the first day of November, but I had lived in New England long enough to know it could go from warm to frigid overnight. I shuddered and wrapped my arms around my shoulders.

"Eeeps!" My foot slipped and my hands flew to the air as my next step met unexpected ice. I hit the ground with a soft thud. I glanced at the girls farther down the path. No one had heard my outcry. Looking out over the field in front of me, I was surprised to see small patches of ice and snow on the ground, as if winter had come and gone and spring was near.

Beyond the field, a few lights flickered from the small town. The girls huddled together and crept down the hill. Two of them entered one of the larger houses. The others scurried to various homes nearby, each entering quietly like a cat returning from a night's prowl.

I didn't recognize the town. The houses were not like any I had seen before, except in books and in the older parts of Danvers. I had never spent a night alone outside and wasn't sure what to do. My mother would be worried sick by now, especially with the hunters bringing Seth home alone. I pulled my cell phone out—fully charged, but no bars. *Figures.* I crammed it into my back pocket. No doubt someone would have a landline I could use.

The troublesome episode in the woods haunted me. Maybe I had dreamed it. *Yeah, keep thinking that, Bess.* I held my throbbing head. The blood had dried, but the gash was still painful. *Hitting my head on that boulder—could that explain the strange visions?* I nodded. *Probably. Dang.* I was going to need lots of therapy.

I wondered which house to approach. Only three had flickering lights coming from a couple windows. One was the bigger house that two of the girls had entered, the other a small, hut-like shed behind it.

As I got nearer, I realized there were no streetlights in the town. There wasn't a single traffic light, either. *Where am I?* The light in the bigger house went out, narrowing my prospects. I sighed and walked to the hut, where I knocked lightly on the door. It opened a crack and two wild eyes looked out at me as if they had seen a ghost.

"I'm sorry," I said in reply to the woman's frightened gibberish. Her boney fingers wrapped tight around the edge of the door as if she was getting ready to slam it. "Excuse me. May I use your phone?" I asked in my most polite voice. "Phone?" I repeated, taking mine from my pocket. "My cell doesn't seem to be working here." I had barely gotten that out of my mouth when she waved her arms like a crazy woman, screamed, and fell backward.

"Whoa, lady!" I moved past the door and tried to catch her but was too late. As she fell, she slammed her head onto the corner of a wooden box behind her. "Oh, no!" I gasped. "Are you okay?" She didn't move and her eyes were closed, so I knelt down and checked her pulse. Strong and steady—at least she was alive. "Hello? Is there anyone here?" I called. "She's hurt. Hello?"

From the first-aid classes my mother made me take each summer, I remembered that unconsciousness from a head injury requires a doctor's attention. Where would I find one this time of night? I unfolded the woman's twisted body, then covered her with a quilt I found draped over the back of a chair. Then I searched the house for a refrigerator, wanting to find something frozen to place on what I was sure would be a nasty bump on the side of her head.

No refrigerator. Not even running water. Where the heck did she use the bathroom? I shook my head in disbelief. How could anyone live like this? So simple—too simple for my taste. Was she Quaker or Amish or something? There was not a single piece of modern furniture in the room, let alone a phone. The light I had seen from outside was a small candle, and it had nearly burned out. Soon there would only be the dim light from the fireplace. *Great.*

I placed a rolled-up blanket under the woman's head and ventured back outside. Just as I'd hoped, the remaining snow against the house held a slab of ice. I dug at it and broke off a piece. Inside the house again, I wrapped the ice in a rag and placed it on the lump forming on the woman's head. She moaned. That was good. The candle went out. That was *not* good.

I sat beside her and gently rearranged the melting ice, then wiped off the trickles of water that had escaped onto her face. My eyes adjusted to the darkness, and I surveyed the room. It was small, orderly, and clean. The wall facing the front entry held the fireplace. Otherwise the walls were bare, except for a cross made from two sticks tied together.

The woman groaned again. I felt bad for her, though for the life of me, I couldn't understand why she had flipped out when she saw me. I leaned forward and caressed her arm, and then a song came to me—one I had learned as a child. I stared at the rough cross on the wall, the soft flames flickering against it, and sang the words. It had a calming effect on her, and on me, too. I sang every song I could think of. My eyes felt heavy and after a while, I let them close. I needed sleep, so I didn't fight it. Hopefully morning would bring a better day, with news of Seth and Trent.

The next thing I knew, I opened my eyes to find the woman standing there, staring down at me. She held a piece of wood in her hands and raised it quickly. I rolled out of the way, but she tossed it in the fireplace, then squatted beside me.

"Ye are no devil, lassie."

"Uh, thanks," I said, a little perplexed.

"Though ye dress like one." She gestured to my clothing.

What's wrong with my clothes? I wore blue jeans, and a bright-orange tank top under a white blouse tied around my waist. I glanced at her clothing. "Are you Amish?"

She only frowned, so I said, "You know, Amish—they dress kind of like you."

"I do not know what ye speak of."

A knock came at the door. The woman's eyes opened wide, and she gestured for me to remain silent. She stepped to the door and opened it slightly, just as she had when I'd knocked.

"Fine morning, Goody O'Brien," a man's voice said.

"Top o' the mornin' to ye, Parson," the woman said with a nod. She didn't open the door farther, which meant I couldn't see the man and he couldn't see me.

"My dear wife believes she heard you scream last night, Martha," he said.

Martha cleared her throat. "Aye, Parson, it was me." She did not say more and appeared to be waiting for him to continue.

"What shall I tell her was the reason?" he asked coolly.

"Tell her not ta mind herself—it was jist a bear that got too close ta the house." She pointed to something outside. "It startled me, to be sure, but me scream sent it off on its way."

"Oh, I see." He sounded a little disappointed. "Well, be sure that you stay inside after dark, Goody O'Brien—especially with the strange events of yesterday."

She shuddered and pulled her shawl tighter. "Aye, I've heard."

"Of course you did! There was not a soul in Salem Village that did not."

"Aye, aye," she said with a nod, then closed the door without another word. She turned to face me, some of the old fear back in her eyes. Just as quick, her countenance softened. "Nah, the devil never sings." She helped me up off the floor. "So who be ye, lassie, an' where do ye hail from?"

"Danvers." When she did not seem to know where that was, I said, "Salem Village?" That's what it was called before it was known as Danvers.

"Ye are from Salem Village?" She looked at me incredulously. "I've not seen ye before."

Danvers has a population of about 26,000, and she thought she would have known me? "Yeah, okay. Well, we've lived in Danvers, er—Salem Village—forever, ever since my grandparents emigrated from England and Ireland."

Her eyes lit up. "Irelan' ye say? Then we be family!"

"O-kay," I said, relieved at the happy look on her face.

She frowned again as she studied my outfit. "Well, ye cannot wear the likes of those, me love." She went into the next room and came back with a long dress the color of sand. "This is me niece's. Here, ye can have it." Martha thrust it into my arms. "Go put it on an' be quick about it."

It was an order, so I figured this must be a community of super-conservative people, like the Amish. With thick Irish accents instead of German. Hmm . . . that part puzzled me. Still, I could play along until I found a phone.

I wore my orange tank top under the dress because the fabric felt like scratchy burlap. But the dress fit me almost perfectly. I pulled my cell phone out of my jeans and checked the bars again—nothing. I folded my jeans and placed them on a wooden stand. Seth's knife bulged in the back pocket, so I removed it and slipped it and my phone into the dress's deep side pocket. I returned to the front room, where Martha nodded her approval. She gestured to a chair and then began running her fingers through my thick hair.

"Do ye mind if I comb yer hair a bit?"

"No, go ahead."

She worked quickly and I wondered if I was getting a French braid like the one I sometimes wore.

"What is yer name, lassie?"

"Elizabeth Martin, but I go by Bess."

"Elizabeth is a grand Christian name," she said, pulling at my tangles.

"I guess so." I shrugged. I liked Bess better. "Is your name Goody or is it Martha?"

"Goody Martha O'Brien, but ye can call me Aunt Martha," she said softly.

Wow. She must really like me to want me to call her my aunt.

"For yer protection, wane," she said. "Strangers are not trusted in these parts."

"Where exactly am I?"

She raised a brow. "But ye said yer from 'ere, from Salem Village."

Yeah, but I never call it that. I lived in Danvers— former day Salem Village. It wasn't my choice Danvers had at one time been the butchering block for strong willed women and men who stood out in an overly pious community. I had really gotten into the history of Danvers when I was in 8th grade—had dug deep too, and what I found astounded and disgusted me. That was the beginning of my distaste for tourism—for anything, that propagated lies instead of truth. Of course, I was being a little hypocritical. After all, I did own one of the snazziest witch's hats in Danvers—orange and black with lots of shiny bling.

"Where do ye live in Salem Village?"

I pointed behind the house up the hill. "Somewhere out there. I got lost in the woods." I jumped up. "Oh, shoot! Seth and Trent! I have to find a phone, Aunt Martha."

She shook her head. "I have no idea what yer blatherin' about, lassie."

"You don't have a cell phone?" I already knew she didn't have a landline. She gave me a blank look, and I wondered how long had she lived in this technologically isolated community. I reached into my pocket. "I'll get mine."

"What's that ye got, lassie?"

"It's my phone." I showed it to her. She looked at it nervously, but with some admiration, I think.

"What's it do?"

"Well, I talk to people on it."

She laughed uneasily, like I was a "blatherin'" idiot, or maybe she thought I was kidding. I grinned and turned on the phone. As always, it played an annoying jingle while booting up. Aunt Martha jumped up. Her face turned pale and she looked terrified. Her hands shook as she pointed at the phone.

"Devil! Devil!"

"What?" I stepped back from her and lowered the phone to my side. The jingle had not quite finished though, and Aunt Martha was nearly in fits. For the first time, I realized that not only did she not own a phone, but she probably had never seen one before. This place was worse than I thought. "It's not the devil," I said firmly. "It's just a phone."

She slumped back against the chair, nearly falling backward over it before sitting. Her crazed eyes scared me—was she going into shock? "Aunt Martha," I said softly, approaching her.

"Stay away from me!" She held her hands up as if to block me from her view.

Now I was really freaking out. I shoved the phone down the front of my dress. "Aunt Martha, what's wrong?" I had not meant to let tears slip down my face, but I'd had a rough two days and this was just too much. As I thought about my little brother fading into the mist, I tried to swallow the ache in my throat. Had I really seen that happen? What was going on? I broke into sobs.

Martha's wary expression changed to concern. "There, there, wee lassie," she said gently. She motioned for me to come near and sit on the floor by her feet, and then she rubbed my back with trembling hands. "Now, I want ye ta tell me what that fierce quare box is ye have."

I was afraid to answer, but I knew I must. "It's a phone."

She stopped rubbing my back. "Ye say ye blather ta people in it. Do ye know how fierce quare that sounds?"

I guess for someone who had never seen or imagined a phone before, it would sound "fierce queer" to talk to people on it.

"Where ye get it?" she asked.

I bit my lower lip. "How much do you want to know?"

She paused for several seconds, then softly said, "Everythin'."

I turned to face her. "Well, phones have been around for a long time, since way before my grandmother's time, even." Aunt Martha's eyes went wide and it looked like she had stopped breathing. Finally, a gasp of air escaped her throat. "Um, I guess my voice travels through the air," I continued. Her eyebrows furrowed, so I quickly added, "Like it is right now. My voice is reaching your ears by traveling through the air." She shook her head slowly. "Only on a phone, my voice travels a lot farther." Her face was expressionless. *Great. She has no clue what I mean.*

"What about the fierce quare sound it makes?" She shuddered.

"Oh, the jingle—yeah, that is weird." I meant it as a joke, but she must have taken me seriously, because her head nodded vigorously. "No, no, I mean—" I sighed. "It's called a jingle." I had meant to change mine but had not taken the time. "It's just silly music somebody recorded and then made available for cell phones." She gave me another blank look. "Um, it's just music, recorded. Oh, you probably don't know what that is, either. Well, recordings have been around for years, too." I let out another long sigh. With her bewildered expression, I realized this was going to be more difficult than I had fathomed. I did not understand recordings myself. "It's just where someone's music is . . . recorded." I slumped forward. "Oh, I don't know how they work. They just do."

"If it doesn't come from Heavenly Bejesus, then it must come from the devil 'imself!"

"What is a Bejesus?" I asked slowly.

She gasped and looked at me like I was clueless, which I was. Her lips pressed together tight, and she firmly pointed to the cross on the wall.

"Ohh, that Jesus." I took in a breath. "Well, it does come from him—sort of." Though I had not been to church for years, I believed in Jesus and attributed anything man had ever invented straight back to him. Why wouldn't he guide us to great discoveries like the technology behind cell phones? He certainly was smart enough. Aunt Martha's eyes narrowed as if she did not believe me. "You're making it sound like Jesus is only as smart as you are," I said. "He's far more advanced than anybody on this earth."

Her eyebrows rose. "Ye are right about that, me lassie—ye speak the truth."

I wanted to pull the phone out and show her all my cool apps. Of course, there probably would not be any internet in this secluded part of Massachusetts, and if the jingle freaked her out, the videos and pictures on my phone would send her over the edge.

She slapped her knees and stood up. "'Tis time for breakfast. Are ye starved?"

"Yes, I'm famished!" I said.

"Go into the barn an' gather the eggs." She pointed out the window to another building and handed me an empty basket. "Wait, put yer bonnet on first." She grabbed one from a peg and tossed it to me. "Never go outside without yer bonnet, lassie. 'Tis not proper." She eyed me sternly. "An' if anyone asks who ye are, tell them ye are me niece, Elizabeth Bowley, from across the water, come ta stay with me for a while. Say ye came by ship last fortnight. Do ye understand?"

"Okay," I said, wondering why she wanted to create an alibi for me. I tied the bonnet string beneath my chin and opened the door. It was beautiful outside—a little cold, but still very nice. I looked down at my long dress and shawl and couldn't help but skip to the barn, having seen several reruns of *Little House on the Prairie*. It was kind of hard to skip on the slushy path, so I soon slowed down to a walk.

I lifted the wooden latch and pushed open the door of the large barn, which looked like most of the older ones I had seen in Danvers. It reminded me of my Uncle Charlie's barn. Only Martha didn't own a tractor like he did, or even a lawn mower. No surprises there.

Chickens ran helter-skelter, squawking and pecking at the dirt floor, as I walked through them to a small room with a wooden shelf strewn with straw. Since we had chickens at home, I knew where to look for stray eggs. Sure enough, I found one or two where they shouldn't have been and gathered them up with the others. I turned to leave and nearly dropped the basket when I saw a young man about my age, standing in the open doorway.

The sun behind him made it hard to see his face, but I could make out his tangle of black curls silhouetted against the morning light. He must have seen my startled look, because he held his hand out in a gesture of friendship. At least, I thought it was friendship.

"Who are you, and what are you doing in Widow O'Brien's barn? Speak!"

Three

Afflicted

Speak? Did he just tell me to speak? I fumed as he stepped closer. He probably expected me to run like a thief, but I stood my ground. Once he moved away from the door, I could see his face—his gorgeous face. Still, how dare he command me to do something? I glared at him. "Excuse me?"

He drew his head back in surprise. He must have been used to women jumping at his ridiculous orders. His fists balled to his sides. "I said, speak!"

I rolled my eyes. "What planet are you from? Get out of my way." I pushed past him and heard him repeat my words in a daze, as if they were the strangest thing he'd ever heard.

He raced to the door and pulled it shut. "You will tell me who you are."

So, I did what any red-blooded American girl would do. I threw an egg at him. It smashed into his shoulder and the insides dripped down his shirt. It wasn't one of my brightest ideas—after all, he was blocking the door. I pulled out another egg and tossed it a few inches into the air, caught it, and tossed it up again. He stared at me with the greenest eyes I had ever seen. Well, next to Trent's. In fact, he looked a lot like a younger version of Trent. I wondered if they were related, maybe cousins or something.

The door opened and Martha peered in. "Excuse me, Hezekiah," she said in her thick accent, then gestured for me to come with her.

"Goody O'Brien, you know this woman?"

She gave him a strange look. "Of course, I know her. She's me sister's child come ta visit me from afar."

Her words seemed to pacify him, though he glared at me as he wiped the egg off his shoulder. I tried to pass, but he put his arm out to block me. His green eyes locked onto mine. "What is your name?" he asked with a slight edge to his voice.

Martha quickly reached under his arm and took my hand. "Come along, Elizabeth, we've got ourselves a breakfast ta make."

Once we were back inside the house, she closed the door behind us. "That's one ye don't want ta get on the bad side of, lassie." She pointed out the window at Hezekiah, as he walked away. "Comes from money, he does, an' he knows it."

I knew a few people like that in Danvers too, unlike my best friend Trent, whose grandfather owned most of Dorchester. If I read Martha right, Hezekiah had passed judgment on me. I liked him even less now, if that was possible.

I ate quietly, mostly because Martha frowned every time I opened my mouth to speak. She gestured back to the food. *Bizarre.* Finally, she put her fork down and smiled. I shoved the last bite into my mouth. Now to find a phone. "So, Martha—"

"Aunt Martha," she corrected.

"Aunt Martha. How far are you away from the closest city?"

"Boston is a day's ride from 'ere."

A whole day? How could that be? I didn't go that far into the woods. Danvers was only a half an hour drive at the most. She must have noticed my confusion.

"'Tis true ye need ta be gettin' home, lassie. What can I do ta help ye?"

"I just need to call my mother. She'll pick me up."

Aunt Martha frowned. "How can ye call yer ma? Is she nearby?"

I reached for my phone, but stopped. "No, she is not nearby. I guess I need to look around this town for a way to call . . . er, to get a hold of her."

"She is in Boston?"

"Yes, she works there."

"Yer ma works?" Martha sounded surprised.

"Well, yes, she has to." I felt a little uncomfortable, but continued, "My father's ship went down . . ." I couldn't speak. The look on Martha's face brought back the anguish I had learned to suppress.

"Ye need not say more, lassie. 'Tis me lot too." She let out a long sigh that was more like a moan, and I realized her husband must have died at sea as well. She shook her head slowly. "So, yer ma—she is a servant?"

I nodded. It was kind of like that. My mother worked as a housekeeper.

"Ah, ye poor child." Her eyebrows rose. "What do ye do with yer time?"

"I take care of my little brother, Seth." I felt a sudden pang at the mention of his name. "We got separated in the woods." I gripped the fabric of my dress. "I saw some hunters take him, but they did not see me."

"Awful, jist awful." Aunt Martha patted my arm. "How did ye find yerself lost in the woods?"

I explained everything to her, except for the strange parts I had no explanation for.

"Ah, me sweet child—what a time ye have had of it. Ye stay with me until we find yer ma an' yer wee brother." She stood and gestured for me to come near and wrapped her arms around me. "Ye mustn't tell the others what ye have told me, lassie. 'Tis an unbelievable story an' one that would bring suspicion upon ye." She released me, but gave me a stern look. "Till we solve this mystery, we'll keep the story that ye are me sister's child."

"From across the water?"

"Aye, lassie. Me sister, Mary Bowley from England."

It was strange that I couldn't just be me, but I said, "Okay, I will be Elizabeth Bowley. And you'll help me go home?"

"Aye, I'll help ye, me lassie."

We went back to the barn, where Aunt Martha showed me the chores she wanted done before I could walk around the town. She gave me one last warning. "Do not speak unless ye are spoken to, an' be brief with yer words." She grimaced. "An' don't be sayin' anythin' about that fierce quare phone."

How was I going to find a phone if I didn't ask about it? I figured I would ignore that advice, though something told me it might be a big mistake.

It took me quite a while to do the chores, so I pulled out the phone to check the time. For some reason, however, the time wasn't showing. I scrolled through my phone and discovered almost all the apps were frozen. When I tried to open them, they disappeared—except the ones that didn't rely on the internet for updating. At least my pictures and videos were all there. My mother would be livid when she found out my phone wasn't working. I'd promised her if she let me have a smart phone I would treat it like gold. Turns out it was not so smart after all.

I stuck it back in my dress, threw a wool shawl over my shoulders, and headed out the door. The sun was high, so I figured it must be 1:00 or 2:00. I saw buildings farther down Martha's street and walked toward them. It was a tiny town and very old-fashioned. I did as she requested and spoke to no one first. But I got plenty of stares, and two girls about my age soon approached me.

"Good afternoon," the taller one said, extending her hand. "I'm Mercy, and this is Betty."

"Hello," I replied, trying not to stare at their yellow, decayed teeth. Maybe the girls were rehearsing for a play and were wearing fake teeth. No one had teeth that bad.

Betty stepped forward. "You must be new here. I've not seen you before."

"Aye," I said, trying to mimic Martha. "My name is Elizabeth, and I'm visitin' me Aunt Martha."

"Martha O'Brien?"

Theresa Sneed

"Aye." I felt my face go red. I had told my share of lies before, but nothing like this.

"Oh," said Mercy. "Well, if you'd like to come with us, Elizabeth, we're going to the meetinghouse to bring the reverend a message."

I nodded and fell in step with them. From that point on, they spoke as if they'd forgotten I was there.

"Yes, Mercy—tonight." Betty looked over at her and grinned.

"Oh, all right, I guess so, but something about all of this gives me the frights."

"Don't you want to know if John will be your future husband?" Betty giggled. "It's just a game, Mercy—a harmless, fun game."

"We are not supposed to play that game," Mercy declared, her voice so low I almost couldn't hear her. "Remember what the reverend said?"

Betty scowled. "That's ridiculous, Mercy. It's not evil. It's just a silly game."

Mercy shrugged. "Perhaps."

We arrived at a large house, one of the nicer ones in the neighborhood. The door opened and a young man stepped out. "Good afternoon, ladies," he said, giving a slight bow.

"Reverend Lawson." They curtsied, so I did too. He gave me a strange look.

"I don't believe I've made your acquaintance."

"This is Elizabeth," Mercy told him. "She's Martha O'Brien's niece."

I curtsied again. "Reverend Lawson."

"Pleased to meet you." He turned to Betty. "You bring me word?"

"Yes, sir," she said. "Dr. Griggs would like to see you as soon as possible."

Mercy leaned in to me. "Dr. Griggs is Betty's uncle." She pointed across the street and down a few houses. "He's at Reverend Parris's."

"Very well." Reverend Lawson passed by us and walked down the road.

As he went, the girls watched him, seeming mesmerized. I broke the silence. "Your uncle is a doctor?"

"Why yes, Elizabeth. Do you need a doctor?"

I didn't need a doctor, but I needed what I was sure that every doctor had—a phone.

"Let's take a stroll by the Parris house." Betty chewed on her fingernail and glanced Mercy's way. They were quiet as we walked. Soon we stopped in front of the house Reverend Lawson had entered. Betty pressed closer to Mercy, clutching the folds of her dress tight.

A mournful wail filled the air, followed by piercing screams. Mercy pulled Betty under the window then dashed back to get me. They were shaking like they were scared to death. I figured it was probably a horror movie turned up way too loud, but the way the girls reacted to it totally freaked me out. Mercy pushed me toward the open window.

"Stop! Leave me alone!" I slapped her hands away.

She shoved harder. "Tell us what you see."

"Why?" I struggled to get away, but Betty joined in and forced me up alongside the windowsill. I looked inside.

Reverend Lawson and a couple men stood over two girls who lay side by side on a large bed, pressed up against the headboard. I recognized one of them as the girl in the woods who asked me to come play. Beads of sweat gathered at her brow. Her messy hair was matted against her head, and dark circles swelled beneath her wild eyes. The younger girl had the same sweaty brow and tangled hair, but her face was white as snow, her pupils narrow pin dots.

"What is wrong with my daughter, Dr. Griggs?" One of the men pointed at the younger girl.

"I should think it is quite obvious, Parris. Your daughter is afflicted by the evil hand of witchcraft."

Parris paced the room. "I will send her away until this passes."

His daughter wailed and rose two feet off the bed. Fear shot up my spine, and I clutched the windowsill. The men grabbed her, but could not pull her down. All at once, her body jerked. Her head spun to her back and her torso bowed in the opposite direction, while the older girl's body rolled in a violent spasm.

That is not humanly possible! My hands went to my throat. I turned and stumbled to my knees, then threw up on the ground. Mercy grabbed me from behind.

"You really do need to see my uncle," Betty said, her voice trembling.

"No!" I pulled away. Mercy clutched the windowsill and peered inside, her face full of fear. My body shook violently. I had to get away—far away. I sprinted toward the trees, not looking back. *Fading brother. Strange, backward place. Girls possessed by evil.* My head swam. *I must be going crazy.*

I found a flat boulder and climbed on top. The sun beat down and warmed me, but still my body would not stop trembling. I lay back and closed my eyes, keenly aware of everything around me, the sounds, smells, the warm sun— and the approaching footsteps sloshing in the melting snow.

I jumped up.

"You ought not to be here," Hezekiah said.

I noticed that what was left of the egg had dried on his shoulder.

"Elizabeth, these woods are dangerous," he continued.

Yeah, right. I knew all about the woods, having practically grown up in them. "Do you think I can't take care of myself?"

He rubbed at the egg. "I do not doubt that you can." He looked me over. "But not out here." He repositioned a rifle on his other shoulder.

I grimaced but then remembered what Martha had said—that he came from money. If so, he would have a phone. I gave him my sweetest smile, but stopped when his rough expression didn't soften. "Okay," I sighed. "Hezekiah, do you have a phone?"

He shook his head. "I do not know what you speak of."

I pursed my lips. "You've never heard of a telephone before?"

"No, I have not."

I brushed my dress off. "I can't believe it. Martha . . . um, my aunt Martha . . . said you were—" I stopped, remembering her warning. "Oh, never mind."

"What is a phone? Is it something you eat?"

I stared at him in shock. If he had money like Martha said, he'd know all about phones, even though he lived in a totally backward community. "Turn around," I said sternly. I wasn't about to stick my hand down the front of my dress with him watching. "Please?"

He shrugged and spun around.

"Okay, you can turn back around now."

He slowly turned to face me.

"This is a phone." I held it up for him to see.

Hezekiah tilted his head to the side. "I have not seen anything like that before."

That much was evident. I hesitated to turn it on for fear that he'd react the way Martha had.

"May I see it?"

I handed it to him. He turned it over several times and then passed it back to me. "It is interesting, Elizabeth."

"Come on, Hezekiah—you're playing me, right?"

"I do not know what you mean. Where did you get this thing, and what is it?"

"I got it from my mother, and it's a modern device you talk to people with." I shook my head. "It's not working here though—no bars."

"Bars?"

"Yes, little lines on the screen that . . ." I could see my explanation was going nowhere. "I have pictures in it, though. Would you like to see them?"

Hezekiah held his hand up while pulling a small bundle out of the folds of his jacket. "Like this?" Inside the bundle was a book. I couldn't read the title. It was in Latin, I think, but when he opened it and showed me the illustrations inside, I gasped. "Wow! This has to be ancient!"

"Yes, it is over two hundred years old," he beamed. "It is part of my father's collection."

"Where's it from?"

"My father brought it over from Germany."

We sat against the rock and thumbed through the book. The images were amazing—all hand-drawn and probably created from some kind of stamp. I pointed to two that were similar.

"Yes, they often reused the woodcuts for different characters."

Woodcuts—it really is old. "What's it called?"

"*The Nuremberg Chronicle.* It is the history of the world from the Creation until 1493."

"Oh, so this is a copy."

"Copy?" Hezekiah gave me a dumbfounded look.

"You're kidding." I gasped. "This is not one of the original copies made from the woodcuts!" That would make it over five hundred years old and priceless.

"Of course it is authentic. My father purchased it himself."

Martha wasn't kidding about him coming from money. "Why do you have it out here?" I gestured to the trees.

"The reverend requested to borrow it, and I am delivering it to him. I got here late last night and stayed at my cousin's house. I was on my way to the church when I saw you dash into the woods."

"And you followed me?"

Hezekiah looked embarrassed. "You seemed upset."

Oh yeah, I was. I swallowed hard. "And that?" I pointed to his gun.

"I thought I'd do some hunting before heading home." He patted his rifle. "But your improper behavior sidetracked me. These woods are no place for a lady."

Polite, controlling, and weird. I've entered the world of bizarro. It was time to change the subject before I hit him with a slushy snowball on top of the dried egg. "Your father's book is kind of old to be lending out to someone."

Hezekiah nodded. "I told Father that, but he insisted that Reverend Parris would take excellent care of it."

I bit down on my finger, remembering what I had just witnessed at the reverend's house.

"Now it's your turn. Show me your pictures." The corner of his lip turned up in a grin—very nice, like Trent's. I shook off the thought.

"Oh, all right." I glanced down at my phone. What would he do when I turned it on? A cool breeze blew through my hair so I pulled the wool shawl tighter and tied the ends together. "Hezekiah," I began slowly, "do you believe that there is more to life than what you know?"

"What a strange question, Elizabeth." He was silent for a while then said, "I can only hope that there is."

I brightened. "Well, there is." I held up my phone. "Promise me that you will remain calm and not run away from me. Okay?" He looked at me and chuckled as if nothing I could show him would frighten him.

"This is not magic, Hezekiah, or the devil," I explained. "It was invented by some really smart men and women."

"Someone you know?"

"Uh, no." Clearly my world was a lot bigger than his. "But most everyone I know has one of these." I tapped my finger on the phone. "I'm not the only one." I knew I was dragging it out, but I finally said, "Are you ready?"

He shrugged. "I guess so."

I looked sideways at him. "Lay your gun down first. This thing is going to make some strange sounds—I'm just warning you." He smirked as if I was being a little too wary of him. "Okay, here goes . . ." I pushed the button on the side of my phone and it came to life.

Hezekiah jumped back, tumbling off the rock. "AAAHHH!"

"I told you!" I muted the phone to stop the jingle.

He placed his hands on the rock and approached me slowly, which was a lot better reaction than running away or grabbing his gun. "What is that?"

"That is my phone powering up."

"Powering up?"

"Yes." I turned the phone off and removed the back cover. "That's a battery." I took it out. "It's where the power comes to run the phone." I slipped it back in. "When I push this button, my phone draws power from the battery—like this." I turned the phone back on and unmuted it.

Hezekiah's face was pale, but at least he didn't bolt. Within seconds, my phone was fully on, but still no bars.

"It's not working out here away from any cell towers," I told him, "but I can still show you the pictures and videos I have. Oh, and I have a few movies saved on my phone, too."

"Movies?"

"Yeah. Let's see . . . movies are images of people acting—kind of like opera." He tilted his head to the side. "Oh, never mind," I said. "Let's just start with pictures." I gestured to the spot next to me on the rock. He hesitated then sat beside me. I opened my phone's photo gallery.

He scooted off the rock. "What is this magic?"

"It's not magic, Hezekiah, remember? It was invented by men and women." I pulled up a picture of Seth. "This is my brother." Hezekiah came near. "He's only six years old."

"How is this not magic? Is this not him?"

I knew I could get Hezekiah to believe the still pictures were just pictures, but I wasn't sure about showing him videos yet. "No, it is not him right now, but an image of him a few weeks ago." Suddenly, it came to me—the best way to show him. "Come closer." I tugged on his arm. "Just trust me." Holding the phone in front of our faces, I took a selfie. His expression was one of complete fear at seeing himself on the screen right before I snapped the picture. He grabbed the phone and threw it into the woods.

I slapped my hands to my head. "Why did you do that?" I scrambled off the rock and stumbled to where I had seen the phone land in a bramble of dried weeds sticking above the melting snow. "Oh, my mother is going to kill me if it's broken, or ruined from the wet snow." I looked up to see Hezekiah staring off into the distance, a worried look on his face.

He held his finger to his lips, then grabbed his gun and hurried over to pull me down into the tall weeds beside him. He did not need to tell me to be quiet, since his bizarre behavior scared me into utter silence. I huddled closer to him, and he put his strong arm around my trembling shoulders.

I expected to see a bear or a mountain lion or something like that, so I was thrown off guard when two men dressed as Indians crept toward the rock. Their faces were streaked with war paint, and their scantily dressed bodies moved with the stealth of a panther. I could see the pages of Hezekiah's book flapping in a sudden breeze and felt him tense beside me.

FOUR
Abducted

This was silly. What were two grown men doing running through the woods, dressed like Indians? I jumped up and was surprised to see them raise their bows at me. The points of the sharp arrows glistened in the sun. This was no game. The surprise on their faces was quickly replaced with fury.

There was no time to run, and in seconds they were on me. They bound my hands in front of me, then stuffed my mouth with some horrid thing that looked, smelled, and tasted like a small animal skin with the fur attached. I twisted and turned my head, trying to dislodge it, but my assailant had tied a thin piece of leather around my head to hold it tight. At first I gagged, which only made it worse, as there was no place for the bile to go but back down.

One of my captors grabbed the book and pushed it into a pack slung over his shoulder. I looked around frantically for Hezekiah. To my great horror, I realized he had fled, and I was alone with these men. Each had a short, dagger-like knife hanging from his side. I had learned in a self-defense class to be submissive when the odds were stacked against you. They were definitely stacked against me now. The guys pulled me along roughly. I was in serious trouble.

I was grateful for the wool shawl, but my hands soon went numb from the cold. We moved on, sometimes stopping briefly. Most of the time, though, my kidnappers insisted on hurrying as if we were being pursued. The thought gave me hope, but by the time night approached, I began to think I was doomed.

Too soon the sun disappeared, and darkness engulfed the forest. Finally, we stopped. I didn't like the way the men looked at me, like they had decided I was slowing them down. Suddenly, the taller of the two—the one who seemed like the leader—started yelling at the other guy. I could not understand his words, but I got their meaning. He shook his fist, spat on the ground, and shouted some more. The other man nodded. He turned to me and took out his knife.

Run, Bess, run! I told myself. *He's going to kill you!* He pushed me down against a tree and then wrapped a long strip of thin leather around the trunk and me several times. He backed away, and he and the other guy took off into the dark woods, leaving me tied to the tree.

I struggled to remove the gag, but couldn't twist it off my chin. Several minutes passed. Cold, confused, and scared, I let my shoulders slump forward. My quivering chin fell to my chest. *I might die right here.*

My head snapped up when I heard movement in the distance. I shook with fear as whoever it was—whatever it was—got closer. Suddenly, my captors broke through the trees with four rabbits hanging from their belts.

Delirious with cold and fear, I wondered what was really going on. I mean, these guys were one hundred percent getting into this Indian thing. Maybe there was a weird convention going on in Boston. A new reality show where the participants have to abduct an innocent citizen and scare her out of her wits on live television. I half expected a makeup artist to jump out from behind a tree and fix the guys' war paint before the camera person continued filming them.

They skinned the rabbits, and I was morbidly engrossed in watching the fur fall away from the flesh. Soon, the guy who seemed to be the leader had a small fire going at the base of a couple of good-sized rocks. They tossed the rabbit meat into the fire. It didn't smell too bad, and if I closed my eyes tight, and forced myself not to think, I could almost imagine I was back home having a barbeque with my family. Yeah. Right. Like that imagery lasted long.

After the men finished eating, the one that had tied me up brought over a piece of the rabbit. With a quick slice of his knife, he cut the leather strap tied around my head. I spit the gag out before he had a chance to touch it. He seemed amused. I wanted to spit on him, but more than that I wanted to eat. He shoved the rabbit meat into my mouth and I chewed. Seeming pleased, he pushed another piece in and then pressed a water gourd to my lips. After a long drink, I turned my head away and he got the message, grunted, and went back to his friend.

I continued to watch them as they sat by the fire. The leader laughed a few times at whatever the other man was saying. How could two men be having a great night together after abducting a woman and dragging her deep into the woods? Of course, I did not want to think about the answer.

As the fire burned down to embers, the men slumped back against the rocks. I couldn't tell if they were sleeping, but either way I spent the next few minutes struggling with the cord before finally realizing it was useless. I rested my head back against the tree and stared at the starless sky. Gloom, thick as night, settled over me like a dark, heavy blanket. I was sinking into a place in my mind I knew would protect me from mental anguish, but a place I also knew I would not return from with ease.

"Bess," said my mother's soft voice. "Where are you?" I could see her face wavering dimly before me and remembered the circumstances well—my father's funeral.

"We can survive this, sweetie," she said, pulling me out of myself. "No matter what, under no circumstances are we helpless." Her image faded before me, along with her last word. "You can do this, Bess. Don't give up."

I gasped for air now, as if I was rising above water and breathing again. I would survive. I would escape. My mind worked furiously. I would head back the way we came, following the sun. Trent had shown me how to stay alive— by foraging berries, leaves, roots, and grubs. I even knew how to whittle a fishing spear from a twig. I was grateful for the knife hidden in the deep pocket of my dress. I remembered thinking Trent was a little weird—one of those fanatical survivalists—but wished I had his weirdness with me right now.

I had no idea the woods surrounding Danvers were this dense and had such weird people living in them. Were these men involved in some kind of ritual? They made convincing Native Americans for sure, but not like the ones I knew in Danvers. My history teacher was a Native American and a great man. These men were not.

I shivered throughout the cold night, falling asleep only when I could no longer keep my eyes open. The sun had not risen when one of the men nudged me with his foot. I struggled to get up, but then stopped as he cut my cord again. This time he wrapped each wrist individually so that my arms were free to swing as I walked. Of course, it wasn't for my comfort, but for theirs, as I could move much faster now.

We stopped twice that day and the next. Early in the morning on the third day, we reached what turned out to be our destination. Nestled in a valley below us was a small village of teepees and thatched huts. It looked like something right out of the movies.

As we entered the village, a cry went up. Dark-skinned children peeked out from behind leather flaps or clung to their mothers' legs and pointed at me. It was surreal—like a dream, only it was punctuated with unfamiliar smells, sore muscles, and unquenchable thirst. I wet my lips and stared at the water a woman poured from a gourd into a large bowl.

Soon we stopped at a hut, and one of the men pushed me inside through the leather flaps. A scowling older woman approached me. She was not as gentle or quick with cutting the strap, and the point of her knife sliced the top of my wrist. I did not cry out, but I flinched as she squeezed the cut then pinched it tight. She mumbled something, and a girl about my age brought over a basin of water. The woman shoved my wrist into the basin and I watched the blood seep into it, creating a swirl of red in the clear water. The water felt wonderful, and if it hadn't been spoiled with the blood, I would have stuck my face in it.

The older woman took my hand out of the water and patted it dry, then wrapped it in a tight cloth. I licked my dry lips and gazed at the dirty water. She snorted as if disgusted and motioned for the girl to take it away. Shortly, she returned with fresh water and handed me the bowl. Hoping it was for me to drink, I brought it up to my lips. They both laughed and the older woman took the bowl from me. She said something in her language, and then motioned for me to stick both of my hands in the water and wash up, while the girl took a gourd off her hip and handed it to me. She brought her hands to her face as if she was drinking—a universal sign in any language. I grabbed the gourd and drank the cool water. The girl patted my arm and ran her fingers through my matted hair. She frowned and said something to the woman, who nodded.

The girl gestured for me to follow her. Outside the hut, she led me quickly through the village, not stopping to answer any of the comments thrown our way. We went to the end of the village, which was right next to a beautiful lake. In one small part of the lake, close to the village, a bubbling steam rose from the water's surface—a hot spring, no doubt. The girl giggled and jumped into the warm water, then stripped down and scrubbed at her clothing. My clothes smelled awful, and I longed to be clean. I sat down on the edge of the hot spring, stuck my legs in, and then slipped into the water. I hadn't realized how heavy my dress would become in the water and struggled to remove it. The girl laughed as she watched. Finally, I maneuvered the dress down and let it slip off my floating legs, but I left on all my underclothing. The girl gave me a funny look and then began scrubbing her hair and body with some kind of crude soap. She handed it to me and I rubbed it into my hair.

My new friend patted her chest. "Awenita," she said slowly. "Am Awenita."

"Am" was an English word. I wondered where she had learned that. Probably in a public school ESL program. Except as I looked around, I didn't see any roads connecting the village to anywhere. I pointed to her and repeated, "Awenita?"

She nodded and then laughed again. From the rush of unfamiliar words that followed, I figured she probably wanted to know my name. I was right as the last word she said was "You?"

"Me?" I said. "I am Bess." I went with my nickname, thinking a one-syllable name was a lot easier to remember than Elizabeth.

"Bess," she said. "Bess, Bess, Bess."

I smiled. "Awenita, Awenita, Awenita."

She seemed pleased that I understood her name. Then, she pointed back to the village. "Come," she said, pulling at my arm.

Shivering in the cold air, I gathered my wet dress and dragged it out of the hot spring. Awenita wrapped a cloth around her slender body, then spread her wet clothing over a large rock nearby. She motioned for me to do the same. I was careful to fold the layers of the dress over the bulge in the pocket and knew that soon, I would come back and retrieve the knife.

Wrapping my arms around my cold shoulders, I gestured to the water dripping off my underclothes. My teeth chattered. "Awenita, I'm cold."

Smiling, she handed me a thick piece of wool like hers. She showed me how to wrap it around my body and tie it. She seemed intrigued by my bright-orange tank top, cocking her head to the side as she studied it. "Pretty," she said in her thick accent.

"Yes." I took the tank top from her and laid it on the rock next to the other wet clothing. We walked into the village and back to the hut. Awenita wove her hair into a thick braid, while I twisted mine into a mess. She shook her head, then undid my hair and started over.

"Ouch, Awenita!"

She patted my shoulder soothingly but continued to pull at my hair. I knew it wasn't her fault—she didn't know about conditioner. She sat back and examined her work, then reached past me and grabbed a hair pick with three long feathers and turquoise beads hanging from thin pieces of leather. "Nashota," she mumbled softly, then pushed it into my hair. She smiled and picked up a beautiful mirror with an intricately carved back and a slender silver handle. It was definitely not Native American. I gave her a questioning look and she blushed. "Ayiana . . . is Ayiana."

"Ayiana?" I repeated. She giggled and held it in front of me. I drew in a quick breath. The feathers framed my pale face, and the long turquoise beads brought out the blue in my eyes. She took my hand and led me out of the hut.

We turned more than one head as we walked through the village. A young woman around our age ran up to us and hugged Awenita. She spoke excitedly, occasionally glancing at me.

Awenita put her hand on the woman's shoulder. "Magena," she said, patting her on the arm. She likewise patted my arm. "Bess." And then pointed to herself. "Awenita."

"Oh." I pointed to her friend. "Magena." Then I pointed at her. "Awenita." I linked my two pointing fingers together and switched them back and forth for the sign for friend. "Friends." I smiled, repeating the sign. They laughed and made the sign with me. Someone called for Magena. She gave us each a hug and ran off.

Suddenly, from behind us, someone yelled, "Awenita!" We turned, and I froze. It was the leader of my abduction party, and he was not smiling. He stomped toward us. I took a step back and cringed as he and Awenita exchanged heated words. It seemed she had some kind of influence over him. He reached for the feathers in my hair, held them up, and said the same word she had— "Nashota"—then dropped them and turned away. I watched as he stormed off, still apparently unhappy that Awenita had befriended the enemy. As if to further demonstrate her defiance, she looped her arm through mine and we continued our walk through the village.

Finally, we came to a stop in front of the largest hut in the village. On either side of the door, a few tin frames stamped with the royal crown of England were crudely lashed together, overflowing with an abundance of dead vines—last year's flowers, no doubt. In front of the hut was a small statue of Jesus, unlike any I had seen before. My mother would love it.

Awenita stepped through the door and pulled me after her. "Ayiana!" She threw her arms around a tall, white woman with long, graying braids. Awenita pointed to me, her words coming out fast. Ayiana brought her eyes to mine and gasped.

"Who are you?" she asked in perfect English, although thick with tribal accent.

"My name is Bess Martin." I gave my real last name and not the one Martha had given me.

"Bess," she repeated, not taking her eyes from me. She gestured to a wooden chair with a fur tossed over it. "Come sit, my child," she said softly. She turned to Awenita and said something in their language. Awenita nodded. "I see," Ayiana said with a touch of sadness. Again, she spoke to Awenita, who quietly left. "I asked her to find her brother, Honovi—the one who brought you here."

Ayiana must have seen the fear in my eyes, for she took my trembling hands in hers. "How well I remember the fear you feel. I know it is hard to believe, but you are one of the lucky ones, like me. Honovi chose to keep you alive for a reason—Nashota." She gently touched the beads in my hair.

"Nashota? What is that?" I asked.

"It means twin. Nashota was Honovi's sister—his twin."

I frowned. "I remind him of his twin?"

A sharp puff of air escaped Ayiana's throat. "No, you cannot remind him of her. You look nothing like her. You sound nothing like her." Ayiana's voice took on a bitter tone. "You will never be her." She clicked her teeth. "And I will never be their Anevay, but they have replaced them with us—it is their way."

I stood up, suddenly feeling the need to flee. Ayiana had been abducted too, and this crazy woman believed she was doomed to live here and never go back to her own home. "You know how insane this sounds?" I said.

She looked at me curiously.

"That something like this could happen in this day and age is absurd!" I clenched my fists to my sides. "Why don't you walk out of here?"

She sighed. "I tried. I tried more than once."

I threw my hands in the air. "And then what? You just stopped?"

She blinked. "No. It wasn't like that." She glanced out the window and bit her lip. "I was young." She looked back at me. "How old are you?"

"I'm seventeen." *Like that matters right now.*

"I was eleven." She looked down at her hands. "They raided our village."

My eyes widened. "These men?"

"Oh no, not them. Another tribe—one of their rivals. They left me to die, but Elan watched from the trees, and after they left, he found me."

My head spun. Indian warfare in the twenty-first century? "Who is Elan?"

At the mention of his name, a smile played upon Ayiana's lips. "He is second in command here."

"Oh. Then surely he would let you leave?"

"Yes," she said softly. "I believe he would, but where would I go? The small settlement I lived in was burned to the ground." She looked around the hut. "Elan was able to retrieve a few things and has purchased others from Frances Small."

My mouth went dry—burned to the ground? "Who?" I asked numbly.

"He is a white man who is friendly to us. We trade with him."

Of course, yeah. Why not? Every remote village has a white man who trades with them and keeps their identity completely secret. I tried not to show my sarcasm with my words. "Um, this white man—will he be by soon?"

"Frances has not been here for a while. He is getting old. Some say, he has settled at last. I doubt it, though. He is a true wanderer."

"The statue?" I gestured to the door.

"Yes. We traded much for that. Though I am a part of their tribe, I am still an English woman at heart."

"There is a whole wide world out there! Why don't you just leave and go back to it?"

The flap on the door parted and a dark-skinned man came in. He glanced briefly at me and then approached Ayiana. His tender expression threw me, as did the way he brushed a loose strand of hair from her face before his lips met hers. I understood now. They spoke softly with an occasional glance my way, and then he left.

"Elan?"

She nodded. "He is my husband."

I expected as much. "Cute." She gave me a strange look, as if she did not understand what "cute" meant. "Oh, I mean, he is an attractive man."

She smiled. "Yes, he is."

Now I knew why she would never leave the village, but would she understood why I had to? "Ayiana, I don't want to stay here."

She knelt down by my side. "After a while, you won't want to leave." She placed her hand on mine.

I tensed. *I will never feel that way.*

"It will be good to have you here with me. I've missed my English side, especially since Frances stopped coming by. So, tell me everything that is going on out there."

I pulled my hand away, hardly believing she thought for even one second that I was going to be like her. "I'm going home."

Her countenance darkened. "No, you're not, and it's best you learn that now and stop any ridiculous notion of escaping." She stood as Awenita came through the door with her brother, Honovi. Relief washed over me. Her brother was not the leader after all, but the other man. He stared at the feathers in my hair.

"Nashota," I said for him.

His eyes narrowed and a jumble of words spewed from his lips. I must have offended him by saying her name.

"I'm sorry," I said.

Awenita's face went pale, and Ayiana motioned for me to be quiet. "Do not speak until you have permission—especially a name so sacred to him."

I bit my tongue. What was with this place? First Hezekiah in the barn, and now Honovi. Boy, did they need to join the twenty-first century! I dropped my head in bogus submission while fuming inside and biting my tongue so hard it hurt. One thing was for sure, I would not be the next one to speak.

I did not need to worry about that. Honovi completely ignored me and moved close to Ayiana. Magena entered the hut and smiled at me, then stood close to Honovi. He grinned at her as she handed him a bundle. Honovi unwrapped it and handed Ayiana a thick book—Hezekiah's.

I raised my eyes enough to see her reaction—full of happiness and gratitude toward the thief, my abductor. "That is not yours to give," I said sternly, then turned to Ayiana. "Nor yours to receive!"

The room went dead silent. Ayiana's and Magena's eyes widened in fear, and Awenita gasped. Honovi grabbed me by my hair. He ripped the feathers from it and dragged me from the hut.

Five

Honovi

Honovi pulled me kicking and screaming through the village. The path was lined with people dressed like Native Americans, but no one made an attempt to stop him. Near the cold lake, he threw me down and unleashed a strip of leather. He forced me back to my feet, tied me to a post, and ripped open my cloth, exposing my bare back. One of the younger Indians ran up to him carrying a long whip.

"Stop! Oh, stop! You're really not going to whip me." He was probably just trying to scare me—yeah, that was it. I looked around for the camera, expecting some Hollywood personality to jump out and say, "Surprise!" There was no way this guy dressed as an Indian would follow through with an actual whipping, especially with all the other actors watching.

But he did. And the first strike brought a searing pain like I'd never experienced before. My screams filled the village as the cruel lash ripped through my skin, slicing my flesh over and over again. When Honovi finished, he cut the ropes that bound me, and I sank against the pole. He left me there to bleed and stomped off to the calls of the hooting spectators.

Awenita rushed to my side with a basin of what appeared to be water and poured it on my back. Whether it was meant to heal or hurt, I didn't know, but when it touched my back it burned like fire. I didn't think I had a scream left in me, but I was wrong. I shrieked until my throat was raw. Weakened beyond my capacity to endure, I let my head fall forward as my mind stopped working.

When I awoke, I was lying face down on a fur rug inside the hut. Awenita lay beside me. I groaned and her eyes shot open. She said some soothing words in her tongue and then "Bess . . . Bess."

My back felt as if it had a hundred knives stuck in it, and I couldn't move without terrible pain shooting throughout my body. This strange village was real—there were no paid actors here. I lay there groaning and sobbing pitifully as Awenita caressed my arm. By morning, the wounds on my back had stopped seeping. The cloth had stuck to the dried blood, which was stuck to my wounds, so even though Awenita was careful, it hurt like crazy when she pulled off the cloth. Then I watched her take different kinds of dried leaves and a ground-up root and mix them with mud. She gently spread the mixture all over my back. The stuff smelled awful, but it eased the pain a bit.

Trent knew these woods so well—well, not these woods, wherever we were. I was so confused. How could he—outdoorsman Trent—not know about this village or the strange Amish-like town so close to Danvers? How was this kind of stuff not on the news? My head hurt too much to think about it.

I lay on the rug for most of the morning, trying hard to hold still, but eventually I sat up. "Awenita." I reached for her. She draped a light cloth over me and tied it loosely, leaving most of my back bare. That was the worst part, as some of the cloth brushed against my sore skin like a steel-wool pad. I cried out in agony with every movement.

Still, when I stepped out into the sunshine, I was determined to not show my suffering. I would not let Honovi defeat me. I held my head high. Even though it hurt like crazy, I walked without moaning, although I silently screamed with each step.

Awenita took my hand and leaned close. "Igasho watches you." I looked up to see the guy who had helped Honovi abduct me. He had a huge grin on his face as if he was happy about my injuries. In defiance, I tried even harder to ignore the pain.

I saw the amusement at my public chastisement slowly slip from the faces of those I passed. They must have expected me to wail and cry. I would show them all. One by one, their expressions changed to wonder and maybe even respect, but I wasn't buying into it. I was getting out of that place as soon as I could. I might die trying, but it would be better than living in a place that thought whipping women into submission was acceptable. I was glad my mother and a good English teacher had taught me to write, and boy, was I ever going to. This secret society was going down. My anger fueled my strength and I walked tall.

Theresa Sneed

In the long weeks that followed, it was different in the village. Almost everyone was kind to me, offering me dried fruit and meat, and gifts such as miniature animals carved out of wood or buffalo bone.

The wet, spring-like weather baffled me. According to my calculations, it had to be mid-January, but it couldn't be, because the grass turned green and flowers pushed up through the moist ground.

I hadn't added anything to my secret stash in days. I didn't feel the urgency, though I still planned to leave. I breathed in the delicious aromas wafting through the air. The womenfolk, which now included me, had spent the better part of the day preparing a feast for the evening's tribal gathering. Honovi and Ayiana talked in a corner of the meeting place, but when he saw me watching them, he left. Ayiana came over to me, her high-strapped moccasins making impressions in the soft ground.

"The men will be leaving soon. They are going on a great hunt." She studied my face. "I probably shouldn't tell you this, but Honovi feels bad for whipping you."

"Really? What a shock," I said with disgust. "So that's supposed to make it all okay now?"

Her lips twisted. "Sometimes you say things in the strangest ways, Bess."

"You act as though I should forgive him." She glanced toward the statue of Christ by her hut. I knew all about the forgiving thing, but this went way beyond that. Honovi stole me from my home—well, from the forest outside of the town I stumbled into—and then he whipped me when I reminded him that he was a thief. Some nerve.

She sighed. "Bess, have you considered your part in this? Your quick tongue got you in trouble."

I huffed. "You're going to turn what he did back onto me?"

Ayiana grimaced. "According to tribal rules, you were insolent and out of order."

I couldn't believe she was taking his side. "Speaking my mind is out of order?"

"Yes. In this tribe, it is." She folded her arms. "I just thought you would want to know that he has changed the way he thinks about you."

My eyes narrowed. "In what way?"

"What do you mean?"

"In what way has he changed? He's not going to expect me to like him back, is he?"

"Like him back?"

"You know, like you and Elan."

She laughed, but when she saw my scowl, she stopped. Her fingers remained over her quivering lips. "Oh, Bess! You thought—" She laughed again. "Sorry. It's just that, well, the change is that he respects you, but the romance part, no. Couldn't you tell?" Ayiana became quiet. "It's so apparent." She pointed at Magena, who hovered around Honovi as he stood outside the gathering place.

"Magena and Honovi?"

Ayiana nodded.

"And he feels the same way?"

"We see signs that he will return her affections soon."

I watched closer and saw him steal a glance Magena's way. Still, something was not right, because he looked my way too. "What's wrong with Honovi?" I asked Awenita, who had joined us. Someone called for Ayiana, and she hurried away. Awenita fidgeted beside me. I wasn't sure she understood my words. "Honovi," I said, pointing to him.

"You like?"

"What? No!"

She looked at me funny. "You no like?"

He was my abductor; of course I didn't like him. Her countenance fell. It seemed as important to her as it was to Ayiana for me to forgive Honovi. "Okay, I like him," I lied. I put my hands over my heart "But just not in that way." *Not in any way.* She smiled wide and jumped up from where she had been sitting cross-legged.

Ayiana returned. "What was that all about?" She tilted her head toward Awenita.

We watched as Awenita approached her brother and relayed something to him. He shook his head and looked our way. I felt like I was back at Danvers High. Ugh. I hated that kind of who-likes-you and who-doesn't-like you school game. "She asked me if I liked Honovi."

Her eyes widened. "And you said?"

"What do you think, Ayiana?"

"Well, as long as you were very specific with her. She doesn't understand a lot of English."

I thought back to my exact words and bit my lower lip. "Well, I guess I said yes."

Ayiana gasped.

"But not in that way!" I added.

"She will not understand that, Bess."

We watched as Honovi walked toward us. He motioned for Ayiana to leave. I grabbed her arm. "Don't go far."

He took my hand. I fought the urge to slap him or at least pull my hand away. Even though I had noted his tender kindness toward Magena and his willingness to do whatever was asked of him in the village, it was hard to forget what he had done to me.

He gazed into my eyes. "Bess."

It was the first time I had really looked at him. His deep-brown eyes were nothing short of gorgeous. Wow. How had I not seen that before? *Yeah, girl. He abducted you, remember? Focus. He is the enemy.* "Yes?"

He said something in his language that I could not quite make out. I motioned for him to stop and pointed to Ayiana with a questioning look. He nodded, so I gestured for her to return. He repeated his words.

Ayiana's eyes popped open. She turned to me. "He says he will do the honorable thing—that which he has seen his father's oldest brother do."

"Who is his uncle?"

She bit her lip. "Elan."

Yikes. I swallowed. Gorgeous eyes or no, there was no way I would marry him. My mind worked quickly. I glanced over at Magena, who wrung her hands and bit at her lower lip. I turned back to Honovi but spoke to Ayiana. "Is it honorable to be dishonest?" Ayiana flinched at my words. "Your heart belongs to another. I have seen it. You long for Magena."

His eyes widened at the mention of her name, and he grinned as Ayiana translated my words. Obvious relief washed over him as she repeated my refusal of his offer. "I would be most pleased to see you happy. Your heart belongs to Magena. Honovi, my wish is for you to wed her."

"WHOOP!" He threw his arms around me. I winced from the pain at the contact with my wounds, weeks old but still tender, and he pulled away. He hesitated, then brought his hand to my face. "Nashota." The sadness in his eyes startled me. He spoke in a low voice.

"He says you are much like his sister," Ayiana explained. "She was strong and fearless. You have brought back her memory, but in his treatment of you, he has dishonored that memory. For that, he is sorry."

A peace settled over me that I could not deny. "All right." I nodded. "Okay." I stood still as he pulled Nashota's feathers from a bag across his shoulder and wove them into my hair. Then he grinned and raced off to Magena's side. Soon, the whole village knew and could talk of nothing else, or at least that's what Ayiana told me.

It was an exciting time, the women readying for a wedding and the men leaving on a hunt in the next few days. A sudden pang of sorrow wrenched my heart. I would make my escape as planned, never to see Magena or Awenita again. Of course, that might not be true. Once I wrote my breaking story, all of America would be seeking their village. I frowned. Could I really do that to them? I twisted a strand of hair around my finger, unsure of the future in many ways.

Magena and Honovi came to see me. He handed me a small bundle as she giggled softly. "For Bess," he said in broken English.

"Thank you." I unwrapped the cloth and drew in a breath. It was beautiful. Honovi had carved a bear out of some kind of red wood and had fastened on blue stones for its eyes—tourmaline, I think. "I love it!" I said with a smile. Honovi beamed. Magena held onto his arm, grinning.

I spent a good part of the evening studying the bear, then carefully placed it in the leather bag Ayiana had given me for my treasures. I had a separate pouch inside the bag where I stored dried foods and meats, along with my knife, for my escape. But as the days passed, I thought less about fleeing and more about Magena's upcoming wedding, which would happen when the men returned from the hunt. In the past, I would have just gone to the store, but now I understood that hunting was critical to their survival. Meat was one of their staples—and one of mine now. Me, an avowed vegetarian. Amazing.

The morning of the hunt finally arrived and the women, older men, and younger boys stood in a long line while the hunters rode past us. Magena stood tall and erect as Honovi bent down and passed her a feather. She smiled and then stuck it in her hair. Everyone gathered while the hunters rode out of the village and disappeared over a knoll.

We spent the better part of the day cooking food, mostly flat breads and seed cakes for the big celebration at their return. We would skin their catch and dry most of the meat, but the night of their return we would feast. I could almost smell the sweet-tasting venison and savory vegetables we would prepare for the sumptuous meal.

Ayiana took me aside. "There is something different about you." She searched my eyes. "I am not the only one who has noticed it."

"Oh, really?" *Must be my living-in-the-twenty-first-century city upbringing,* I mused.

She slapped my shoulder, probably because of the smirk on my face. "No, Bess. You are different."

"You and who else think so?"

She titled her head to the side. "Meda," she breathed out slowly. "She has requested your presence."

"Oh." I had seen Meda around. She was esteemed as one who had wisdom beyond her years, which was something, given that she appeared to be ancient. "The prophetess?"

"Yes." Ayiana nodded.

No one messed with Meda. Her word was always the last one, with no questions asked—that's how revered she was. *She wants to see me?* I gulped.

Ayiana led me by the hand to Meda's modest hut in the center of the village. She parted the leather flaps, ushered me inside, and then spoke to Meda in their tongue—a formal greeting, I surmised. Meda stared at me with deep-set eyes. Normally I would have been creeped out, but I was actually okay—her eyes reflected sincere kindness.

We waited for several minutes before she came out of her trance-like state. She spoke in quiet tones, gesturing for us to sit. Crossing to a corner of the hut, she picked up a small wooden flask. It held a slippery oil, which she dabbed across my forehead while chanting in a soothing, lyrical voice.

I looked to Ayiana for an interpretation, but her eyes were closed as if she was praying. So, I closed mine and breathed in the oil's fragrance. After a while, the chanting stopped, and I opened my eyes. Meda stood in front of me, holding a wool shawl. She draped it about my shoulders and recited yet another verse of the previous song. Only this time, her words came out in a soft, melodious whisper. Then she paused and looked at Ayiana as if waiting for her to speak.

Ayiana cleared her throat. "She says you are a child of the sky—one who came from a distant land of days not yet seen."

What does she mean by "days not yet seen"? I wondered. Meda walked in a circle around me. She spoke slowly, keeping her hand within inches of my head. A strong energy came from her gnarled fingers, invisible but real. It made my head spin, while at the same time my mind cleared and seemed sharper than ever before.

"Onida," she repeated over and over, followed by a long line of words I could not understand.

Ayiana drew in a breath. "She has given you an ancient name. Onida." She paused, as if further processing Meda's words. "She says you have been sent by the ancients for a wise purpose."

Really? Okay, I could live with that. I had no idea what the wise purpose might be, but figured if it was wise it had to be good.

"You worry about returning to your strange land," Ayiana said, still interpreting for Meda.

I nodded in agreement. *And I'm not entirely sure I want to leave this world,* I admitted to myself.

". . . and to your family. Meda sees a young boy with golden hair. He seeks for you."

I gasped. Had I forgotten Seth? Of course I wanted to go back to him. I tensed, a jumble of emotions raging within me. Meda stopped talking. I searched for her and found her in an intense stare with Ayiana. Finally, she spoke again, and Ayiana stumbled over her words.

"She says you will leave here soon, and great danger awaits you. She warns you to keep your tongue silent, or you will never return to your home." Ayiana's voice broke. "If you are not careful, you will suffer the same fate as a distant-yet-near ancestor."

A chill went up my back. My mother had always told me that my quick tongue would one day get me in trouble, and now Meda—prophetess of this people—had confirmed it.

"You are Onida—the one searched for. They are looking for you, and they are coming."

Six

Attacked

We returned to our hut, the wool shawl still draped over my shoulders. It was a gift from Meda, along with a clear stone the size of a Robin's egg. I folded the shawl and placed it and the stone in my bag. Though my mind was full, I fell asleep almost immediately with very little thought of fleeing. If I didn't leave, her prophecy couldn't come to pass.

The next morning, the air was cooler than usual, and I felt a heavy foreboding. I supposed it was Meda's words that bothered me, but later that morning, I felt an uneasiness, like someone was watching us.

Suddenly something whizzed past me. Magena's grandmother let out a series of screams, holding onto her aging husband. An arrow had pierced his chest, and deep-red blood seeped through his shirt. I clasped my hands to my mouth. Surely, this was an accident. I rushed toward her, but stopped as several arrows flew by. We were under attack and the men were gone! I sprinted to the closest hut.

Ayiana huddled in a corner, rocking back and forth. "Ayiana, we must fight!" I grabbed Elan's extra bow and nocked an arrow against the taut string, grateful Trent had taught me how to use a bow a lifetime ago. Ayiana looked at me blankly. Our unprotected village was suffering the same fate as hers had those many years ago. I lowered the bow and gently covered her with a blanket, then pressed my trembling lips to her ear. "Hide," I whispered. "Hide!"

The air filled with horrifying screams. I rushed to the open door and drew back the bow. The attackers shot their arrows from under cover, but I could see the outline of one behind a bush. I raised my bow and released it. It met its mark. I had never killed anything before, and fear and adrenaline gripped my soul. Suddenly, a flaming arrow sailed through the air and landed in the teepee next to us. Within seconds, the sky filled with fire, and flaming arrows hit the huts and teepees two and three at a time.

It was unreal, like being caught in a movie. I slapped my hand behind me and searched for an arrow. There was only one left.

"Bess! Look out!" Ayiana stood in the door of the hut, a bow raised and an arrow drawn. She released it, and it sailed through the air. I followed its arc to the young Indian whose bow faced me. His arrow sliced through the side of my arm, tearing my flesh. I hit the earth, my body twisting toward Ayiana. Before she could raise her bow again, an arrow pierced her chest.

"NO!" My scream mingled with the sound of gunfire—not coming at us, but aimed at our attackers. I pulled myself up from the blood-soaked ground and rushed to Ayiana. Pain ripped through my arm as I dropped down beside her. "Ayiana!" I grabbed her limp hand. "I told you to hide! Why didn't you hide?" I fell over her and wailed.

"Bess!" a voice called from the edge of the woods.

My head snapped up. "Hezekiah?" Relief washed over me, but even he could not subdue my agony. "Hezekiah!"

I jumped up and fell into his embrace, wincing from the open gash on my arm.

"Bess! You're hurt!" He spread the seared cloth aside and examined my wound. "John!" He gestured to one of the white men to come to him. Pointing to my arm, he grimaced. "Get a cloth bandage out of the bag." He turned to me. "I'm going to tie it above the wound to keep it from bleeding."

"You'll do nothing of the sort!" Being CPR certified, I knew all about tourniquets and had no desire to lose my arm. "Just pad it good and tie enough pressure over it to hold it in place."

He studied my eyes. "All right, but if it keeps bleeding like it is now, I'm tying it off."

I gulped. He looked like he meant it, but what did I care about my arm? Three white men had rushed past us while Hezekiah tended to me, and now they returned, shaking their heads.

"Dead. They are all dead."

"No!" They were not dead—I would prove it. Numb with grief, I stumbled toward the next hut.

Hezekiah stepped in front of me. "No, Bess. You do not need to see this."

He would not let me go farther. I slammed my fists into his chest, frustrated because he was too late to save them, and angry because he wanted to keep me away. I pushed past him, but stopped in my tracks. The bodies of the villagers lay strewn around like ragdolls. In the midst of them were Awenita and Magena, their bloody arms entwined. I dropped to my knees, a long wail escaping my throat.

Hezekiah knelt down beside me. He wrapped his arms around me and held me for a long time. I stood, he turned me away from the village, but as we passed by Ayiana, I ran to her. The white men had covered her with a blanket. She was free. I grimaced. She was never captive.

I went into the hut and picked up my leather bag. My eyes fell to Hezekiah's book. I wrapped it in the dress Martha had given me a lifetime ago and carried it close to my heart. Ayiana had loved that book, and I had loved her. Hezekiah picked up her long woolen cloak and draped it over my shoulders. I had not noticed the cold.

We hiked into the night, the white men afraid of retaliation for something they had not done, but would have. Hezekiah told me they had received word from a fur trader about a young white woman in an Indian village who matched my description. Fortunately for me, they had arrived during the raid on our village. The idea of an Indian raid in 2015 baffled me. Everything was so primitive and surreal as if I had gone back in time, but that was impossible. Nothing made sense.

I imagined what it would be like when Honovi returned, and my heart broke for him. My former life as a student at Danvers High seemed a lifetime ago, like a book I had read or a movie I had seen. I was Honovi's twin, and Awenita, Magena, and Ayiana would always be a part of me.

The farther south we traveled from my village, the deeper my sorrow became at the destruction of a people I had learned to love as my own. Yet how could I have remained? I needed to get home—to my real home, to Trent and my mom and brother.

We stopped hiking in the early hours of the morning. "Sleep," Hezekiah encouraged me. "We won't be here long." He led me to a moss-covered area and gently coaxed me to the ground, then covered me with the warm cloak.

I was worn out from the long walk, my arm throbbed, and my eyes were heavy, swollen from constant tears. It didn't seem like we slept long, which turned out to be true, since the sun was barely up when Hezekiah nudged me. He helped me stand and then surveyed my attire. "You might want to change into your dress."

I sighed. The simple cloth I wore was much easier to walk in, and the cloak kept me warm.

He seemed to carefully choose his next words. "Bess, you could get shot for dressing like an Indian." He slipped his book out of Martha's dress and held it out to me.

I pointed to my arm. "And just how to you think I am going to get that dress over this?" He took it from me and ripped the sleeve up to the shoulder. "Oh." I went behind a large boulder and stared at the dress. It took some effort to slip it over my injured arm, but after a while I had the dress on. I stepped out from behind the rock and handed the Indian cloth to Hezekiah. "To wrap around your book."

"Thank you, Bess." He ran his fingers down the feathers in my hair and frowned.

"Oh, yeah," I said without feeling. I reached up and pulled out the hair pick, smoothed the feathers, and placed it in my bag.

He watched me with an uncomfortable look. "Bess, you should not keep that."

My eyes met his. I knew he saw the fire in my gaze, because he backed off. *Remember your tongue, Bess.* "You're probably right," I forced myself to say, "but can we deal with that later?"

His countenance softened. "Yes, of course."

I imagined he thought he had won that battle, but he had not. I would never part with Nashota's feathers. I would keep them forever. Somehow.

It rained that day and into the evening. Right before dark, we found a cave and settled in for the night. "Are you all right?" Hezekiah asked. He helped me to the ground and covered me with Ayiana's cloak. "I won't be far away." He pointed to his bedroll and then left me alone. Clutching my shoulders, I fell into a restless sleep. I awoke to a clattering outside the cave and the faint rays of morning light breaking over the horizon.

The men were up and cooking something—fish, from its strong aroma. I pressed my fingers into my empty stomach and turned away from the smell. I couldn't eat. I didn't want to. Footsteps came up behind me.

"You need to take some nourishment, Bess," Hezekiah said.

I groaned and drew Ayiana's cloak tighter. "No."

He placed his hand on my shoulder. "If you do not, your body will weaken and your way will be harder."

I pulled myself up to a sitting position, shaking off a wave of dizziness. Hezekiah held a piece of fish to my parched lips. After a few bites, I put my hand up to stop him from giving me more. I shook my head.

"All right, Bess." He stood and looked down at me with a startling tenderness. "We're leaving as soon as we finish eating."

"Okay."

He crouched down. "Can you walk? You're looking a little pale."

I nodded, hoping he would leave before I threw up the fish. I scooted over to the wall and used it to help me stand, then leaned against it until I found the strength to walk out of the cave.

The wound ached deep within my arm, like a dull gnawing on the bone. I held my arm and made my way to the nearby stream, then worked my way down to the water's edge. I stooped down and ran my fingers through the clear water, then dug up a handful of greenish-gray clay from the bank. I worked it into a ball then pressed it flat against a nearby rock. I sat on the rock and peeled the bandage off my arm.

What I saw made me draw a sharp breath. The skin around the wound was rimmed in bright red—infection had set in. No wonder I felt dizzy. I lay the clay compress on top of the open wound. Right away it cooled and soothed, starting to work its medicinal magic. I wrapped the bandage several times around the clay, relieved I remembered part of Awenita's remedy.

"Are you ready, Bess?" Hezekiah scooted down the embankment toward me. He reached for my hand and helped me up.

He was careful to not push me faster than my strength allowed. I felt overwhelmed with grief, my mind weighed down with painful memories that overshadowed all others. I longed to only think of the peaceful and pleasant times with Awenita, Ayiana, and Honovi, and prayed that eventually it would be so, but my thoughts kept returning to the fiery arrows and my friends' dead bodies. Soon, we would be back to Salem Village, and there would be questions, the answers to which I could not give. I would heed Meda's warning and watch my tongue. I knew if I didn't, I wouldn't survive.

I wondered why we hadn't come upon a real civilization—one with a phone. I shook my head, realizing my phone had been in the bramble of weeds for a couple of months and must be damaged beyond repair. When we were alone, I told Hezekiah, "I'd like to try to find my phone."

He grinned, two distinct dimples just like Trent's framing his lips. "I hid it."

"Thank you, Hezekiah. That means a lot."

He moved in front of me and blocked me from going farther. "Don't get mad, Bess, but I think we should hide everything." He patted the bag across his broad shoulder.

I opened my mouth to protest, but then stopped. "I guess so."

"That is a yes?"

"Yes."

Just then, some of the men came up behind us. "No one's following us," one of them reported.

Hezekiah relaxed, but I didn't. *No one is following after me.* The revelation crushed me. Of course, it was better that way. Honovi would be mourning the loss of his village for the rest of his life, and so would I. I couldn't explain what had happened—it just didn't make sense. I trembled and forced myself to not think.

Later that evening, we broke through the dense trees. The setting sun cast an array of brilliant colors across the evening sky, framing several buildings and dozens of lamp-lit streets below us. My heart skipped a beat. "Where are we?"

"Boston," Hezekiah said. He took a deep breath.

I could smell the ocean too. We hurried down the hill. My long journey had ended. I would finally be able to find a phone and get back to Danvers. Though my arm no longer throbbed, it would need to be looked at by a doctor. I had no idea how I would explain my injury to anyone, let alone my mother. She was going to freak out for sure.

I looked out over the buildings as we neared them. Although I had been to Boston many times, I didn't recognize this part of it. The woods were thick, the roads unpaved. Weird. The city must be forking out big bucks to be doing such major repaving.

The men said their goodbyes and headed off in different directions. Hezekiah led me down a street lined with elegant homes. We stopped in front of a large estate at the end of it. "What is this place?"

He looked up at the flickering lights in the windows. "It is my home—well, my parents' home."

"Oh," I said in surprise. I should have been thrilled with seeing such splendor, but it frightened me. Hezekiah's family was obviously wealthy, and he didn't have a phone. He hadn't even known what one looked like. Something strange was going on, and I was sure I would eventually unravel the mystery. Time travel passed through my mind, but that was utterly ridiculous. There had to be a *sane* explanation—totally believable. *Yeah, right. Keep thinking that, Bess.*

Maybe Hezekiah's family belonged to a group that shunned modern technology—archaic for 2015, though perfectly within their rights. I bit at a fingernail. Living without technology in the village hadn't been so bad. Hezekiah's family—part of a radical, dissident group— might explain the weird-clothing-and-lack-of-modern-conveniences thing, but nothing could explain the Indian tribe. My tribe. Did I really need an explanation for them? I repressed the thought and followed Hezekiah through the lavish entryway.

We were met by a butler, or at least he looked like one. Hezekiah spoke to him and then motioned for me to follow.

"Can I have my things?" I asked. Hezekiah took his book out of my bag. He unwrapped the Indian cloth and handed it and my bag to the butler.

"Have Charles fetch Doctor Griggs for her arm." He turned to me and gestured to the butler. "He will draw your bath and lay out fresh clothing. Join me in the parlor after you dress properly," Hezekiah said with an edge to his voice.

My eyebrows rose. Was he back to commanding me again? The twinkle in his eye said otherwise. It seemed he thought playing the authoritative beau was somehow attractive. I scowled and his twinkle faded.

"What I meant to say is, if you feel up to it." He turned and walked away.

I was glad he had changed his tone, but wondered if he really did mean it. I followed the butler up a long flight of stairs and into a beautiful bedroom with lace curtains and antique furniture. I marveled at the intricately carved bedposts and marble fireplace carved with humming birds. Amazing. The butler set my bag on a table, draped my cloak over a chair, and left the room. I slipped the moccasins off my sore feet.

A short woman entered the room. From her odd clothing and that of the butler, I figured they must be getting ready for some kind of a costume ball. Everything was so weird—even in this older part of the city. I couldn't wait to talk to someone about my experience with the Indians. It was so confusing. Maybe a lost tribe could live in the deepest jungles of Africa, but not in the woodlands of Massachusetts.

The woman carried a towel and a pitcher of warm water. "Won't you sit, my lady?" She pointed to a chair by the bed, so I sat. She removed a small basin from the nightstand and set it on the floor by my feet. After filling it with the water, she bent down and placed my feet in it. She began scrubbing them while five or six maids filled a freestanding tub in the adjoining room with hot water. *Yeah, I could live like this.*

"Your dress, my lady." She gestured to my dirty clothing. Two maids stepped close to me and worked the dress over my head, careful not to dislodge the bandage. Okay, a little weird for me, but I was a huge fan of *Downton Abbey*, so I let them. They helped me into the tub, then proceeded to wash my shoulders. I held my arms to my chest and shook my head. I could wash myself there. At least I had that much dignity.

The woman unwrapped the bandage, revealing the homemade poultice on my wound. She gasped. "My lady?" I didn't want to be the topic of gossip down in the galley, so I simply frowned. She glanced at my scarred back and grimaced, and suddenly I felt truly naked in front of her, with all of my secrets revealed. I wept.

They treated me like royalty. The woman wrapped my arm with a clean bandage and helped me into a dark-blue silk gown covered in delicate lace. I was grateful for the wide sleeves that lay over the bandage. The lace was a bit much for my taste, but I was happy to be out of the soiled dress I had been wearing for several days.

The woman sat me in front of a large, ornate mirror and brushed my hair, then pulled it into a bun with long ringlets framing my face. "What is your name, my lady?"

"Bess—er, I mean, Elizabeth. What's yours?"

"I am Mrs. Fayette." She reached for a stubborn strand of my hair and tucked it back into the bun. "Lady Elizabeth," she repeated, placing a gem-studded hairclip adorned with hanging pearls into my hair. It was beautiful, but even as I stared at it, I longed for Nashota's feathers. "There. You are done." She smiled at me in the mirror.

I nodded my approval and stood. "Where is the parlor?"

"I will take you there."

I followed Mrs. Fayette down the stairs and through a long hallway. The shoes she had slipped on my feet were stiffer than any I'd ever worn. My mother had told me that when she was young, all new shoes had to be broken in and took several blisters to do so, but that was long ago. These were just bad shoes—cheap, I'd say, if it weren't for the pearls sewn into the tops.

We walked past a large room with carved double doors propped wide open. I glanced inside at the splendor—rich tapestries, oil paintings, and ornate trim running up red velvet walls. The most exquisite figurines and flower vases adorned every table and mantelpiece. I drew in a sharp breath. An antique harpsichord with gold decorative molding sat in the far corner. "Oh!" I said, gazing at it.

"Do you play, my lady?"

"Yes, I do." I'd had years of piano lessons and once had the opportunity to play a harpsichord on display in the museum. I had to wait in line, and they sanitized our hands before they allowed us to press its keys, but it was astounding—a highlight of any of my frequent visits to Boston.

Mrs. Fayette motioned for me to come near the harpsichord. I was more than happy to oblige. Maneuvering the dress around the bench was difficult, but she helped me, and soon my fingers flew across the keys. I played "Pachelbel Canon in D."

"My, but you play beautifully!" She clapped her hands together.

The music had also caught the attention a young girl, who stood in the doorway, mesmerized. When I finished playing, she ran up to me and asked, "Who are you?" Her big blue eyes were filled with wonder.

"My name is Elizabeth." I said, holding my arm, which had started to throb just before I stopped playing. "Who are you?"

She curtsied. "My name is Isabella Hanson."

Of course she would be a Hanson. I hadn't thought to ask Hezekiah about his brothers and sisters, or even if he had any. She bent forward and ran her fingers over the keys. "You play very well."

"Thank you." I scooted over and patted the bench. "Do you play?"

She slipped in beside me. "Yes." She had to be around twelve, but she played as though she was much older.

"Wonderful!" I clapped my hands together after she played a piece. Then my stomach started its flip-flops again, so I motioned to Mrs. Fayette to help me up. "Well, I've got to go, but it was nice meeting you. Goodbye, Isabella." She nodded, then turned back to the harpsichord.

We stepped out into the hall, walked the length of it, and rounded a corner. There stood Hezekiah. He looked handsome in his fancy clothing, like something straight out of a Jane Austen novel. Leaning back against the door frame, he glanced my way, and there were those signature dimples and fantastically green eyes. But the look he gave me was one of surprise and then something deeper. I felt the heat rise in my cheeks as he moved toward me and reached for my hand.

"Elizabeth, I have someone I want you to meet."

He twirled me around as a beautiful young woman approached us. "Oh, your sister?"

"No."

Hezekiah seemed a bit uncomfortable.

"A cousin?"

She laughed and took his hand. "Hezi," she said in a rich English accent. She nuzzled her nose into the nape of his neck.

Oh. "Hezi?" I said coolly.

She looked down her nose at me. "Yes, he is my Hezi." *Calm down, Bess. Hezekiah was never yours.* Still, I couldn't resist. I grabbed his hand and pulled him outside onto the deck. I looked behind him and saw his girlfriend gaping at me like I had leprosy. "Are you her Hezi?" I demanded. In my world, being direct got you answers a lot quicker than playing games.

He pulled the stiff white collar away from his throat. "Yes," he said, though he didn't sound very convincing.

I was shocked. We hardly knew each other, but I would have told him if I had a boyfriend. I stared at him, waiting for an explanation.

"I've have not seen Arabella for several years."

I frowned. "And she's your girlfriend?"

"Well, she's a little bit more than a friend. I'm supposed to marry her."

My eyes widened. "What?"

"Have you not heard of arranged marriages?"

"Yeah, in the Dark Ages, maybe."

"Well, apparently they still happen today, Bess. Our marriage has been arranged since we were infants."

"Is that even legal? I don't think it is." I leaned against a stone column. "How can you marry someone you don't know, let alone love?"

Hezekiah tried to take my hand, but I wouldn't let him. His eyes twinkled. "My future bride and I will come to love each other."

"Right." By the way Draculette had attacked his neck, I doubted it would be love. Fortunately, she had wandered off to chat with the other guests.

Hezekiah stepped so close I felt his warm breath on my cheek. His green eyes held a strange intensity. "I must explain, Bess."

I put my fingers on his chest and gave him a gentle nudge. He stepped back. Suddenly, everything started to spin.

"All of my life, I have known about Arabella," he continued. "It has been our parents' wish that we marry."

Barely able to breathe, I leaned back against the column.

"Even though my father is set on the marriage, my mother told me it would be my choice."

"Oh." A hard wave of dizziness hit me. "I need to sit down, Hezekiah."

"What's wrong?"

"I don't know." I grabbed his arm to steady myself.

Hezekiah led me toward a bench. Everything closed in around me. I held a hand to my head and squeezed my eyes shut just before my knees buckled beneath me.

Seven

Mamm

Hezekiah carried me up the stairs and laid me on top of my bed. "Mrs. Fayette!" he yelled, then hurried from the room.

I don't remember much after that—only that a few of the maids changed me out of the formal gown and into nightclothes and covered me with a blanket.

When I awoke, a man with a bushy beard and beady eyes stood over me. He looked vaguely familiar. Hezekiah stood beside him with a woman I did not recognize.

"She's waking up, Dr. Griggs," the woman said.

The doctor bent over me. He smelled of pipe smoke and mints. "Elizabeth, can you hear me?"

"Yes." My mouth was dry, my lips thick and cracked. Hezekiah took my hand.

"She's still feverish." Dr. Griggs frowned. "I'm afraid we need to remove it."

Remove what?

"She has been through too much already, Doctor," Hezekiah snapped. "I will not allow you to take her arm."

I wanted to jump up off the bed but was too weak.

"Then I'm afraid there is no more that I can do." Dr. Griggs put his hat on and turned to leave. "I'll be back in the morning, in case you change your mind." He shook his head. "If she survives the night."

Like I needed to hear that. He gave the woman a strange look and then left.

Hezekiah grimaced. "Well?" He swept his hand toward the woman. "Go ahead. See what you think."

The woman stepped close to me and studied a small cut on my arm. I couldn't remember where it had come from.

"'Tis not a good practice to bleed them like that."

What is she talking about?

She lifted the sheet covering the rest of my arm and gasped. "You ought to have come for me sooner, Mr. Hanson."

Hezekiah folded his arms across his chest. "Can you heal it?" he asked grimly.

She reached into her bag. "I can try." She pulled out some small pots filled with dried leaves and herbs, then ground them together into a fine powder. She looked closer at my infected wound. "Did you take a bath, dearie?" She waited for me to respond, then added, "In a tub filled with water?" She glanced over at the freestanding tub.

What a strange question, I thought, but I nodded.

"That was your mistake," she said with a frown. "One with an open wound should never bathe in dirty water—the grime will seep right into the wound."

Oh, right. I didn't think about that.

"This will sting." She looked at me with sad eyes. "Hold her hands," she told Hezekiah, then sprinkled the powder over the gaping hole.

I clenched my teeth tight, refusing to scream. My head pounded and my arm felt like it was on fire again. I squeezed Hezekiah's hands so tight it must have hurt him, but all he did was whisper soothing words into my ear.

"I cannot marry her, Bess. I will not."

I looked up at him through teary eyes, wondering if I'd heard him right.

He turned to the woman and said, "Please stay on until tomorrow." She agreed and left the room.

Hezekiah said no more to me, and I wondered if I had heard him at all. Maybe I was hallucinating. Maybe he didn't say anything. But then he bent down and kissed me, and for a moment the pain and the world stopped spinning.

Dr. Griggs stopped by the next morning. He seemed pleased when he lifted the sheet and saw my arm. "Well, well, well," he said in surprise. "I must admit, I did not think you would make it through the night, Elizabeth. Praise be to God. You are one blessed woman."

Later that morning, Hezekiah came to see me. He leaned over and kissed me on the forehead. I was a little disappointed, wanting a better kiss, but I understood, as Mrs. Fayette was nearby dusting the shelves and seemed to be listening. He saw me look at her and dismissed her with one wave of his hand. As soon as we were alone, he took my hands in his. "How are you today, Bess?"

"I'm okay. I think I can get up."

He frowned. "Not yet—you need to rest." I scowled, so he added, "At least wait until afternoon."

"No, Hezekiah." I rose up on my elbows and quickly fell back with a wave of dizziness.

"You see?"

"My arm is much better." I looked down at it—the redness was nearly gone. "Who was she?"

He gave me a questioning look.

"The woman who put the powder on my wound."

"Oh, her." He leaned close and his voice dropped low. "She is the town witch."

I slapped him on the shoulder. "Cut it out. Who is she? You don't really believe that, do you?"

He shrugged. "She healed you, didn't she?"

I rolled my eyes. "She used plants that have medicinal properties—everyone knows that."

"Well, I had to smuggle her in, so don't tell anyone about her."

He sounded serious, so I asked, "Where did you smuggle her from?"

"Marblehead."

I raised an eyebrow. "And her name?"

"Wilmot Redd. She goes by Mamm, though."

I titled my head to the side. Why did her name sound so familiar?

Later that day, Hezekiah helped me get out of bed and walked me around the room. It was amazing how much better I felt, and by the next morning, the redness was completely gone. I had a surprise visitor too—Martha.

"Oh, wane, ye had me so worried! Ye were gone for so long. An' then ta find out ye were taken by Indians!" She moaned and wrapped her arms around me. After a long hug she spoke again. "They are treatin' ye grand 'ere?" She glanced in wonder at the fancy decor.

"Oh, yes." Mrs. Fayette stepped out of the room, leaving Martha and me alone. I told her about Honovi and Awenita.

Martha shook her head. "Ye are mighty blessed, me wane, but do not forget that Honovi took ye away from yer family."

I nodded, a knot forming in my throat, and then I told her about the raid on the village. Her eyes widened when I showed her my arm. I could not show her my back, fearing she would judge Honovi unfairly. I was not condoning the whipping—I knew it was wrong. Honovi knew it too.

"Yer arm seems ta be healin' well," Martha said after examining it closely.

"Yes. A woman named Wilmot Redd put some powder on it—"

Martha jumped up and her hands flew to her face. "The witch?"

A puff of air escaped my throat. "You too?" My indignation left quickly, as Martha truly had a look of fear on her face. "Aunt Martha, why do you think she is a witch?" I said slowly.

"The words of a witch's curse came from her lips, they did." I'd never seen Martha so animated, her voice rising in pitch and volume. "She had a disagreement with a lady an' the lady became pure shuk, jist as Mamm said."

"Shuk? What is that?"

"Shuk—like ye are. Shuk." Martha made a gagging sound and held her hands to her throat, stuck her tongue out, and pretended to roll her eyes back into her head.

"Oh—sick." Did I look that shuk? I shrugged. So, Mamm had cursed someone over an argument, and then the woman actually got sick? *Huh. I wish I had that power.* I twisted my lips. *Just kidding.* Everything was so freaky weird, even Martha and Hezekiah now. I leaned back on my elbows, wondering if I had stumbled upon a scientific experiment the government was funding, like Area 51 in Nevada.

As much as I wanted to hang around, especially with Hezekiah, it was time to make my exit. I was sure I could find my way back here to continue whatever it was I had with Hezekiah, but I'd had enough of everything else. "Would you excuse me, please?" I swung my legs over the side of the bed and sat up. "I'm going home now."

"Aye, yer ma is 'ere?"

"Actually, she would be getting off work right now." There was a light rap on the door, and Hezekiah entered. "How close are we to Dorchester?" I asked him.

"This is Dorchester."

"No, it isn't." I stood up and smoothed my nightclothes. I knew Dorchester almost as well as I knew Danvers. I practically grew up there in the summers when I was younger. Mom would take Seth and me to work with her. He was a baby and stayed in the nursery on the estate where Mom worked, while I got to roam anywhere I chose, as long as I showed respect to the owner's property and privacy. That's where I had met Samantha, and a few years later, her cousin Trent. Saddened at the memory, I frowned. I really missed him.

Hezekiah gave me a strange look. "I think I would know where my house is, Bess." He spread his arms out. "This is 110 Sturbridge Ave, Dorchester, Massachusetts."

I fell back against the bed, my heart pounding. "No. It isn't. My mother works at 110 Sturbridge Avenue." Both

Hezekiah and Martha looked at me like I was crazy. I moved to the large windows facing the long driveway and sighed in relief. The riding stables and large swimming pool were not where they should have been. "See? This isn't 110 Sturbridge!"

Martha's and Hezekiah's wide eyes and blank expressions frightened me. "I'll prove it to you!" I declared. My heart raced as I stepped down the stairs with Hezekiah right beside me.

The front entryway seemed similar, but then again, why wouldn't it? A lot of the mansions in Dorchester probably had the same parquet-inlaid entryways edged with marble. I stumbled to the front door and threw it open, tripping over my feet.

I strode down the walk, my nightclothes swishing against my bare legs, and then turned to face the estate. A scream swelled in my throat. Trent's grandfather's home on 110 Sturbridge Avenue was much larger, but this was without a doubt the same place. I fell to my knees. Hezekiah reached my side quickly.

My mind filled with a soft drumming, and a distant voice, like a whisper in the wind. "Onida, child of the stars, heed my warning." I pressed trembling fingers to my head. Everything made sense as I recalled Meda's words—"One who came from a distant land of days not yet seen."

Hezekiah wrapped his arms around me, and I forced myself to stop shaking. I stood and brushed off my nightclothes, keenly aware of the stares from staff and family. "I–I must have been mistaken," I lied.

Hezekiah led me back to the estate. I heard the words the staff whispered as I walked by. "It's the high fever—causes delirium." "Looks like she's coming out of it."

Hezekiah helped me back upstairs and into bed. He spoke to Martha, "Would you mind staying for a few days? I would feel better knowing Bess has fully recovered before you take her back to Salem Village."

"Aye, ta be sure, I will."

He turned to Mrs. Fayette. "Put her in the bedroom beside Elizabeth and open the connecting doors."

I forced myself to remain calm, until everyone had left my room. Air sputtered from my throat and my body tensed. I was in the past, but how far back? From the clothing and the . . . *Oh, dear.* I groaned. I wasn't insane or in some alternate reality—I was a *time traveler*, which was the craziest explanation of all. It was even hokier than witches. I shivered in realization.

Mrs. Fayette came back into the room and crossed to my bed. She looked down at me pitifully, like she believed I was a nut case too.

"Do you have anything I could read?" I asked with quivering lips.

She drew in a deep breath and squared her shoulders. "The Hanson family has one of the best libraries in Massachusetts Bay."

I blinked. *Massachusetts Bay?* "Yes, of course." But books were not what I was looking for. I chose my next words carefully. "My mind has been a bit scrambled lately." I touched my arm, and she nodded in agreement. "And I've lost track of the date. What day is this, please?"

The hard lines on her face softened. "Today is Wednesday, my lady."

"Wednesday," I repeated. "In the Indian village we had no calendars or clocks, so I became very disoriented. What month is it?"

She patted my hand. "April."

"April!" I gasped. I really had lost track of time. I had to ask. "What year is this, Mrs. Fayette?"

"It is 1692, my lady."

My blood turned cold in my veins and my heart nearly stopped. "It is 1692?" *No, it can't be!*

Eight

Another World

My body took to uncontrollable tremors, making my teeth chatter. Every time I thought I'd gained control, my mind locked onto my bizarre circumstances, and the tremors returned. It could not be 1692. No matter how much I tried to process it, my mind refuted it at every turn. It simply was not possible.

Over the next few days, I receded farther within my mind, shut off from the living and nearly too weak to live. Locking my words behind my tongue, I felt neither the need nor the desire to speak. The doctor came often and left without encouragement. On some level, I was aware of Hezekiah and Martha, but unable to offer them any hope. How could I accept a life in 1692, the very year I abhorred the most? I lost the desire to live and waited only to die.

Bitter tears streamed down my face as I realized I might share the same death date as my long-deceased grandmother. I let that thought seep and fester, when suddenly my eyes popped open and my mind cleared. It was only April, and Grandma Martin was hanged in July. She had not even gone to trial yet. *Maybe I was sent back in time to save her!* I pushed the blanket off and swung my legs over the side of the bed.

Mrs. Fayette came into the room and dropped the stack of sheets she was carrying. "Lady Elizabeth!" She hurried to my side and tried to force me to lie down again.

I held up my hand. "No, no, I'm okay now." She took a step back. "I am hungry, though." I pressed my fingers to my stomach.

"I will get you something from the kitchen." Her eyes lowered. "At the least, let me help you to the chair, my lady." She pointed to the lounger beside the bed.

I nodded and allowed her to steady me. She helped me sit, pushed a pillow behind my back, and placed a small blanket over my legs. I pointed to the windows. "Would you open the curtains, please?" Without a murmur, she obeyed and then rushed from the room.

It was a beautiful day, and I longed for some air. Looking across the room to the window, I slipped off the lounger. I was steadier than I'd expected. I made it to the window and pulled the lever down. With a pop, it released and opened a small crack. I pushed on it, and it swung partway open, allowing a cool breeze in. I breathed in deep and returned to the chair, covered my legs, and pressed my head back into the pillow.

I heard footsteps and turned to see Hezekiah dash in. His face twisted in horror—not exactly what I had expected from him. He went to the window first.

"Incompetent woman. I will have her fired for this!"

He turned to me and his face sobered. He slipped his arms under my body and lifted me back to the bed. "Mrs. Fayette will hear from me about this. You should not have air on you right now."

I reached up and put my fingers on his tight lips. "She did not open the window, Hezekiah. I did." I searched his eyes until I saw them soften.

He smirked. "No doubt you did."

"Now, either you help me back to the lounger and open the window, or I will do it myself."

"Bess, I almost lost you. I can't, I just can't . . ."

I reached up, pulled his face to mine, and pressed my lips to his. A bold move for a 1690's girl, but not one in 2015. I quickly pushed him away. I could not be a twenty-first-century girl, not if I wanted to blend in. "I'm sorry. That was impetuous and rash of me."

His eyebrows rose. "Yes, it was."

Not exactly what I hoped he would say, but I resigned myself to it and lowered my eyes.

"Bess." He scooped me up in his arms. "You are so different from the other girls I know. It's almost like you are from another time." He looked down at me as if deep in thought and then carried me back to the lounger, where he carefully sat me down.

I bit my fingernail. "What makes you think that?"

Hezekiah crouched down and played with a strand of my hair. "Your mannerisms, the way you speak, and" — he looked into my eyes— "your phone." He sat down on the floor beside me. "It is from another world, Bess, and so are you."

I was shocked. I wanted to confirm everything he said, but remembered Meda's warning. "I am not from another world."

He grinned. "That's good, because I wouldn't have believed you anyway."

"So, you didn't mean what you just said?"

He leaned back on his hands. "Oh, I meant it, Elizabeth Martin. After they took you, I went back and found your phone, and while John gathered some men for me, I studied it."

I drew in a breath. "What did you discover?" I asked slowly.

"Pictures. I saw pictures of places I've been to in Europe—only they were filled with outlandishly dressed people and strange things."

Those would have been the pictures my mother took on her trip last summer. I had let her use my new phone, because hers didn't have the internet. It was a long two weeks for me, but she came back with some awesome pictures.

"Bess, they were undeniably pictures from a future time," Hezekiah said with a quiver in his voice.

"Why would you say that?"

"People got inside carriages that moved without horses—moved, Bess. And the pictures moved too!" His voice was full of wonder and tinged in urgency.

How do you explain videos and automobiles to someone who had never imagined anything like them? Except for him. He had seen pictures from the future. He was now the most knowledgeable man on the face of the earth.

"They are called videos and movies," I said, "and the horseless carriage is called a car." For the next hour, we

Salem Witch Haunt

sat side by side while I answered as many of his questions as I could. I still didn't know how cars ran, other than by using fuel.

"Incredible. Just incredible." Hezekiah grabbed at the sides of his head and shook it.

Information overload, I guess. "O-kay. I think you've had enough . . ."

"Oh, no, you have to tell me everything!"

I made a face. Everything would take more time than I wanted to spend. Trent was the go-to guy in my life. Needed to know something? He had the answer. He never ceased to amaze me with the amount of knowledge he had crammed into his brain. Me? I had to google it or ask him. Fortunately, we were interrupted by a knock at the door. Mrs. Fayette and Martha entered.

"We brought you some breakfast, my lady," Mrs. Fayette beamed. She carried a tray overflowing with fruit, cheeses, and meats, while Martha carried a tray with two pewter mugs of frothy milk.

"Aye, we were expectin' ta see ye here, Master Hanson," Martha said with a twinkle in her eye. They set the trays down on the table next to us and left the room.

I ate silently, relishing every bite. The delicious, frothy milk with some kind of dark chocolate swirled in it could rival Starbucks back home. I sighed, realizing back home did not exist for me anymore.

"Ah, you like the chocolate?" Hezekiah asked. "It is very rare indeed."

Yes, of course it would be in 1692. I groaned. I could live without a lot of things, but chocolate? Life was so cruel. A pang of sorrow gripped me. I came back to the past, which was in effect, the present. My family hadn't even been born yet, and I would be long dead before . . . It was too much to think about. "Where is the chocolate from?"

"My parents brought it back with them on their last trip to Europe," Hezekiah said.

"Oh. Do they go there a lot?"

He nodded. "That is where they are presently. I would have accompanied them as I usually do, but upon my father's orders, I was to welcome Arabella to our home. They have not seen her since she was an infant." Hezekiah grinned suddenly. Perhaps we should tell them that you are Arabella."

Yeah, right! And what, pay the entire staff to be silent? It was hard enough being Elizabeth in 1692. "Where is Arabella?" I wondered what part of the estate they were keeping her in—probably as far from me as possible.

He leaned his head against the wainscoting. "I sent her back to England."

I sat up straight. "You did what?"

Hezekiah turned to me. "How can I marry her, when my heart belongs to another?"

Ooooh, good answer. My heart fluttered. *Focus, girl.* "Your parents—well, at least your father—is going to kill you. And me too, probably."

He looked at me funny. "Kill us?"

I realized my meaning was lost in the vernacular. "Not really, Hezekiah—it's figurative language."

"Oh. So my father is not going to kill us?" He smirked.

"Well, I don't know," I said playfully. "How bad does he want you to marry Draculette—er, Arabella?"

"Draculette?" Hezekiah threw his head back and laughed.

I wasn't about to explain that one, although Dracula had already lived and died in Romania in the 1400s, if my memory served correctly, which it usually did.

"Oh, I see." Hezekiah touched his neck as if my meaning had dawned on him. His face sobered. "You are right though, Bess. My father is not going to be pleased at all."

Not good to hear. "When will they return?"

"I expect them in about six weeks. Mid to late June, if the sailing is good."

I was relieved. At least I had time to bathe and go back to Salem Village with Martha. "I'll get ready and leave immediately."

Hezekiah grabbed my hand. "No." He pushed a loose strand of my hair behind my ear. "Strange things are happening in Salem Village. I'd rather you not go back there."

I swallowed. *If he thinks things are strange in Salem Village now, wait until the hangings begin.* I had about two and a half months to change the course of history for my grandmother, and much less time for some of the other victims.

Later that night, I lay awake thinking about how I could stop the tragedy brewing in Salem Village. Who would be hanged first? I searched my memory. Sarah

Good would die in jail in May. So soon! I clutched the sheet to my chest.

There was only one hanging before my grandmother's in July. Bridget Bishop would be hanged on June 10. I bit my lip, trying to remember everything I had studied about her. Tavern owner, flashy dresser. Standing out as she did—being different, and to some people, strange—probably made her an easy target. *Dang, am I ever in trouble.* Fortunately, I had given my bright-orange tank top to Awenita, but I wondered what had become of my other modern clothing.

"Martha, are you awake?" I whispered.

"Aye, me dear, I am." I heard her shuffling around in the adjoining room and then saw her standing in the doorway. "What is it that ye need, me wane?"

"What happened to my things—my belongings?"

"Ye mean yer odd clothing?" She paused, looking uncomfortable. "I burned them."

"Thank you." I breathed out a sigh of relief. With the evidence gone and my phone hid, I felt much safer. "I am glad you did."

"I do not understan' ye, but I know ye are a good person." She turned back to her room.

"Wait! What is happening in Salem Village?"

Martha turned slowly around. "Rank things, me wane, rank things."

"Is there no way to stop it?"

She shook her head sadly. "Nah, me lassie. Those that do are thought ta be in league with the devil."

I shuddered. Two of the accused had tried to stop the madness by turning it back on the accusers. John Proctor, a successful and prosperous man, had spoken out against the hysteria, and John Willard actually resigned as the constable. Both men declared that the young girls were the real witches and should be the ones punished. Proctor and Willard were both hanged on August 19, 1692.

I had to be super careful with my words or that was exactly what they would do to me. Suddenly, I felt ill as I realized I had met two of the accusers—Betty Hubbard and Mercy Lewis. My head swam. I had observed one of the first bizarre episodes—the twisting girls writhing and screaming through the Reverend Parris's window. They must have been Betty Parris and her cousin Abigail Williams. Abigail had come to live with the Parris family after her parents died in an Indian raid in Salem. I gulped and was glad Martha had returned to her room, as the violent tremors started again—fear for something I could not explain but had seen with my own eyes.

The next morning, I allowed Mrs. Fayette and Martha to bathe me, while I kept my arm high, out of the dirty water. Martha let out an audible gasp when she saw the scars on my back. I did not need to tell her what happened, as it was pretty easy to guess.

"The heathens, they did this ta ye?" A cross look covered her face. "Then they deserved what happened ta them."

I squeezed my eyes shut. *No, they did not.*

They helped me get dressed, and then Martha did my hair in a thick braid hanging down my back. Mrs. Fayette watched with pursed lips. I could tell she wanted to do something a bit more elegant. I had already won Martha's heart, and now I needed to win Mrs. Fayette's.

I sighed. "It is very nice, Aunt Martha." I made a sad face, and Mrs. Fayette perked up.

"Would you like me to redo it?" she asked brightly.

I faked a smile. "Would that be okay with you, Aunt Martha?"

She frowned but stepped aside, letting Mrs. Fayette go to work. Before long, my face was framed in soft ringlets. Even Martha approved. She grinned and gave Mrs. Fayette a nod.

A faint knock sounded. "May I come in?" Hezekiah called from behind the closed door.

I bit my lower lip and looked from Mrs. Fayette to Martha. "Do I look okay?" Martha reached over and adjusted a hairpin.

"Ye are a bonny lady," she said proudly.

"Yes, you are beautiful," Mrs. Fayette chimed in. She reached over and pinched my cheeks. I'd seen that done in the movies and it worked, because I looked in the mirror and saw my cheeks flush.

"Thanks!" I hugged both of the ladies. Then they went into Martha's room and closed the door. "Yes, Hezekiah," I said finally.

The door opened, but I didn't see anyone. Curiosity got the best of me and I stepped to the partially opened door. I gasped. The hallway was lined with the servants—all carrying vases and pots filled with sweet-smelling flowers. They bowed or curtsied as they passed by me, and before long, my entire room was overflowing with color. I thanked each one as they left. I'm not sure if that was proper protocol, but I was sincerely grateful.

I put my hands on my hips and scanned my room, then bent over and stuck my nose in the nearest bouquet. I wasn't a showy person and didn't need to be showered with gifts, but I could bend a bit—just to blend in, of course.

Hezekiah came up behind me, and I turned to greet him. Without thinking, I threw my arms around his neck and kissed him on the cheek. I quickly pulled away. "Sorry," I said, wondering if he could see me blush through my pinched cheeks.

He smiled and reached for my hand. "I thought you might like to go for a ride before breakfast." He gestured outside, where the morning sun crested the horizon with muted pastels.

"Oh, I would love to," I said, excited beyond words to be well enough to venture out. I tried to maintain a semblance of proper decorum. Hezekiah led me down the steps and out the front door. We were greeted by a servant, who opened a low door for me on a horse-drawn carriage without a top. I brushed my fingers over its ornate trim.

Hezekiah helped me in, then walked around the carriage and got in the other side. "We brought this coach back from Hungary just last year." He patted the cushioned seat.

We faced the front of the coach, where a driver dressed in a fancy suit awaited Hezekiah's command. Soon we were off to see a city I had always loved, 323 years before my time. The first thing I noticed were the roads, or lack thereof, and the potholes created from the harsh winter. One bump sent me at least two inches into the air. I suppressed a groan.

When the driver took us past an apple orchard in blossom, Hezekiah said, "Stop the coach!" He jumped out and came around to my side to help me out.

With my arm looped through his, we strolled down a road that ran alongside the orchard. Now that we were away from the driver, I could talk openly. I cleared my throat. "I have something important to tell you."

Hezekiah patted my arm. "We have plenty of time—a whole lifetime ahead of us."

"Yes," I said, hoping it was true for not only us, but for my grandmother and others as well. We neared a crude bench made from two rocks and a thick plank. He tried to pull me down beside him, but I resisted. "I can sit down myself." I remained standing. He frowned, but I waited several seconds before sitting down on my own.

He started to reach for my hand, but then stopped. "Sometimes I do not know what to make of you. I'm sure it has much to do with where you came from and your upbringing."

"What was wrong with my upbringing?" I may not have come from money like he had, but at least I wasn't a snob.

"Nothing."

I tilted my head. "Really?"

He kept his hands in his lap. "Really." He seemed unsure of himself, a quality I'd not seen in him before. "It's just that modern girls—" he glanced my way "don't want men to—"

"Control them?" I finished.

"Control? Is that what you think I do?"

I swallowed hard. This conversation was not going the way I'd thought it would. He stood and motioned for the driver to pull the coach forward.

All the way back to the estate, Hezekiah didn't say a word, didn't reach for my hand, and didn't even acknowledge me. He did help me out, though he hesitated before doing so. Then it came to me. *I'm ruining a good thing by trying to push a 2015 feminist attitude on a 1692 proper gentleman!* "Wait!" I called out to him as he neared the door. He stopped but did not turn around. "I'm sorry. I like everything about you, Hezekiah—your smile, your gorgeous eyes, and especially your manners. It's just that I'm not used to a man being so—"

"Controlling?" He turned and studied my face.

"No, so polite, and kind, and . . ." I stammered.

He frowned. He wasn't buying it.

"Okay, maybe you are a little controlling, but I think I get it now."

He folded his arms in front of his chest and waited.

I drew in a breath. "Maybe it's where you came from and your upbringing."

A tiny grin played at his lips. I knew I had him, so I forged ahead. "Maybe what I see as controlling is nothing more than chivalry and really good manners."

"Maybe. And maybe I have to try a little harder to trust that you can do things on your own without my help."

"Yes." I pushed a loose ringlet back into place. "But don't try too hard." I waited for him to get the door.

Nine

Salem Village

Just inside the front door, Martha and Mrs. Fayette were talking anxiously. Martha wrung her hands and looked over at me, then pointed to a lady standing off to the side. I recognized her immediately as Wilmot Redd, the woman who had saved my life with her knowledge of medicinal plants.

Suddenly, I realized why her name had sounded familiar when I first heard it. Wilmot would be hanged as a witch on September 22! My heart caught in my throat. *She saved my life.* I couldn't take my eyes off her. I had to warn her to flee—and quickly.

Martha broke into my thoughts. "Yer Injun came lookin' for ya an' now he's thrown in the prison with them other witches. Mamm came all the way here from Salem Village ta tell ye."

"Honovi!" My hands flew to my mouth. "Is he okay?" Wilmot shook her head.

"Aye, yer Honovi." Martha scowled. "An' the only reason he's alive is he had a cross hangin' about his neck. They figured him ta be a Christian, but still threw him in the prison, till they could figure out what ta do with him."

The cross must have been Ayiana's. I'd never seen her without it. "I must go to him."

"Whoa, you're not going anywhere!" Hezekiah grabbed my arm and pulled me back. "Do you have any idea what's going on in Salem Village right now?"

I groaned. "Yes. Yes, I do!" All three of them stared at me like I was insane. "But we cannot leave him there!" I started to cry and turned into Hezekiah's chest. He pressed his lips to my ear and mumbled something I could barely hear.

"I'll get him."

I looked up at him through a veil of tears. His solemn green eyes filled with sadness. He stroked my hair. "I cannot bear to see you cry."

I realized he probably had not wanted Martha, Mrs. Fayette, or Wilmot to hear him, so I remained silent against his chest while wondering about the power of a woman's tears—a useful tool indeed, and one I would have to subdue, now that I had discovered it.

I followed Hezekiah into the next room and he closed the door behind me. I grabbed his hands and looked into his eyes. "How will you do it? Break down the doors, cut a hole in the side of the prison, dig a hole under the floor?" My eyes widened with apprehension.

Hezekiah laughed. "I don't need to rescue him, Bess."

My heart fell.

"I'll buy him."

I was horrified that he was going to buy Honovi like he was a piece of furniture or a horse. All at once I remembered. I had been thrust into an archaic time in the history of man—a time when men and women were sold as slaves and indentured servants. The practice would not change for hundreds of years.

Hezekiah put his hand on my shoulder. "He will be my gift to you."

I'd never received a man as a gift before. I bit my lip. But once Honovi was mine, I could do with him what I wanted—release him. I suspected that was Hezekiah's intention. "Thank you," I said to him.

He said goodbye and went to change into his riding clothes, telling me he would see me in about a week. I rushed up the stairs and pulled out the dress Martha had given me. The servants had washed it and mended the torn sleeve. It was a plain dress compared to the fine clothing Hezekiah had given me. I slipped into it, then pulled the hairpins out of my hair and braided it in one long braid. I crept down the stairs.

Years of working in the stables at the estate had taught me how to saddle and ride a horse. I knew Hezekiah's horse was in the front of the barn, so I chose the one farthest away, a mare. I had no desire to use a sidesaddle, especially one so archaic, but if I rode down the street astride, I would become the talk of the town and be considered an unsuitable choice for Hezekiah. I had ridden sidesaddle in competitions and even in a parade just last October—or in a few hundred Octobers from now. I knew what to do.

I pulled the saddle off its perch, set it on top of the horse, and fastened the cinch and the girth strap under her belly. Getting on the sidesaddle was another story. I tethered her to the posts, then climbed onto the wooden railing in the stall. "Hold still, girl," I cooed into the mare's ear as I positioned my body just right. Then I basically let myself fall back onto the padded saddle. The horse skittered sideways a few inches, but came right back. I reached over and took the whip off a peg, using it to steady myself on the side of the horse where I couldn't use my leg to signal her.

I remembered what the trainer had told me about how women often used sidesaddles unsafely, and not just in the past. The horns on the saddle trapped the rider. If the horse fell, it usually landed on top of the rider, resulting in the rider's death or paralysis. I studied the way I sat, knowing I'd have to have my wits about me until I got somewhere where I could dismount safely.

I walked the mare to the barn door and peered out. I only had seconds to get in place before Hezekiah saw me. I trotted the mare out, pleased with her easy gait, and hurried down the road toward Salem Village. I didn't go far, just far enough to hide and wait for Hezekiah to ride by.

When I saw him approaching on his horse at a fast clip, my heart fell. How could I keep up with him? I knew I had to try. As part of a competition, I had galloped sidesaddle, but of course the trails in 2015 were much better maintained. Still, Hezekiah was pulling farther ahead of me with each passing second. Fortunately, a passerby distracted him and he stopped to chat, allowing me to catch up.

Resigning myself to the fact that this was yet another of my foolhardy ideas, I rode up beside him just as his friend was leaving. Hezekiah appeared shocked to see me in the saddle, though I did note a pleased grin on his lips.

"Elizabeth, I had no idea you could ride." He switched the reins to his other hand.

"It's one of my hidden talents," I replied with a smirk.

"What are you doing?"

I loved how he always got right to the point. "Well, I planned to follow you, but you're going a bit too fast for me."

He shook his head. "Elizabeth, it's a rough trail and a long ride to Salem Village."

"Yes, I'm figuring that out." I waited for him to tell me to turn back and was prepared to do just that.

"I suppose I could go a little slower," he offered.

"Really?"

"You're safer with me than trailing behind on your own." He looked concerned. "These woods are full of danger. Do you know how many Indian attacks we have had in just this month?"

I hadn't thought about that. Last time I went from Danvers to Boston, my only fear was getting a flat tire and not making it to the Mugar Omni Imax Theatre on time.

Hezekiah motioned for us to go forward. For the first several minutes, we simply enjoyed the ride. It was late afternoon, and I was famished, our breakfast having been cut short earlier. My stomach growled. "Hezekiah, did you bring any food?"

He reached into his saddlebag and pulled out a chunk of bread. He handed half of it to me.

"Thanks." I ate silently, planning my next words.

He must have been doing the same thing, because he said, "We need to talk." He kept his eyes on the road ahead.

"Yep," I said between mouthfuls.

"We never did get to finish our conversation from yesterday, about the phone and the . . . pictures." He glanced in my direction, concern and wonderment etched in his handsome face.

I licked my lips. He had pretty much guessed the truth yesterday, but would he be able to handle it? "Okay, so here it is." I figured it would be a lot easier to tell him if I rode ahead. That way I wouldn't have to look at him when I blew his mind. "I was born on June 30—"

"Oh, what a coincidence! Me too."

"Hmm. That's nice." I pushed a loose strand of hair behind my ear. "Well, I was born on that day . . ." I hesitated, blew a puff of air across my lips, and then blurted out, "In the year 1997." I could only imagine Hezekiah's expression. "I'll be eighteen this year." We rode on in silence. "Are you okay?" I stopped my horse and waited for him to catch up, but Hezekiah wasn't even beside me. He was several yards behind me, looking pretty dazed. I turned my horse around and galloped back to his side. "It doesn't make me a freak or anything," I said, my voice shaking.

He looked over at me. "What's that? Oh, no, of course not, Bess," he mumbled. "Give me a moment." He swung out of the saddle and led his horse to a nearby tree, where he tethered it. Then Hezekiah sat on the ground, pulled his knees up to his chest, and wrapped his arms around them.

I could see the struggle within him as he fought to make sense of it all, but I kept my distance. I would not have been able to get out of the sidesaddle without his help anyway. I trotted off to give him some space. I worried while I watched him from afar. Even from a distance, I could see the deep anguish on his face, and something more. Amazement, I guess. But who wouldn't be amazed, right?

After a while, he mounted his horse and rode up to me. "If I hadn't seen those pictures, I'm not sure I would have believed you." He pulled his horse up close to mine and took my hand in his, his eyes full of astonishment. "I had heard theories, and I have read books about things like this, but I never believed it could be true." His brief look of wonderment turned to worry. "Bess, you must promise me that you will not tell anyone else what you told me— anyone, do you hear?"

I bit the side of my mouth. I understood his fear, but still struggled with being told I had to do something—or not do something—rather than making my own choice.

Hezekiah sighed. "I'm being controlling again, aren't I?"

I gave a slight nod. "Yes, but I agree with you. I know the people in this time are superstitious. They would not understand me at all."

"No, they would not."

"And you, Hezekiah? Do you understand me?"

"That's the easy part, Bess. I feel as if I have known you forever, if that's possible."

Right at that moment, an image of Trent came into my head—his smile, his freakishly green eyes. They even shared the same dimples, and I didn't need to wonder where Trent's physical characteristics had come from. I had wondered if they were distant cousins, and now I knew without a doubt that they were related—separated by hundreds of years. They shared the same surname and the same home. Trent's family had owned their land for generations, straight back to Massachusetts Bay Colony times. These times. "How much land does your family own? Do you own any land in Dan—uh, Salem Village?"

Hezekiah's eyebrow rose. It was a strange question, given the timing. "My father owns a large parcel of land east of Salem Village, right up to the coast."

A chill crept up my spine—so did Trent's family.

"But he's thinking of selling it."

"No!" I exclaimed before I realized they obviously hadn't sold their land. "Never mind." I paused. "So, you're okay with the time-travel thing?"

"Time travel—is that what you call it?"

I shrugged. "I really don't know how it happened, but one moment I was in 2015 minding my own business, and the next I was in Salem Village, 323 years earlier."

Hezekiah's eyes widened and then he relaxed. "Three hundred and twenty-three years in the future," he muttered. He turned his horse in the direction we needed to go and motioned for me to follow. "Are there others?" he asked after a minute. "I mean, is this something people do in the future?"

"Oh, no, no, no, no." Not that I knew of, at least.

"You must miss everything from your life there."

I swallowed hard, unable to answer right away. "Yes, Hezekiah—very much so."

"I'm so sorry, Bess. I can't even imagine."

The tenderness in his voice touched me, and I was grateful to have someone to talk to.

"But this must be the last time it is mentioned."

I turned sideways and stared at him. "What? I need to talk—"

"You need to stay alive, Elizabeth," he said firmly, "and from now on, no more Bess, but Elizabeth. You're in the past now, and you need to forget the future."

I sighed. He was right of course. If anyone ever heard our "from the future to the past" conversations, they would hang me as a witch, or worse yet, hang Hezekiah for aiding and abetting a heretic. "Yes, of course," I said, hoping to be spared the painful memory of a life I could no longer live and a family I could no longer speak of. "They say time heals all things." The words fell off my lips bitterly.

We rode for several hours. Hezekiah had said we would be there by nightfall and could stay at his cousin's house. An hour outside of Salem Village, Hezekiah pulled his horse up short. He held very still and motioned for me to stay quiet. An owl hooted and then another. Hezekiah reached for his musket.

Wait. I recognized that sound! I cupped my hand over my mouth and returned the call. Hezekiah looked at me in bewilderment. All at once, two Indians stepped out of the woods beside us, and five behind us. I clapped my hands excitedly and reached for the closest one. "Elan!"

127

He took my hand in his. "Nashota." His eyes filled with sadness. He spoke in his best, broken English. "Honovi come rescue you." He glared at Hezekiah, who kept his hand resting on his musket. "They throw him in jail."

"She does not need to be rescued," Hezekiah said firmly. The Indians moved closer.

"Is true?" asked Elan.

An Indian behind me spewed out a string of harsh words. I turned and saw Igasho pointing and glaring at Hezekiah. Igasho would not look at me, but I could see greater anger in him than ever before. I wondered if he blamed us for the loss of his village.

Elan gazed at me with searching eyes and then at Hezekiah. He held his hand up to Igasho and spoke swift words to him. Igasho backed off. Elan turned to me and said, "Igasho say he—" Elan pointed to Hezekiah "—with you before. Is he husband?"

I felt the heat rise in my face. I knew if I said no, they would want me to go with them. There was a big part of me that wanted to go with them, and I would have, if it hadn't been for Hezekiah. Still, I could not lie and opened my mouth to give him my answer. "I—"

"Yes." Hezekiah spoke up. "She will be my wife."

I hoped the shock registering in my mind was not evident on my face.

Elan looked from me to Hezekiah and then back again. He nodded. "Is good," he said, then slowly turned away.

"Wait! What about Honovi?" My heart raced. I knew they would never leave him in a white man's jail. He wouldn't have been there if it hadn't been for me. I was altering history already!

Elan turned back to me. "We fight."

Hezekiah lifted the butt of his musket, and Igasho swung his bow around. Hezekiah patted his gun and set it back on the saddle, and Igasho's bow relaxed. I waited for Hezekiah to explain our plan, and when he didn't, I ventured forward. "We are on our way to Salem Village to get Honovi." I felt Hezekiah tense beside me.

"How?" Elan questioned.

I saw the uncertainty in his eyes, but knew if I told him we were going to buy Honovi, the offense would be too great for a man like him. "He came looking for me. I am returning to Salem Village to tell them why." Hezekiah gave me a surprised look. "Honovi," I breathed out, ". . . is my brother."

Elan nodded and stepped aside. From the corner of my eye, I saw the others move back into the woods. "I will bring him to you soon." With that, I took the reins and coaxed my horse into a gallop. I didn't slow down until we had almost reached Salem Village. I could tell by the appearance of houses and the wider road.

Hezekiah pulled up beside me. "You know you cannot tell them he is your brother."

I sighed heavy. "I know." I had been thinking of nothing else but that. Contempt for Indians went deep— the standard textbook reason being their differences. Most Puritans thought of them as heartless heathens, but I knew better. What if the Puritans had lived on this continent first and the Indians had pushed them out of their land? It seemed more than a little hypocritical that professed Christians thought it was fine to claim lands they didn't own, in the name of a king who had never set foot on it, from a people who had lived there for thousands of years. It was guilt and greed that drove the Puritans to hate the Indians. They refused to acknowledge the guilt, and the greater sin of greed they would not confess.

"It is no secret I was abducted and kept captive in an Indian village." By now, I was sure everyone had heard. "I will tell them God wants me to reform the heathen." *Eeks, where did that come from?* "And then you will buy him, so the indigent can earn his keep as my slave."

The words slipped from my tongue like a hiss from a snake. Samantha would be proud of my acting, but my body trembled with fear as I realized this was no stage with phony smoke and bad lighting. This was the real thing.

Ten

Goody Martin

Hezekiah and I trotted our horses up to a nice house—nicer than most in the neighborhood. "Is this where your cousin lives?" I asked.

"Yes." Hezekiah dismounted, then led my horse to a short wall and motioned for me to scoot onto it while he steadied the mare. He had helped me off the sidesaddle three times on the trail, but this time was much easier. He reached up and put his hands around my waist and lifted me off the wall. I wished the moment could last longer.

Once he had tethered our horses, we approached the house together. "Hezekiah!" A stout man with a long nose opened the door and took him by the hand.

"Zebulon!" Hezekiah clapped his arms around him.

"Come on in," Zebulon said, then looked out at me. "Oh, I see you've brought someone with you." He gave Hezekiah a wink and waved his arm for me to follow them inside.

His face suddenly sober, Zebulon gestured for us to sit and poured a thick drink into three mugs. He handed us each one. "Aye, Hezekiah, you have come at a bad time. They are examining the accused at Ingersoll's in the morning—the poor wretches." Seeing my shocked look, he added, "No one is safe, my lady. Everyone has gone mad!"

A series of shivers ran up my neck.

"So what brings you here?" He sat back and studied Hezekiah's face.

"Justice, my dear cousin. Justice."

"You don't say." Zebulon seemed intrigued.

"I'm here to buy an Indian."

Zebulon's eyebrows rose. "What do you mean?"

"I heard tell an Indian is locked up in the watch house, and I want him."

"Whatever for?"

Hezekiah glanced sideways at me. "A gift for my lady."

He was laying it on a bit thick, and I tried not to smirk.

Zebulon stared at me. "Your lady?" A grin broke out across his unshaven face, revealing a mouth full of badly stained teeth. "Well, I'll be! At long last a pretty lass has caught your eye." He leaned forward over the table. "But I'm afraid someone has already beat you to the Indian."

"What?" I jumped up, but just as quickly sat back down, remembering the need to act properly.

"Did someone buy him?" Hezekiah asked.

"Seems like the Reverend Parris would like him another slave," Zebulon explained. "Hasn't paid for him yet though, so you might be able to get him first if you hurry."

Hezekiah turned to me. "Elizabeth, why don't you stay—?"

Yeah, right. I jumped up again and gave him a defiant look that said, "Don't even go there."

Hezekiah sighed. "Let's go."

The watch house, or jail, was across the street and down a few blocks. All the way there, Hezekiah coached me, telling me what to say and what not to say. In the end, I agreed to let him do the talking.

I wasn't prepared for what I saw inside. The jail was packed with prisoners and reeked of human waste. I stayed close to Hezekiah's side as he waited for a man sitting behind a desk to acknowledge us. The man scratched something down on a ledger with a quill. My eyes wandered as we waited.

The small cells had little room for anyone to sit without pressing up against his or her neighbor. However, in one cell, the few occupants were crammed into a corner, leaving most of the space for one lone woman and an Indian—Honovi.

My heart leaped within me. He looked horrible, like he had taken a few beatings. *How ironic.* I pushed that thought aside. I wanted to run to him to let him know I was there, but I remembered Meda's words to keep my tongue silent. Honovi's back was turned to me as he spoke to the woman, who seemed to understand his words. I marveled at her and wondered who she was.

"May I help ya?" said the man behind the desk after clearing his throat.

"Yes, Mr.—"

"Name's Colin O'Donovan." He patted his chest.

Hezekiah pulled out a bag of coins and sat it on the desk in front of Colin, whose eyes widened. "I've come to purchase a slave," Hezekiah said, "and I understand you have acquired an Indian of late."

Theresa Sneed

Colin licked his lips while keeping his eye on the bag. He tilted his head. "I'm afraid this one is headin' out tomorrow mornin'." He pointed to Honovi.

I swallowed hard.

"Has he been purchased yet?"

"Well, nah, not yet, but I heard the parson is comin' in the mornin'."

"Has he signed any legal papers or given his word on it?"

Colin hesitated but then shook his head. "Nah, the man has not." He reached for the bag of coins, but Hezekiah slapped his hand down on top of it.

"How much?"

Colin stroked his whiskers. "Well, there is the matter of his stay and the fine." He held up his fingers for as many coins as he deemed necessary. I would have given him the whole bag just to be done with it. Colin tapped the counter with his rough fingers as if unsure of the transaction.

Hezekiah was quick. "Well, I don't need that one in particular, and I suppose I could find another one easy enough." He took his bag off the counter, but then counted out the exact amount Colin had held up with his fingers and a few more off to the side. Without a word, he gestured to Honovi and patted the coins to purchase him, and then he pointed to Colin and pushed the second pile of coins toward him. Colin nodded and grabbed the keys.

We followed him toward the cell. Colin looked back over his shoulder at me. "Are ye a Martin?"

I drew in a breath. "Why do you ask?"

88 Salem Witch Haunt*

He pointed to the woman talking to Honovi. "Yer identical ta Goody Martin's granddaughter, who was jist in here to see her grandma."

I fell back against Hezekiah. "Take him out," I whispered. I stepped aside and watched as Colin unlocked Honovi's cell and led him to Hezekiah. They kept the claps on his wrists, which was a good thing until I got a chance to talk to him. Hezekiah looked back at me with questioning eyes, but took Honovi outside while I hurried to my grandmother.

Colin had left the door ajar, and I slipped in. She sat alone facing the small window with a Bible on her lap. I glanced down at it and saw that it was open to 1 Samuel 28. I fell to my knees beside her, restraining myself from wrapping my arms around her neck. She glanced up at me with light-blue eyes, old and tired but still keen, and I was blown away with how much she looked like my dad's sister, Aunt Ellen, only twenty years older.

I sucked in a breath. "Susannah Martin?" It came out soft, like a whisper.

Her head tilted and her eyes softened. "Yes, sweetheart, I am she."

The life flowed from me, and I collapsed on her lap in a fit of sobs. She didn't push me away like the stranger I was, but caressed my hair instead. An idea came to me— if she confessed, she would not be hanged. I knew she wasn't guilty, but I wanted her to live! I looked up at her. "Won't you confess?"

135

She clicked her teeth. For a split second, I thought she might toss me from her lap, but instead she looked out the window. "I will not. I dare not tell a lie."

A puff of air escaped my throat. I admired her courage and integrity. I studied her eyes through my tears—strong, faithful eyes, soon to be closed forever. Was there no way I could help?

Colin tapped me on the shoulder. "Yer not allowed in here." He pulled me away before I could say another word.

I looked back, but Susannah had already returned to reading. I couldn't believe her calm demeanor. Where did her strength come from? Tears streamed down my face.

"Do ya know that lady?" Colin asked in a rough voice, as if she was a criminal.

"No." I shook my head. "I've never met her before."

He chuckled. "Yer a fierce quare one, wane."

Yes, I've heard that before. I wiped my nose on my sleeve as Colin pushed me through the open door.

"Over here, Elizabeth!"

Hezekiah and Honovi stood in the shadows. Holding up the hem of my dress, I hurried to them. Honovi was not a hugging kind of man, so I was surprised when he pulled me close. I felt the pain of the past few weeks flow from him to me and hoped somehow I could help ease his suffering.

"We cannot stay here now," Hezekiah said. "Not with Honovi." He studied my eyes. "We can take him to Elan tonight, or otherwise face the wrath of Parris when he finds out we got the jump on him."

"It's best to ride under cover of night," I said. "Go get our horses and say goodbye to your cousin. I'll wait here with Honovi."

Hezekiah shook his head. "No. I'll wait here. You can lead both horses, yes?"

I nodded. I hurried down the road toward Zebulon's house. It couldn't have been later than eight o'clock, and the streets were nearly empty.

All of a sudden I heard a voice from behind me. "Elizabeth?"

I turned to see Mercy giving me a strange look. If she was who I thought she was, she was one seriously sick girl, responsible for helping send twenty innocent people to their deaths.

"Mercy, what brings you out this time of night?"

"I'm meeting Betty and a few others. Do you want to come?"

Heck no. "Right now?"

"Yes—well, soon."

"Oh, um, I don't know. I have an errand to run."

"Oh. Well, maybe another time."

I nodded and hurried down the road, but I could feel her watching me, so when I got to Zebulon's house, I went right in instead of knocking. I had been so flustered, I never even thought of how improper that looked.

"Elizabeth?" Zebulon hurried into the room.

I held my hands to my beating chest. "I'm sorry—I was frightened."

He parted the curtain and peered outside. Mercy stood erect, right where I had left her.

"No doubt, my child. No doubt."

I told him about Honovi and how we were going to take him to Elan. Zebulon didn't seem too pleased, but he agreed that having Honovi out of Salem Village was a good thing. "I'll help you," he said. "Just in case Ol' Witch Eyes is still watching."

I shivered. She gave me the creeps too.

"Mercy Lewis—she's a strange one," Zebulon declared. "Now, I know her parents were killed in an awful Indian raid back in '89, but she's been well taken care of. First to the Reverend Burroughs place, and now at Thomas Putnam's. She ought to be more grateful."

It *was* Mercy Lewis. That freaked me out. I didn't believe in witches, but I knew of the power of a scornful, malicious woman. I wondered about her choice of the accused, knowing her former master, Reverend George Burroughs, would become one of her victims. In addition, her new master was one of the prominent feuding families in the Salem witch hunt tragedy.

"You ready?" Zebulon opened the door.

"Yes." I hoped Mercy was gone, but I had a feeling she wasn't.

Zebulon untethered the horses, saddled Hezekiah's, and handed me the reins of the other one. I wondered why the sidesaddle was gone but didn't question it. We walked slowly down the road toward where Hezekiah and Honovi waited. We didn't see Mercy until she popped out from behind a tree.

"Evenin', Zebulon," she said with a mock curtsey. "Elizabeth." She gave me a look that sent shivers up my back. "Nice evenin' for a ride."

I drew my hands to my chest. "You frightened me!" *Freaked me out is more like it.* I smoothed my dress and forced a smile. "Yes, yes, it is a nice night for a ride."

She looked from me to Zebulon. "You two know each other?"

I shrugged. "Not really. We met earlier this evening."

Her judgmental look turned to one of curiosity then disbelief. "And yet you're taking an evenin' stroll."

"I'd hardly say this was an evening stroll." I didn't want to cross Mercy, but she was getting on my nerves. Part of me wanted to smack her or at least pull her hair—unbecoming behavior for a girl from any generation.

Her eyes narrowed. "So, what's going on here?"

I clenched my teeth. That was none of her business, and I was about to tell her so. "Mercy—"

Hezekiah came up behind me. Honovi was not with him.

Mercy's demeanor changed. "Why, Hezekiah Hanson, how are you this fine evenin'?"

Did she seriously just bat her eyes?

"There you are, Cousin," Zebulon said, handing Hezekiah the reins of his horse. "I was—"

"We've been wondering where you've been keepin' yourself, Hezekiah," Mercy interrupted. "Especially Elizabeth."

I barely held back my gasp. Did she know about Hezekiah and me?

"And not this Elizabeth. Elizabeth Hubbard—Betty," Mercy said.

I clenched my fingers into a fist at my side. Betty Hubbard was a key player in the Salem mishap, maybe even more so than Mercy. But what was Hezekiah's connection to Betty? Just as I thought it, he put his arm around my waist and pulled me to his side. "I only have eyes for one Elizabeth," he said without hesitation.

I cringed. Hezekiah had no idea whom he was talking to and what she could do.

Mercy's eyes went wide and then filled with envy. "Elizabeth, are you still coming with me tonight?"

A tremor raced through my body. I should go— otherwise I could become a target. Then my name would show up in history books alongside my grandmother's!

Hezekiah lowered his eyes. "I'm afraid she has other plans." He took my hand in his.

Mercy scowled. So, I did the only thing I could, after squeezing Hezekiah's hand to warn him. "Oh, Mercy! What shall I do?" I exclaimed. "I really want to go with you." I feigned a sad expression, then said in a low voice, "Do you think Betty will be terribly upset with me?" Then I let myself look worried, which I really was. "I don't want her to be angry with me." *True, that.* "What should I do?" It was the perfect question to ask a new best friend.

Mercy's eyes softened. "You're right about her being mad—she's so infatuated with Hezekiah." Mercy batted her eyes at him again, and I knew I was out of hot water, for now at least. "I suppose I could talk to her," Mercy continued. "They were not betrothed, after all."

Only a best friend would say that. Mercy hugged me, then hurried down the walk away from us. I sighed, thinking how low I had sunk. I was best friends with Mercy Lewis, who was the accuser of dozens and the indirect murderess of twenty—only to save my hide, forgetting all about my own soul.

Eleven

Mercy Lewis

Zebulon shook his head. "A strange one that is." He clasped his hand on my shoulder. "Stay far away from her, Elizabeth, for your own good."

"Yes, I will. Thank you."

Zebulon shook Hezekiah's hand and then pulled him into a hug. "Sorry you didn't get to meet my new wife, Sarah, but next time you're in town, please visit."

After the goodbyes, Hezekiah and I led our horses out of town. I wondered where Honovi was, but suspected we'd run into him soon.

Not too far out of town, I heard a rustle and then saw him run toward us. Soon, we were in the saddle, Hezekiah and I on one horse, and Honovi bareback on the other.

No one said anything. It was as if we were focused on fleeing, which truth be known, we were. I hoped I would never see Mercy again, but feared Hezekiah might get a knock on his door with a warrant for my arrest, after having been wrongfully, but willfully accused as a witch by my new best friend. I pressed my face into his back, unable to control the violent quivers rippling through my body.

We slowed down to a gentle gait when we neared the place we had last seen Elan and the other members of Honovi's tribe. Suddenly we heard a loud "Whoop!" and they rushed out of the woods and surrounded us. Honovi swung off the horse and stepped over to me. He lifted up his eyes to mine and offered me his hand. I felt Hezekiah stiffen in front of me. I looked around at the Indians. There were quite a few, but they did not have their bows raised. I allowed Honovi to help me down.

He took me aside and said in his broken English, "Come me."

Looking into his brown eyes, which were full of longing, I took his hand. "Honovi, I—" My voice broke, my eyes welled up with tears, and I looked back at Hezekiah.

Honovi brought his rough thumb to my face and wiped the tears trickling down. I pulled away. He gestured to Hezekiah with questioning eyes. I swallowed and gave a quick nod. Honovi wrapped his arms around my shoulders and held me for a long time. "Nashota," he whispered, then released his hold and led me back to Hezekiah.

Elan took my horse's reins and handed them to Hezekiah, then turned toward the woods with the others. Before I could say another word, Honovi leaped up the embankment at the edge of the forest. He looked back and gave a small nod, then disappeared into the dense trees.

Hezekiah turned the horses around and headed back toward Salem Village. My heart went to my throat. I tapped him on the shoulder. "Why are we going back?" I had hoped to be as far away from Mercy as possible.

He slowed the horse to a trot. "Elizabeth, it will take us all night to get home. We haven't eaten and we need sleep, not to mention the horses need to rest too."

He was right, of course. We could get up before sunrise and leave then. "All right." I was not used to a trip to Boston taking so long, when in my other life it took half an hour.

By the time we arrived in Salem Village, I was napping against Hezekiah's back. He hadn't suggested riding the other horse bareback, and although I could have, I preferred having my arms around Hezekiah.

He slipped out of the saddle and reached up to help me down. I was starting to like this chivalry thing. After tethering the horses in Zebulon's barn, we knocked on his door. He was there to greet us.

"Expected you'd be back." A stout woman stood beside him. He put his arm around her waist and announced, "This is my wife, Sarah."

Hezekiah grinned. "Welcome to the family, Sarah." She nodded shyly. "Congratulations, Zeb."

Hezekiah ushered me into the house and closed the door. He pulled me around and looked into my eyes. "Did you see them?"

The eeriness in his voice frightened me. "No."

"On either side of us, coming into town—Mercy and her girls, standing at the edge of the woods watching us."

I shivered even though the room was toasty warm. Hezekiah stepped over to Zebulon and Sarah and said a few words I couldn't make out. She went into the next room and came back with a pillow and blanket, then set them on a bed in the corner by the front window.

"You may sleep here, Elizabeth."

Hezekiah took my hand in his. "I will stay at the tavern on Beverly Street, but I will be back early in the morning."

I smiled in understanding. Sleeping under the same roof with him here in Salem Town would turn a lot of heads.

Sarah's hands flew to her face and she let out a short scream. She pointed at the window with a shaky finger. "There, right there. Did you see that?"

I gulped. For a brief second I had seen Mercy's head, wild eyes staring into the window, but she had disappeared like a flash.

"What is it, Sarah?" Zebulon rushed to her side.

"Did you not see it?" Sarah's body quivered with fright.

"See what?" Hezekiah ran to the window and looked out. "There's no one there."

Zebulon grabbed his musket. "Come on, Hezekiah." In a short while, they returned. "There's no one out there, Sarah."

"We searched everywhere," Hezekiah confirmed.

I mustered the courage to speak up. "She was there. I saw her."

"Who?"

"Mercy," Sarah and I said in unison. Sarah's frightened eyes darted from her husband's to Hezekiah's.

Zebulon pulled the front door open and stepped out on the porch. "I suppose she could have climbed up on that old rain barrel." He scratched his head. "That girl is going to be the death of us all."

"Don't say that!" I gasped.

"I'm sorry," Zebulon replied carefully. "But she's a strange one, for sure.

I stood on the front porch and watched as Hezekiah rode away. "He is a nice man, isn't he?" Sarah said.

"Yes." I didn't take my eyes from him until he was gone. I faced her. "Thank you for letting me stay here tonight."

"You're very welcome." Sarah's smile faded as she surveyed the walkway from her house to the next building several yards down the road from her barn. "What do you suppose she's up to?"

"Mercy? It's hard to tell," I said. It was a lie, of course.

"Well, I'm off to bed now." Sarah stepped to the front door. "Good night."

"Good night." I sat down on a bench on the porch. It was just a matter of weeks until everyone would see exactly what Mercy Lewis was up to. I shuddered. Morning, and the return of Hezekiah, couldn't come quickly enough.

A pebble skidded across the porch. I jumped from the bench and followed the direction it had come. Mercy peeked around the side of the barn and waved for me to come over. I swallowed hard and waved back. *Don't go.* I started back toward the front door, but a force stronger than curiosity stopped me. Perhaps I could get the girls to stop their nonsense. Maybe, just maybe I could change the course of history.

I turned and approached Mercy. "It's kind of late to be outside, isn't it?" I asked her.

She gave me a strange look. "You speak so oddly at times, Elizabeth. It's almost like you're not from around here." She looped her arm around mine and led me toward the woods.

"Well, I'm not." I gulped. Going with her into the trees went against every instinct I had.

"Oh? Where are you from?"

"Across the ocean."

"Oh. Where across the ocean?"

My mind raced. Martha was from Ireland, but her sister lived in England, yet I had neither accent. I didn't think Mercy had received much education, so maybe I could get away with it. "Amsterdam," I said. "Across the water from London."

"Oh." She continued leading me briskly toward the thick forest.

"Where are we going?" I asked, though of course I had some idea.

"Come on. I'll show you." The flame from Mercy's small candle dimly illuminated the way, and too soon, we had reached the end of the meadow.

Don't go into the woods! I resisted Mercy's strong tug, but it was too late. Mercy and I stood at the edge of the trees, and there was no turning back.

Twelve

The Circle Girls

We stepped into the dark forest and could barely see the path from the faint candlelight. "This is scary!" I said truthfully.

"Yes, I know." Mercy's nervous giggle sent chills up my spine. "You will love it!"

I doubted that. We walked in silence for a while before she stopped. A small light in the distance grew larger, and then another light appeared. Soon, we were surrounded by several girls, each carrying a lantern or a candle on a plate. I recognized Abby Williams, one of the two girls in Reverend Parris's house who had caused such a spectacle a few months ago. She looked terrified—what was an eleven year old girl doing in the woods after dark? What were any of them, for that matter? My heart pounded in my chest, *knowing exactly why they were there.*

Mercy stoked a small fire in the center of the circle and then gave quick introductions. The girls seemed surprised and pleased that I had joined their group—all except for Betty Hubbard. She didn't smile like the others when Mercy introduced everyone to me.

We sat together in a ring around the fire, some girls on a fallen tree, a few on rocks, and some cross-legged on the ground. I sat on a tree stump and listened to them chat about their day. It would have seemed so normal if it hadn't been close to midnight, in the dark woods, with just the campfire and candles for light—and if Betty hadn't been glaring at me from across the circle.

I couldn't help but stare at the girls one at a time. Mercy sat beside me. Abby Williams pressed close to her. Sitting on the fallen tree on either side of Betty Hubbard were Mary Warren and Mary Wolcott. Both Marys looked like they'd rather be anywhere else, but especially Mary Warren. She fidgeted and kept looking toward the town, even though it could not be seen through the thick trees. Ann Putnam Jr. sat alone on a rock. She appeared to be deep in thought and every once in a while wrapped her arms around herself as if she was cold, though it was nice out.

According to history, which I recognized could not be completely accurate, Ann was the only one who would formally express sorrow for her part in the Salem witch hunt. I'd chosen her letter of apology, written fourteen years after the hangings, as my speaking competition speech just last year—very eloquent words for one who had helped murder so many:

> *I justly fear I have been instrumental, with others, though ignorantly and unwittingly, to bring upon myself and this land the guilt of innocent blood; though, what was said or done by me against any person, I can truly and uprightly say, before God and man, I did it not out of any anger, malice, or ill will to any person, for I had no such*

*thing against one of them; but what I did
was ignorantly, being deluded by Satan.*

The last two girls, Elizabeth Booth and Susannah Sheldon, huddled together on a fallen tree, chatting as if they didn't have a care in the world.

Mercy stood. An eerie silence fell over the girls. "We the Sisterhood of the Circle girls have gathered here together as instructed by Tituba."

She had everyone's attention, including mine.

"We have been chosen by God to weed the tares from the wheat—to rid our villages of the evil that has befallen us. So, my dear sisters, are there any new offenders?" The girls' eyes widened, but they remained silent, until Betty Hubbard stood. She stepped to the center of the circle close to the fire and then swung her pointed finger around to me. My heart gripped with fear.

"She! She is a witch!" Betty yelled in a high-pitched voice.

All of the girls except Mercy screamed and moved away from me. My mind raced. *Am I going to be their next victim? Not if I can help it.* I jumped up and pointed my finger at Betty. "She! She is a witch!" I did not lower my hand and neither did she.

The girls gasped and looked at Betty with new fear. Although no one had thought to accuse her, they seemed agreeable to it. All at once, her hand shook, and she lowered it, a nervous laugh escaping her throat. She smiled at me as if it had all been a joke. I held my hand up a few seconds longer and glared at her, but then dropped it. I didn't want to accuse anyone of being a witch. I feigned a laugh as Betty threw her arms around me. The girls relaxed, though Mercy looked puzzled, almost disappointed.

Betty pulled me down beside her. I guess we were best friends now too. I cringed inside. Back in Danvers High School, my best friend Chelle and I never had this much drama. My mind turned to Trent—I missed him like crazy. I wondered what he was doing. Of course, in my new world, he hadn't been born yet. I smiled weakly at Betty, who was rambling on about something.

"What's the matter, Elizabeth?" Betty said suddenly.

Drama class kicked in again. "It's Hezekiah." I replied, pretending to be upset.

Her eyes went wide. "Oh? What's wrong with him?"

I grinned. "Oh, nothing. He's perfect."

She nodded.

"It's just, well, how can I keep seeing him now that you and I are such good friends?" I emphasized the word "good."

"That's true," she said, looking off to the side.

I had hoped she'd say something like "Oh, that's all right—you can have him now." I'd have to try something else. My hands flew to my face. "But, oh, Betty, I must see him!"

Looking shocked and a bit angry, she asked, "Why?"

My mind stumbled. "Well, uh . . . I'm teaching his little sister to play the harpsichord." It was a lie, of course—Isabella didn't need my help.

Betty gasped. "You know how to play the harpsichord?"

I nodded.

"Oh! You must teach me! My uncle, Dr. Griggs, just had one brought over from England for my aunt Rachel."

"Yes, I'd love to teach you a thing or two." I suppressed a smirk. "As soon as things are settled, I'll give you a call—er, I mean, I'll come over to see you."

She gave me a weird look. "All right, but don't wait too long."

We were interrupted by Mercy, who again stepped to the center of the circle, the flickering flames casting a ghostly look on her face. "Are there any new offenders?"

Mary Warren jumped up. "Do we have to keep doing this?" She put her hands on her stomach as if she felt sick. "The jails are full from our accusations."

Betty Hubbard stood and moved quickly to the center of the circle with Mercy. "Of course we do. We're not making anything up—there are witches in our midst!"

"Don't you want these horrible fits to stop?" Mercy glared at Mary, who sat back down. "This is the only way we can end them—we must rid our village of the evil!" The girls nodded.

What I saw made me nauseous. Didn't they know that the people they accused had lives—hopes, dreams, and families? *Argh!* I gripped the folds of my dress, squeezing my fists tight and trying to force the surfacing scream deeper into my gut.

Suddenly, an overwhelming sensation settled over me as if a weight had been placed upon my shoulders, pressing

Theresa Sneed

me down and preventing me from jumping up. Meda's words came to me in the sudden breeze—*Keep your tongue silent, Onida.*

Still I wanted to yell at these foolish girls. My grandmother had been dragged from her home and examined twice under cruel and inhumane conditions. One of her neighbors blamed his lack of success on my grandmother, who had "cursed" his cattle twenty years earlier. Another neighbor accused my grandmother of flying to Newbury on a broomstick. I grunted in disgust and wondered if it was already too late to reason with these girls.

"What?" Betty Hubbard looked my way. "Why did you make that sound, Elizabeth?"

"Why indeed." I tilted my head sharply—a mistake on many levels as Betty's eyes darkened and the old tension returned with a fury. I stood. "Of course we want these fits to stop." Betty drew her head back and gave a quick nod.

Mercy looked my way. "Are you having them too?"

"Well, yes," I said, knowing I might not be welcomed into their secret society if I didn't understand their dilemma.

"Oh? Tell us, Elizabeth! Tell us everything!"

The circle of girls moved in closer, and I suppressed a shudder. "I, um . . ." Remembering the words of Mark Twain, I said, "Truth is stranger than fiction." The girls nodded vehemently, so I continued Twain's words, "But that is because fiction is obliged to stick to possibilities. Truth isn't." I sighed. The girls looked at me with

154

curiosity. "Where I'm from," I began slowly, "things are not so different from here."

"How so?" Abigail asked.

I looked from girl to girl. "I had a group of friends like you." I searched for just the right words. "We tried things we shouldn't have."

Betty's lips pressed together. "Such as?"

I swallowed. "The very thing you accuse others of."

Mercy gasped. "Witchcraft?"

"No! Not witchcraft, but what you're doing right now." They gave each other uneasy looks.

"Your friends had fits?"

"Yes."

Mercy's trembling hands came to her face. "Witches caused their fits!"

I shook my head. "No."

From the look in Betty's eyes, I knew I had gone too far, but I couldn't turn back now. "The fits were caused by the girls' themselves."

Betty folded her arms across her chest. "Are you suggesting that we are causing our own fits—or maybe that we are not being truthful?" She glared at me, and for the first time I saw something fiendish lurking behind her eyes.

"I don't think you're lying," I said softly. That seemed to appease most of them, but not Betty, who looked as though she would hang me herself if she could. "The fits my friends had were real, but they were not caused by witches."

Ann huffed. "What then? What could cause something so horrible, if not witches?"

"We played games," I said with a real quiver in my voice. I heard a few gasps and knew from history that the circle girls practiced many games, things they had felt were harmless. In reality, they were calling on powers they should have left well enough alone. My friends and I had done that too, tapping into a power we did not understand.

Mercy grabbed my hand. "Will you teach us? Tituba used to—"

"Don't say her name!" Betty clenched her fists to her sides, but it was too late. Blue flames shot up from the campfire, followed by a cloud of black smoke and an acrid odor. The girls screamed and jumped up, huddling behind me, of all people. "Sit down!" Betty yelled. She pointed to the ground around the fire.

Abby sobbed, burying her head in her hands. I had to admit the whole thing was frightening. I had to be sure, so I asked, "Tituba used to what?" I had barely gotten her name out of my mouth when the flames shot up once more. The girls screamed again, but this time, I saw her do it. Betty had tossed something into the fire. I grabbed her hand and pried it open. To my dismay it was empty, except for a gritty black residue that was hard to make out in the dark. I rubbed my fingers over it and brought it to my nose—sulfur.

She snapped her hand away and stepped back. Her eyes flashed and her nostrils flared. I leaned in to her and whispered, "Be quiet or I will tell them how you made the fire jump high." She pressed her lips tight together.

Susannah Sheldon sucked in a sharp breath. She rose up and then fell to the earth, writhing and twisting and moaning. She held her hands to her gurgling throat.

"She choking!"

Betty rushed to her side. "Who—who is doing this to you?"

I grabbed Betty and pulled her back. "This is a medical seizure! Make sure there is nothing she can get hurt on." I quickly moved a few small logs out of the way of Susannah's thrashing arms and legs.

"What do you think you are doing?" Betty yelled at me. "She is possessed of the devil! Can you not see that?"

I shook my head. "How can you be sure, Betty?" She looked at me like I was crazy for not seeing the evidence right in front of me. "When her head twists around and she starts spewing out green bile, then I'll give the devil his due, but this looks like a common seizure from where I come from." Susannah stopped thrashing and lay still, moaning softly. "There, it's over." I rubbed her back and helped her to sit up and then stand. "Come on, let's put this fire out and get her home."

Mary took her by the arm and helped her sit on a rock, while the other girls threw sand onto the dying fire.

"Do you really think this is nothing?" Betty said.

I could feel her eyes on me. "Yes, I do. But not what you and Mercy and I saw at Reverend Parris's house." Betty relaxed, like she was pleased I supported her, but I wasn't saying it for that reason. I'd read a theory about how grain grown in wet marshlands could cause something called ergot poisoning, which led to seizures. But not even that could explain what we saw while hiding under the reverend's window.

No one spoke as we made our way out of the woods. A chill went down my back, as from Zebulon's porch, I watched the girls break into smaller groups and head toward their homes. I went into the house and collapsed on the bed, terror coursing through my body. *Calm down, Bess—it's over*, I told myself. Yet I knew it wasn't. I closed my eyes tight, grateful to have made it through a long and strange night with the Sisterhood of the Circle Girls.

Thirteen

Strange Happenings

I lay awake for a while, trying to put together the pieces.
If Susannah's fit was caused by ergot poisoning, most of
the villagers would be affected, not just a few—and their
"conditions" wouldn't come and go at leisure, but would
be constant until healed. I hoped to see her again so I could
ask if this was her first fit. Maybe she had epilepsy, like a
friend of mine at school. Outside, the wind howled and
whined. The long branches of the trees scraped up against
the house, and the noise kept me from falling asleep. I
pulled the blankets up over my head, trying to drown out
the annoying sound.

I'm not sure if I got any rest, but I was totally relieved
to see the dawn's muted rays on the horizon. I didn't get
up though, until I heard Zebulon and Sarah come into the
kitchen.

"Good morning to you, Elizabeth," Sarah said with a
pleasant smile.

"Good morning." I sat up and stretched, then ran my
fingers through my disheveled hair. The lack of mirrors in
the late seventeenth century was both a curse and a
blessing. I smoothed my hair and then braided it to the
side. Sarah handed me a thin strip of leather, which I
thanked her for and tied around the bottom of my braid.

She burned the cornmeal grits—our breakfast.
"Sorry," she said with a grimace. I waved it off and held

my dish out. The food was as bland as it was burnt, but I vowed not to let her know.

Halfway through our meal, Hezekiah arrived. He came over and kissed me—on the forehead. *Nice.* I waited for his lips to find mine, but when they didn't, I opened my eyes to find him looking at Zebulon in concern.

"There has been a new accusation," Hezekiah reported. "Betty Hubbard says she was attacked by the specter of Goodwife Rebecca Jacobs, the daughter-in-law of old George Jacobs Sr."

Sarah's eyes widened and her hands flew to her mouth. "Oh my! Rebecca has been unwell in her mind for years— especially since her poor child drowned. How can she be accused of anything in her fragile state of mind?"

I wavered and fell back against the chair. I had just been with Betty last night—the wicked creature! Though I was concerned for Rebecca's delicate sanity, I knew she would not be hanged. Her father-in-law would not be so lucky. My mouth went dry. Using ghosts as evidence was ridiculous, yet that was all the proof needed to convict and hang in that bizarre court. In a little over a month, Bridget Bishop, accused as a witch by Betty, Abby, Mercy, and Mary, would be the first person hanged. I had to try to help. I jumped up. "Isn't there anything we can do?"

Hezekiah placed his hand on my arm. "You cannot bring any more attention to yourself." I bit my lip and rose from the table, asking to be excused. I moved to the door but continued to listen to their conversation.

"Reverend Parris sent little Betty off to live with his cousin until this passes."

Sarah grunted. "It's about time he stepped in to help that confused child."

Needing some air, I swung the door open and stepped outside into the cool morning. I walked in short, quick strides, intending to turn around and walk back as soon as my mind cleared. *Maybe saving Bridget will break the cycle.*

"How dare you call us liars!" a shrill voice yelled, startling me.

I spun around. "Betty! You scared me!" I took a step back. "I did not call anyone a liar, Betty."

She grabbed my arm and squeezed hard. "You will pay for this."

"Ouch! That hurts!" My mouth fell open. I grabbed her arm and squeezed back. "I did not call you a liar, Betty, but you are one and you know it. If you so much as breathe my name, I will expose you for the liar you are."

Her face went white. Releasing her grip, she fell back and muttered, "You are wicked!" Then she turned and ran down the street.

Prickles of fear swept up my back. I had not kept my tongue. Without a doubt, I was at the top of Betty Hubbard's hit list.

"Elizabeth!" Hezekiah called from down the street. I turned and saw him rushing toward me. "Are you all right?" He grabbed my shaking hands. "Elizabeth, what is wrong?" He pulled me into his strong embrace and held me tight. Then he led me back to his cousin's house, where I told them about the night before, and my unfortunate meeting with Betty just moments ago.

Hezekiah circled the room. "We must leave earlier than I planned. I'll take you to England or any place you want as long as it is far from here." Sarah, who had been listening, hurried to the cupboard.

I'd always wanted to go to England, and to be with Hezekiah was tempting, but if I left right now, Bridget, my grandmother, and the rest of the accused would die.

Hezekiah reached for my hand. "Come, Elizabeth."

I followed him out the door and to the stables. Sarah ran after us with a small package wrapped in cloth. "Bread and cheese for your trip," she said softly.

"Thank you, Sarah." Hezekiah placed his hand on her shoulder. "Please let Zebulon know of our departure."

"Of course."

The warm sun beat against my back. Beads of sweat gathered at my brow and trickled down my forehead. Sweltering in my long dress, I longed for the shorts and tank tops of my other life. After a while, the sky clouded over and a low rumble sounded in the distance. I rode sidesaddle beside Hezekiah. An hour outside of Salem Village, we came upon two men arguing with each other. The veins bulged on the younger man's neck. He took a swing, but the older man skipped back before it made contact.

"Whoa!" Hezekiah dismounted and stepped between them. "What's this all about, John?" He directed his question to the older man.

"Truth!"

The younger man jumped forward ready to swing again, but Hezekiah blocked him with an outstretched hand. "Hold on, Samuel."

Samuel balled up a fist and shook it at John. "That cow was fine when we had her!"

John spit on the ground. "Wasn't cursed then." He wiped at the sweat rolling down the sides of his face. "She broke all the ropes fastened to her, and we could scarce get her along. We tied her halter two or three times round a tree, but she broke that too, and when she came down to the ferry, we had to follow her into the deep water." He held his hand to his waist. "And the water was this high!" He made a face. "We had all we could do to get her into the boat."

Samuel pushed past Hezekiah's hand and glared at John. "And for that, you accuse my mother of being a witch?" His nostrils flared.

"Truth is truth, Samuel Martin. Your ma bewitched my cow."

I gasped and fell back in the saddle. I knew this story. John Atkinson accused my grandmother of cursing his cow. I stared at Samuel Martin—wow, oh wow! He was my eighth-great-uncle!

Samuel lunged at John and caught Hezekiah in the jaw instead. He stumbled back, shaken. "Sorry, Hezekiah," Samuel said.

Hezekiah rubbed at his jaw. "Get on home, Samuel, and you too, John."

"Home? And just what do you think that's like with my mother being arrested—taken right out of her home because of vile people the likes of him?" Samuel mounted his horse. "My mother may be a lot of things, but she's no more a witch than that girl." He pointed to me.

I nodded in agreement but didn't like the look John gave me. John grumbled. "Well, what about the Allen's oxen that ran right into the sea and drowned after your mother cursed them? She said the oxen should never do them much more service."

Samuel pulled his horse around to face John. "They were sickly, were they not? My mother saw that they weren't good for anything, and they weren't."

I had read about that too. Susannah had asked for help getting some fence posts back to the farm, but the Allen's oxen were in bad shape—overworked and undernourished—and he refused her.

"Don't be twisting the truth here, lad." John made a fist at his side. "Your mother cursed them oxen just like she cursed my cow."

Samuel jumped down from his horse and was on John before Hezekiah could stop him. "Truth?" he bellowed and pushed his fingers into John's chest. "Let's talk about truth. You threatened to drown my ma in the brook. She barely got away from you."

"She flew over the bridge, now didn't she?" John snarled. Hezekiah grabbed him by the collar and pulled him away.

"She jumped over the bridge into a brook, trying to escape you." Samuel waved his hands in the air. "You should be on trial for a real threat against my ma, instead of her being on trial for a supposed curse. But you just don't get that, do you."

Go, Uncle! I wanted to cheer, but covered my mouth instead.

John stroked his beard. "You saying I'm stupid, lad?"

Samuel smirked.

"Why, I'll—" John lunged at him.

"Leave him alone!" *Oops, did that come out of my mouth?* They both turned and stared at me, giving Hezekiah enough time to step between them and push them away from each other.

Samuel cocked his head to the side. "Do I know you?"

"Um, no."

"You look familiar. Have we met before?"

"Hmm. Can't say that we have."

Hezekiah broke in. "Get on your horse, both of you, and ride on out of here."

Samuel mounted his horse but stared at me for several seconds. "You look like my sister, when she was younger."

I smiled. There was a reason I looked like her—DNA, something that wouldn't be discovered until around 1869.

John grunted. "Don't know as I'd like to resemble that bunch."

Samuel glared at him. "My mother's an honest, hardworking Christian woman, John Atkinson— something you ought to respect."

Hezekiah pointed down the road and gave Samuel's horse a firm whack on the rump. "Off with you."

John turned his horse in the opposite direction. "Be careful whose side you're on." He scowled, pulled the reins up, and galloped away.

"That was weird," I mumbled.

"Yes." Hezekiah nodded. He mounted his horse then pulled up beside mine. "You want to explain that to me?"

"What?"

"'Leave him alone?'"

"Oh, that."

Hezekiah stared at me until I couldn't take it any longer. "You know the born in the future thingy?" I said.

He grimaced.

"Well, if you're born in the future, uh, you must come from someone in the past." I pointed in the direction Samuel had gone.

Hezekiah's mouth dropped open. "What . . . him . . . Samuel?" he stammered. "Does that mean he's your grandfather?"

"No." I shook my head. "Not a grandfather, but an uncle."

"Oh my. Isn't that something."

"Well, there's more." This would be the hard part, but I knew I had to tell him.

Hezekiah pulled his horse close to mine. "What is it, Elizabeth?"

"I don't know how to tell you this, but Salem Village is well known in 2015."

"Really?" He looked surprised and a little pleased.

I licked my lips. "Not for anything good, Hezekiah."

"Oh?"

"Not just Salem Village, but 1692 Salem Village."

His eyes narrowed. "You mean right now?"

"Yes." I lowered my eyes. Some things are best left unsaid and forgotten, but the hangings hadn't even begun yet. They would soon, and there would be no escaping it, even though I was determined to change as much of it as I could.

He pulled his head back. "How has this year in Salem Village made history? And what does it have to do with you?"

Tears came fast, filling the rims of my eyes. "They're going to hang my grandmother, Hezekiah," I whispered.

His face went white, and he stiffened. "Goody Martin?"

I stifled a sob. "Yes, and many more before it ends."

Fourteen

The Witch Trial

"Who is the first to die?" Hezekiah's voice came out soft, like a whisper.

"Sarah Osborn, in a prison in Salem Town. But she wasn't hanged. She was ill when they arrested her, and she died—will die—on May 10th." I tried not to think about her lying sick in a dirty jail without the medical care she needed.

Hezekiah grimaced. "That's just eight days from now."

I gasped. "Wait, does that mean today is May 2nd?"

"Yes."

"Hurry, Hezekiah!" I turned my horse around and took off at a gallop.

"Stop! Where are you going?" I heard him yell.

"To Ingersoll's!"

"Hold on—why Ingersoll's?"

I pulled my horse to a stop. When Hezekiah caught up, I said, "They are holding my grandmother in the watch tower, er, jail, until they examine her at Ingersoll's." I slapped my forehead. "Oh no! What time is it?"

Hezekiah looked up at the sun. "Must be around noon."

I groaned. The questioning started at 10:00 am. "Hurry!" I took off again.

Hezekiah reined his galloping horse next to mine. "Slow down! Why would you want to see such a thing? You already know how it ends."

I shot him a hard look. "She's my grandmother! Maybe I can help her."

"No, Bess, you cannot."

Ignoring him, I rode hard until we reached the jail. Ingersoll's was just across the street. I pulled the reins up, stopping my horse short.

The door to the jail opened and two men escorted my frail, seventy-one-year-old grandmother across the street to Deacon Ingersoll's home, a local tavern that often served as a courthouse. My grandmother passed an old woman being led across the street from Ingersoll's. The woman let out a shrill laugh. "Goody Martin, you must confess, you old witch!"

"Dorcas Hoar, what do you know of it? I'm no more a witch than you are," my grandmother snapped.

Dorcas's expression turned sad. "Aye, but I have just confessed."

My grandmother drew her head back in surprise. "Why would you do such a thing?"

The other woman did not answer.

"Move along, Goody Hoar," said the man leading her across the street.

Hezekiah helped me off my horse but did not release me right away. "If I could restrain you, Bess, I would."

I'd expected half as much.

"At least pull your bonnet over your eyes. Betty Hubbard is probably in there."

He didn't have to ask twice. I tugged on my bonnet and then followed Hezekiah into Ingersoll's. We slipped into a row of wooden chairs in the back, far behind the accusers—the circle girls who sat together in the first row.

Three men behind a high bench faced us. I recognized Reverend Samuel Parris. He had a stack of paper in front of him and an inkwell to write down the words spoken during the inquisition. I had read his transcript of my grandmother's examination many times and knew it well.

I could hardly believe I was in the same room with the notorious John Hathorne—the only judge who never apologized for his part in the Salem travesty. His great-great-grandson, the author Nathaniel Hawthorne, was so disgusted with him that he changed the spelling of his last name to distance himself from his grandfather.

The other judge had to be Jonathan Corwin, whose house known as the Witch House, I had visited many times during school field trips. It was the only house left standing in Salem with direct ties to these trials.

Addressing the front row of girls, one of the men spoke. "Do you know this woman?" I knew it was Hathorne then, as he was the official inquisitor.

A hush fell over the crowd as Abby Williams stepped forward. "It is Goody Martin," she moaned, holding her sides and twisting her face in agony. "She hath hurt me often."

I bit down on my tongue to keep from shouting. My grandmother had not hurt anyone, but I knew Abby had previously claimed my grandmother had left her physical body and, as a specter, had harassed and hurt her. I shook my head. Still, it was hard not to have pity on Abby—she looked even worse now than when she had thrashed about on the bed at Reverend Parris's home. Her thin arms trembled, and her listless eyes sunk farther into her gaunt face.

Mercy jumped up, startling those sitting behind her. A haunting gurgle escaped her throat. Chairs scraped the floor as nervous spectators pushed away from her. Her hand flapped about in a wild jerking motion, until it went limp and fell in a straight line to my grandmother. All at once, Mercy collapsed to the floor like a lifeless rag doll. Along with several other people in the room, I jumped up to get a better look. Half expecting to see her head twist around, I was a little surprised to see her just writhing— any good actress could do that.

Everyone started talking at once, while the judges conferred with each other. Through the noise and confusion, Betty Hubbard called out, "I have not been hurt by her." Though I was familiar with her words in print, hearing them in person surprised me. The spectators quieted down as if wanting to hear what else she had to say, but she didn't add anything.

"I have never seen her," a man called out. I strained my neck to get a good look at John Indian. From reading the transcript, I knew he was one of Reverend Parris's slaves and Tituba's husband.

Judge Hathorne sat back and placed the tips of his fingers together, a sour look on his face. He surveyed the room. His eyes fell on mine, and I lowered my head, tugging the bonnet over my eyes.

A stirring in the front snapped my head back up. Ann Putnam Jr. rose on her seat and arched forward, as if hanging from an invisible cord. In one quick movement, she thrust her glove at my grandmother and slipped to the floor alongside Mercy, whose condition had not improved.

My grandmother gave her a scornful look and laughed.

"What do you laugh at?" Hathorne questioned.

"Well, I may at such folly."

"Is this folly? The hurt of these persons?"

"I never hurt man, woman, or child."

"She has hurt me a great many times and pulls me down!" Mercy cried out in agony.

My grandmother laughed again.

"This woman has hurt me a great many times," Mary Walcott added.

"She has afflicted me too!" Susannah Sheldon pointed at her with a shaky hand.

Judge Hathorne shook his head. "What do you say to this?"

My grandmother scowled. Her fingers balled into fists at her sides. "I have no hand in witchcraft."

The judge pursed his lips. "What did you do? Did you not give your consent?"

Her answer came quick. "No. Never in my life."

Hathorne smirked. "What ails this people?"

"I do not know."

"But, what do you think?"

My grandmother grimaced. "I do not desire to spend my judgment upon it."

"Do you think they are bewitched?"

"No." She shook her head. "I do not think they are." She glanced over at them with a shrewd eye.

Hathorne rubbed his chin with his finger and thumb. "Tell me your thoughts about them."

My grandmother seemed put out with that question. "Why, my thoughts are my own when I keep them to myself, but when I speak out, they are another's." She pointed to the girls. "Their master—"

Hathorne interrupted her. "You said, their master? Who do you think is their master?"

"If they be dealing in the black art, you may know as well as I."

The judge frowned, clearly not pleased with her sharp tongue. "Well, what have you done towards this?"

"Nothing. I desire to lead myself according to the word of God."

Hathorne spread his arms out over the girls. "Is this according to God's word?"

My grandmother gave the girls a look of contempt. "If I were such a person, I would tell the truth."

Hathorne's eyes narrowed. "How comes your appearance just now to hurt these?"

She shrugged. "How do I know?"

His voice rose. "Are not you willing to tell the truth?"

"He that appeared in Samuel's shape a glorified saint, can appear in anyone's shape," she snapped.

Her words pierced me to the bone as all at once, I got it. I fell back against Hezekiah. All of my life, I had wondered what the circle girls had experienced. Was it temporary insanity brought on by ergot poisoning? Had they seen the actual specters of those they accused as witches or had they lied to get attention? My grandmother,

Susannah North Martin, had had the answer all along. *He that appeared in Samuel's shape a glorified saint, can appear in anyone's shape.* Satan, the great deceiver, was responsible for the chaos happening here in 1692, because the people were naive enough to allow him to deceive them.

The circle girls were not lying. They weren't crazy, or deluded, or poisoned. They saw specters, all right—not specters of living, breathing people, but spirits that had followed Lucifer and been cast from heaven. Those spirits had simply taken the form of the accused. The answer had been there all along, in 1 Samuel 28 in the Bible—the very book Hathorne professed to live by. King Saul sought out the witch of En-dor to raise the prophet Samuel from the dead. It wasn't Samuel that appeared, but Lucifer in Samuel's form.

Hathorne's sharp voice pulled me back to the examination. He gestured to the girls. "Do you believe these do not say true?"

My grandmother twisted her lips. "They may lie, for aught I know."

"May not you lie?"

The deep creases on her face hardened. "I dare not tell a lie, even if it would save my life."

"Then you will speak the truth."

"I have spoken nothing else." Susannah gestured to the girls and shook her head. "I would do them good."

"I do not think you have such affections for them, whom just now you insinuated had the devil for their master."

Betty jumped up, holding her limp hand. "Ouch!" She turned to a man sitting beside her. "Goody Martin pinched my hand!"

A piercing scream ripped through the room. Mercy stumbled backward, her eyes wild with fright. "And there! On the beam! There she is!" She pointed to the ceiling. The girls shrieked and ran helter-skelter, pulling at their hair and falling into each other.

This was ridiculous! How could my grandmother be on the beam when she stood before them? I jumped up, but Hezekiah pulled me back down. He seemed to read my mind. "I know she is not one, Elizabeth, but they say that a witch can leave her body."

I leaned into his ear. "Yes. I already know that, but if she left her body, wouldn't it go limp?"

He tilted his head away from me. "I would think so."

Hathorne slapped the desk with his hand. "Pray God discover you, if you be guilty."

"Amen!" Susannah gave him a defiant look. "Amen!" she repeated. "A false tongue" —she glanced at the girls— "will never make a guilty person."

Mercy jumped up, her eyes still crazed. "You have been a long time coming to court today," she snarled. "You can come fast enough in the night!" She lowered her eyes, like a mischievous child trying to punish a parent for not giving her what she wanted.

My grandmother shook her head and then sighed long. "No, sweetheart," she said softly.

Mercy flung herself to the floor. Mary screamed and tried to brush something invisible off her arms. Ann collapsed to the floor alongside Mercy, and Abby joined them. They writhed in a frantic frenzy of twisted arms and legs.

I jumped up along with Hezekiah and pushed past the others toward the front of the room.

John Indian fell into a violent fit. I had never seen anything like it—not even Betty Parris's and Abby's fits could compare. I fell back into Hezekiah's arms and he pulled my trembling body aside. I leaned into him and looked up at my grandmother. She wrung her hands and bit at her lips, looking afraid, but who wouldn't be? This was no game.

"It is that woman!" John pointed to my grandmother. "She bites! She bites!" he screamed.

"Have you not compassion for these afflicted?" Judge Hathorne bellowed.

My grandmother was undone, but quickly regained her composure. "No. I have none."

I understood her apathy for what it was—disgust at what the girls were doing, but I knew I was in the minority.

"Ahh! She has a black man with her!" The girls in the front row jumped back as if transfixed on this invisible being.

"Yes! I see him!" cried a woman in the room.

This is insane! It was a good thing Hezekiah held me tight. Otherwise, I was not sure I could have kept my self-control, let alone my tongue. He moved me toward the door, but I resisted.

Hathorne banged his fist on the desk. "I order this court to have a touch test!"

My eyes widened. "Incredible." I jerked my head around to Hezekiah. I wanted to scream. "Hypocrites!" Oops, did I say that out loud? Two or three people near us whirled around and looked at me. *Tongue, girl, remember your tongue.* I tugged on Hezekiah to bend down and whispered in his ear, "A touch test is witchcraft—they are going to use witchcraft to uncover witchcraft!"

"Bring them forward." Hathorne waved his hand in the air, gesturing for the guard to escort Abby, Mary, and the woman who called out to my grandmother. "Touch Goody Martin and send her wicked spell right back on her!" They drew near, but the closer they came to my elderly grandmother, the more painful it appeared for them—none of them could get close to her.

"I will kill her!" John said in a rage. He rushed toward my grandmother, but before the guard could stop him, he was flung to the floor by an invisible force.

I muttered under my breath just loud enough for Hezekiah to hear. "Excuse me, but didn't they see John Indian just try to kill my grandmother? And they're not trying him in court for that?"

Judge Hathorne's interrogation continued. "What is the reason these cannot come near you?"

My grandmother shrugged. "I cannot tell." She threw her aged arms into the air. "Maybe the devil bears me more malice than another."

Hathorne leaned forward and repeated, "What is the reason these cannot come near you?"

"I do not know, but they can if they will, or else if you please, I will come to them."

Hathorne paused. He studied her. "What is the black man whispering to you?"

She gave him an incredulous look and held her hands out in front of her. "There is no one whispering to me."

Hathorne's eyes narrowed. "Do you not see how God evidently discovers you?"

Her shoulders fell. She let out an exasperated breath. "No. Not a bit."

Hathorne looked out over the crowd. "All the congregation think so."

My grandmother drew her shoulders back and jutted her chin out. "Let them think what they will."

Hezekiah pulled me through the door. "Hurry, Elizabeth."

"Wait, I want to see more, maybe I can do something."

"No, Elizabeth." He held me by my elbow and led me to my horse. "You didn't see, did you?"

"See what?"

"Betty pointed at you just as we left."

Fifteen

Consequences

We rode hard for the first hour. There would be no stopping in Salem Town to help Sarah Osborn now. I shook my head—would I be able to help anyone? After a while, we slowed down, hopeful no one was following us. At first, I did not want to answer Hezekiah's questions about what I knew, but then I decided having another person know the future would be beneficial to my sanity. At least now Hezekiah would understand my moments of despair and anguish, and most of all, help me prevent some of it. There was still time. "Will you help me?"

"I can't, Bess."

I drew the reins back on my horse. "We can stop it. I know we can. We could start with educating the citizens of Salem Village."

"And just what would you tell them? The future? If you did, you'd take Bridget Bishop's place as the first woman hanged in 1692. Or maybe you'd try to preach to them the philosophies of 2015 you told me about earlier." Hezekiah made a face.

I rolled my eyes. I hated it when he was right. "But surely, we can try to save some of them?"

"No, Bess."

"Fine. Don't help me." I pulled my horse ahead and took off at a gallop.

"Bess!" He caught up to me. "That was childish."

I already knew that but wasn't about to admit it. I slowed my horse to a trot. "I'm going to save as many as I can, whether you help me or not." I clamped my mouth shut and kept my eyes on the path ahead.

"Are you then willing to pay the consequences?"

"Consequences? Of saving a life?" I glared at him. "I can't believe how selfish you're being."

Hezekiah reached over, grabbed my reins, and brought my horse to a sudden stop. "You've only read about them in your history books, but I know many of the people that are about to be hanged." Anguish deepened the creases on his forehead.

"Then you agree that just one life is worth it?"

"Which one, Bess? Which life would you save?"

"Well, I—"

"You wouldn't be happy with saving one person, and you would die trying to save them all."

"You don't know that."

A few minutes passed before he spoke again. "What would you say to them? 'Hello, I'm Bess Martin, Goody Martin's ninth-great-granddaughter, from the future, and you're going to die just like her.'" Hezekiah grimaced and I wanted to smack him. "Do you think they will believe you, Bess?"

I huffed. "I wouldn't say it that way. I would say, 'Hi, uh, I'm . . . well . . . you, um . . .'" *Dang.*

He looked at me tenderly. "I know you want to change the future, but there's more to it than just the happy-ever-after ending."

Is he kidding? Happy endings are, well, happy.

Hezekiah shook his head. "If you alter history, you'll have to live with the changes it will make, including within your own family. Several generations will be born and die before your time. If you save one person now, families will be changed so that people you know—even some of your own ancestors— might never be born. Think about it, Bess. Your own family might not exist as you know it. Would you want to give up your brother, Seth? Or your mother and father?"

"What? Of course not." *How ridiculous.*

"Neither do any of the people you would affect by altering history. In many cases, someone would have to give up somebody they have already loved."

My heart plummeted as I realized I could do nothing but watch one of the most horrific pages of history unfold in front of me.

"I will take you away from here," Hezekiah said. "We'll go to London."

Neither of us spoke for several minutes. Bitterness weighed heavy on me, pressing me down into despair. On top of the travesty unfolding in Salem, there was no escaping something else. I was falling in love with Hezekiah—a man who had lived, died, and probably loved *someone else* 323 years before my time.

We rounded a corner and saw the lights of Boston below us but rode on in silence until we reached the mansion. Hezekiah treated me with great tenderness. I wondered if he had figured out as I had that our relationship could go no further. I couldn't alter his future any more than I could alter anyone else's. He, and whomever he chose over three hundred years before my time, had to be Trent's ancestors—that much was obvious and simply could not change. Trent was too important to me. What if my intrusion into 1692 would completely alter Trent's existence in the future? I shuddered at that thought.

Two stable boys met us in the barn and led our horses away. Hezekiah held his arm out and I wrapped mine around it. I loved being close to him. Breaking up with him would be the hardest thing I'd ever done, even harder than time-travel.

Hezekiah opened the door, ushered me inside the large estate, and escorted me to my room. When he tried to kiss me, I turned my face from him, then stepped into the room and closed the door. I leaned back against it and heard his voice on the other side. "Elizabeth?"

"Good night, Hezekiah."

After a few seconds, I heard him say good night and turn to descend the stairs. All at once, the door in the adjoining bedroom opened a crack and Aunt Martha stuck her head in.

"There ye are. I was hopin' ye would return soon an' safe." She came over to me and put her hands on my shoulders. "I was worried about ye, wane."

"I was worried too." I rested my head on her arm while she ran her fingers through my hair.

She dropped her hands to her sides and sighed heavily. "Come an' sit down. I have some bad news for ye." Her eyes filled with pity. "Hezekiah's mom and da' are back from Europe."

Oh. An hour or two ago that would have seemed bad. I sat on the bed. I wanted to meet them, but wasn't prepared for their anger and the questions they would ask when they learned about Hezekiah and me—especially how he had sent Draculette away. Yet what did it matter now? I would never be with him anyway. At least Arabella wouldn't either.

Still, I wondered if I hadn't already sealed Trent's fate. I shook my head. *No. Hezekiah would never have agreed to marry someone like her. He would've sent her back to England even if he'd never met me.*

I patted Martha's hand. "Well, I guess I'll be extra careful tomorrow—first impressions and all."

"Ah, me dear. That is not the bad news." She shook her head. "They brought that English lass back wi' them."

I jumped up. "Really? How?"

Martha pulled me back down. "They met at the docks an' began blatherin'. That's how they found out who she was an' where she was headin'. The wee squealer didn't even tell them Hezekiah had sent her away, but just pretended she was on her way ta Boston for the first time. The servants knew all about it, havin' heard her blatherin' ta herself like she was insane." Martha stood and walked toward the door. "Try an' get some sleep. We have an early start tomorrow."

I sighed. I couldn't go back to Salem Village that was for sure. Betty Hubbard would accuse me the next time she saw me. At least I felt a little safer in Boston, somewhat removed from the hysteria. But who was I kidding? They tracked the Reverend George Burroughs all the way to Maine, finally arrested him on August 2, and brought him back to Salem. Even though he recited the Lord's Prayer perfectly, something a witch was not supposed to be able to do, they hanged him a week later. I trembled and must have cried out, because Martha quickly opened her door again and came to my side.

"What's the matter, wane?"

My voice quivered. "I can't go back to Salem Village right now, Aunt Martha."

She tilted her head. "I was not goin' ta take ye back. Mrs. Fayette an' I shall fix ye up prettier than ye have ever been before. The servants really like ye, and none of them like that fierce quare English lass."

"Oh, all right." I tried to smile.

Aunt Martha kissed me on the forehead and left. I washed my face in the basin and got into my bedclothes. Almost as soon as I pulled the blankets up to my chin, my exhausted thoughts jumbled together, as they often do just before sleep takes hold. Tonight, they morphed into a dream where Hezekiah spoke angrily to a young man around his age who looked like Trent.

They were fighting over me.

Sixteen

Abner Gyles Hanson II

I woke up early and lay in bed thinking about that dream. Most women fantasize about having more than one man after her, but not me. I hadn't realized until that moment just how important Trent was to me. Still, truth be known, I had fallen in love with his grandfather. Life was so unfair—to not be able to love Hezekiah in the way I wanted to, was cruel indeed.

I wondered if I should end it now and give him time to decide about Draculette on his own. It seemed like a good idea. There was a knock on my door. Mrs. Fayette stepped in carrying a light-blue shimmery frock and dainty slippers. Martha followed, her arms stacked with towels and what looked like underthings. A long line of servants came in after them, each with a bucket of hot water. It was bath time. I sighed. It was fun to be pampered, but my heart was breaking with what I needed to do.

After bathing and dressing, I sat on the chair staring into the mirror while Mrs. Fayette arranged my hair. I smoothed the frock down with trembling hands.

Martha leaned over to say, "There, there, me dear, don't fret so. Mr. an' Mrs. Hanson will love ye." She handed Mrs. Fayette a blue hairpin in the shape of a forget-me-not.

How appropriate. I would never forget Hezekiah. The plan brewing in my mind was to go to England without him. I was highly educated for the time, so I could probably find a governess position. I loved *Jane Eyre*. I could live like that, except without my Rochester. I would work hard the rest of my life and not get romantically involved with anybody. I sighed. It was now my sad lot in life to live and die the life of a spinster at the young age of seventeen.

Mrs. Fayette gestured toward the door. "It's time for breakfast."

Showtime. But where was Hezekiah? He had always escorted me. I shook it off, thinking maybe it was the natural course of things. Martha opened the door and to my surprise, there stood a young man whose features resembled Hezekiah's. His eyes lit up when he saw me.

"Good morning, Lady Elizabeth." He offered his arm. "I am to take you down to breakfast. My brother, Hezekiah, is otherwise indisposed."

I rested my hand on his arm, thinking I could guess whom Hezekiah was "otherwise indisposed" with. "And who might you be?" I asked politely.

"Pardon me," the young man said with a slight bow. "I am Abner Gyles Hanson II, Hezekiah's eldest brother."

"Abner. That's a nice name." He couldn't be much older than Hezekiah.

"Thank you. It's not a name I would have chosen. It's so old-fashioned."

I had to smirk at the irony.

"I go by my middle name."

"Gyles?"

"Yes," he said with a formal nod.

"May I ask where you have been?"

"Certainly. I've been abroad with my parents."

"Oh." That would explain why I hadn't seen him before. "Then you must know Arabella." I forced her real name off my tongue.

"Yes." He turned to me suddenly. "How do you know her?"

Oops. Not knowing what Hezekiah had revealed, I had better not mention that she'd been here before. "Oh, I don't know her. I've only heard about her."

"Well," he said as we began to descend the stairs, "Arabella is—how shall I describe her?" He let out a puff of air. "She's rather, hmm, annoying."

I couldn't help but laugh and covered my mouth quickly. Gyles squeezed my hand and grinned. I was really going to like him.

We turned the corner and entered the dining room. Gyles stopped and bowed. Having seen every possible BBC English drama, I gave my best curtsey—the one that dips low with formal dignity, as a servant introduced me.

"Lady Elizabeth Bowley."

"Lady Elizabeth, how nice of you to grace our home," said a woman who had to be Hezekiah's mother. "Mr. Hanson will join us shortly. He's had an unexpected visitor."

"Thank you," I said graciously.

Gyles led me to a chair next to Hezekiah. While I was grateful for that, I wondered what other scenarios Hezekiah had created for me. I decided it best to let him do most of the talking.

Everyone looked at me, particularly Draculette, appropriately dressed in a blood-red gown. She had the seat directly across from Hezekiah and glared my way, no doubt attributing her earlier dismissal to me.

I was taken aback by her beauty. Did I see any of Trent in her? Well, he, like his grandfather, had black hair, not her auburn hair, nor her dainty features. Though that gave me some hope, I still had to let things unfold naturally and not get in their way. Of course, the slight snarl on her upper lip was not helping my resolve.

Breakfast was served. I followed Hezekiah's lead and ate only when and what he did and used whichever utensil he used, delicately dabbing my mouth between bites as needed. I smiled, complimented where necessary, and did not initiate any conversation. Most of all, I held my tongue when Arabella berated the wretches jailed in Salem, though my eyes shot daggers her way when she wasn't looking. All would have gone well if she hadn't pushed things too far.

"Massachusetts Bay should be pleased to be rid of those horrible hags. They are the dregs of society."

I clenched my teeth and gripped the fabric of my gown under the table.

She raised her goblet. "The sooner they are hanged, the better."

Not even Meda's warning could hold me back. I slapped the table and stood. "Do you know how stupid you sound, Arabella?" She snapped her head back and her pretty red lips dropped open. At my side, Hezekiah coughed and covered his mouth with a napkin. I sat back down.

"Humph. They are witches, are they not?" she said.

Hezekiah tensed and nudged me firmly with his foot. I got the hint but kept going. "I personally do not believe that they are, Arabella, and I would think a Christian would need that assurance before condemning and wrongfully hanging someone."

She clicked her teeth. "A Christian would know immediately."

"How?" I demanded. Hezekiah nudged me harder. Arabella glared at me but said nothing.

Mr. Hanson returned to the room. "So, what did I miss?"

Gyles stood. "I will inform you, Papa. Arabella says the women should be hanged because they are all hags." He gestured to me. "Lady Elizabeth questions the authority to judge." He pointed back to Arabella. "And she has no answer for that."

"Fascinating," Mr. Hanson said. "I quite agree with you, Lady Elizabeth." He held his plate up and gestured for some vegetables.

"Thank you, sir," I said slowly. *Wow. Situation defused.* Hezekiah relaxed beside me, and Draculette let out an exasperated breath and pouted. With the way Mrs. Hanson glanced at her husband, I suspected a long discussion regarding their son's matrimonial future would happen the next time they were alone.

Mr. Hanson sat his plate down and picked up a fork. "It is a terrible travesty unfolding, the likes of which we left in England years ago."

"I hope it is not a repeat of the Glover case a few years back, Abner," Mrs. Hanson offered. "That poor Irish-Catholic woman understood very little English."

"Quite right, Victoria, but they examined her in English with no interpreter to explain their questions in her native tongue and hanged her anyway."

Abner studied Draculette and then Hezekiah. He laid his napkin on his lap. "Have you two set a date for your wedding?"

I nearly choked on my dessert. Evidently, Abner had not read Victoria the way I had.

"Abner," Victoria said softly, but it was too late. Arabella latched onto his question like a shark on a fresh piece of meat.

"Yes, Hezi and I will be married soon."

No. I clutched my dinner napkin tightly. *Stay out of it, girl.* I tapped my foot nervously—it was none of my business.

Hezekiah pressed his foot firmly next to mine. "No, Father, we have not picked a date yet." He pushed his foot in tighter and I got it. My little Hezi was not being honest with his dad, but for some reason, he did not want to rock the boat right now.

Arabella reached across the table for Hezekiah's hands, the fine lace on her sleeves carefully draped between the plates of food. "My Hezi, it will be soon, yes?" She drew her lips up in an overly pronounced pout.

Gag me with a spoon. I rolled my eyes and did the first thing that came to my mind. I reached for my goblet, knocking it over onto her lace, and then in my rush to catch it before all its contents spilled, overturned a plate of red beets onto her lap. *Darn. Don't you hate when that happens?* "Oh, I'm so sorry," I said. It was probably my best performance ever.

"Ah!" Draculette's sudden, exasperated breath and narrowed eyes told me she knew what I was up to. She jumped from the table holding her hands, especially the one with the dripping lace, over the table. A strand of unrepeatable words left her mouth before she turned and stormed out of the room.

Strangely, no one moved toward her to help—not even the four servants standing at the front of the room. I stole a glance at one—a petite, brown-eyed girl close to my age, and saw her give one of the other servants a quick grin. Her eyes popped open when she realized I had seen her do that. I did not want to bring attention to her, but made it my mission to speak to her later.

Victoria put her napkin on her plate. "Lady Elizabeth, I hope you do not feel bad about that."

Oh, not at all. "I feel horrible," I said politely. "I do hope I haven't ruined her dress." From the corner of my eye, I saw Gyles put a napkin to his grinning face.

"Not to worry, Elizabeth," Abner chimed in. "We purchased that for her, although she brought four large trunk loads of the finest dresses in London with her on the ship."

"Really, hmm." So, Arabella had money, and apparently lots of it. I looked at Abner. Was this why he was pushing Hezekiah into the marriage?

Abner turned to Hezekiah. "Do you have a rough idea when you intend to wed?"

"Yes." Hezckiah wet his lips. He glanced quickly my way. "November, I think."

"There, now that's better. Arabella's parents and grandparents will need to be contacted as soon as possible to plan for the voyage over here."

Hezekiah nodded. "Yes, but hold off until I actually ask my future bride, all right, Father?"

"Yes, yes, of course."

Bogus or not, I had heard enough. "If you will excuse me, I think I will get a bit of fresh air." I stood and gave a slight curtsey.

"May I escort you?" Hezekiah asked carefully.

"Yes, you may."

He looped his arm through mine and led me to the door. Once outside, I pulled my arm from his and walked beside him toward the extensive gardens. "What are you doing?" I asked without looking his way.

He put his hands on my shoulders and turned me to him. "I thought it best to continue this little ruse to keep the attention away from you."

"And marrying her would do that?" I said tersely, forgetting my resolve.

"I never said I planned to marry her, Elizabeth."

"Yes, you did."

A slow grin spread across Hezekiah's face. "No, I did not. I said to wait until I asked my future bride. I did not say she was Arabella."

I parted my lips to refute that, but his words came back to me and he was right. He never mentioned her at all. His green eyes held an intensity I'd not seen before. *Settle down, girl—you're only seventeen.* "Oh?" I tried to pull away from his stare, but found it impossible. Yeah, in 2015, a young love like ours would be frowned upon, but I was beginning to have a true appreciation for the merits of 1692. *Oh, wait—Trent.*

Hezekiah reached up and brushed his fingers across my lips and I knew this could be the best kiss I had ever had, but right then, Hezekiah's face took on Trent's expression and for a brief moment, Trent came to me. A warning? A plea? I had to end it. I pulled away and rushed into the gardens.

Good timing.

"Hezi? My Hezi?" Arabella's rich voice called out for him.

I stopped dead in my tracks and slipped between the hedges. "Elizabeth!" Hezekiah whispered loudly. He took another step closer to my hiding place.

"Ah! There you are, my Hezi!" Arabella descended on him with her talons open. "How clever to come here away from the rest where we can be alone." She stepped close to him. I waited for him to back away and was surprised when he did not. Running her fingers through his hair, she pressed the side of her face to his. "My Hezi, do not fight me so."

I held my breath. If he kissed her, it was over. *Oh, wait. It's already over. I ended it, right?* At that moment, I thought of every get-even, vengeful movie I had ever seen and almost stepped out and let her have a taste of a 2015 girl. One well-placed sucker punch to the face ought to do it. She'd never see it coming. I sighed. Even in my day I would never do that.

I waited.

Hezekiah brought his hands to her face. I froze. I'd seen that move before, but then he stepped back and dropped his hands to his sides. "I sent you away, Arabella."

"Yes, and why? Why did you do that, Hezi?"

"Why do you think? We hardly know each other."

"What is there to know? I am a woman and you are a man." She stepped forward and ran her fingers down his arm.

He placed his hand over hers and gently pulled her hand down. *Wow. What a gentleman—and I had wanted to punch her.*

"Arabella, let me get to know you first." He took another step back. "If you are to be my wife, I need to be sure we are a good match."

She made a face. "But we are a match—we both come from wealthy families. What else matters?"

He shook his head. "Is that what you want?"

"Of course. Isn't that what you want?"

He put his arm around her shoulder. "My Arabella."

I drew in a sharp breath. *His Arabella?*

"Have you never thought about love?"

"Love," she said with a faraway look. "Yes, of course."

Hezekiah dropped his hand. "I want you to promise me something."

I leaned forward in the hedge, nearly losing my balance. "Yes?"

"I do not want to commit to a marriage unless we fall in love."

"Hezi, do you not think that will happen later?"

"I do not know, and for that reason, I need to be sure."

Her face was to me, so he did not see the catty look she had plastered across it. "Of course, my Hezi. I promise. I can make you love me." With that, she nuzzled her perfect nose into his neck. I had to hold back my anger.

He pushed her away and pointed in the direction of the house. "I need to be alone."

She drew her head back. "Yes, of course." Clearly reluctant, she left the gardens and headed for the house.

"Elizabeth," Hezekiah said. "You can come out now."

Uh, no. That hadn't sounded like him putting a stop to anything with Draculette.

He stepped over to the hedge and parted it.

"Hi," I said sheepishly.

"Hello." He grinned, took my hand, and gently pulled me out. "How much did you hear?"

So that was it. How much did I hear that he had to cover for? I pulled away and said in a husky tone, mimicking Arabella, "Oh, my Hezi, I will make you love me." Rolling my eyes, I then imitated Hezekiah, "I do not want to commit to a marriage—unless we fall in love." Though it was none of my business, I glared at him.

He tried to suppress a laugh. I did not find anything funny and walked quickly past him. "Elizabeth!" He grabbed my arm and pulled me around. "Elizabeth, I will not play that game."

I stopped short—play what game? Was he accusing me of acting childish? "You are the one playing games, sir."

He tilted his head to the side and studied me. "Is this a game?" He leaned forward and kissed me on the forehead.

I pressed my eyes tight. "Um, yes, that is a game."

"And this?" His soft lips kissed my eyelids, one at a time.

I swallowed and nodded.

"How about this?" Hezekiah held his face within inches of mine and paused. His warm breath caressed the side of my face and forced my eyes to flutter open.

"Especially that," I said with great resolve to turn and walk away. *Okay legs, turn and walk. You can turn and walk away now, legs.*

He shrugged. "All right. You win." He walked past me and headed toward the house.

That was it? He was leaving me? I watched him get farther away. "Wait!"

He stopped.

I hurried to his side and waited for him to turn around, but he didn't. Out of breath and nearly in a panic, I asked, "What was that?" I stepped in front of him.

He grimaced. "That, my dear Elizabeth, was a game." He grabbed my shoulders and pulled me to him. "And this is not." He pressed his lips firmly to mine, and at that moment I wanted nothing in the world but him. He ended the kiss—a kiss I wasn't finished with. "But we better not meet like this again." He took me by the arm and led me toward the gates to the gardens.

"What? No—why?"

He pushed me up against a tree and kissed me again. "That is why." He stepped back. "I like you too much."

You could never like someone too much, I was sure of that. "What do you mean?"

"I know your world is different from mine, but I do not think that our values are much different."

Values—oh, wait, he meant . . . oh, he meant that.

"So, I propose we commit to each other to not meet in secluded areas."

Oh. A commitment. Like a promise. I drew my head back. "You asked Draculette to make a promise too."

"Yes. A promise to not expect to marry without being in love."

"And you seriously think she's going to keep that promise."

Hezekiah shook his head. "No. Not at all."

"What?" I threw my hands into the air.

"I wouldn't expect someone like Arabella to understand a promise like that, let alone keep it."

Now I was confused.

"But what I do expect is for her to anticipate that I will keep my promise." He pulled me close again. "How can I fall in love with someone whose main ambition in marriage is to acquire more money?"

That made sense. I nodded.

"And besides," he said, pushing a loose strand of my hair behind my ear, "how can I fall in love with someone else?"

Yes? And . . . I waited for him to continue.

"When I have already given my heart to you."

This would have been a great place for another one of his incredible kisses, but instead he stepped away, took my hand, and continued silently toward the exit. "I realize that we will have times when no one is around, but the kisses—we're done."

My eyebrows rose. Done?

He leaned into me. "Until we're married." He walked past me toward the path to the house.

"Mr. Hanson," I said firmly.

Hezekiah looked around—for his father, no doubt—but I had been addressing him. He tilted his head to the side.

I cleared my throat. "I will not marry you, sir."

His eyes widened slightly then narrowed. "And why not?"

"It is the cruelest game of all to pretend you don't love someone when your heart is about to burst."

"Elizabeth, I am sorry," he said softly.

"And then to merely walk past me and tell me we will be married—it is a total faux pas. A blunder, sir."

"Oh, yes, I suppose that you are right." He got down on one knee.

"Oh my!" I quickly pulled him up before someone could see him. *What if Draculette is watching from the window? Okay, in that case, I hope she did see.* But who was I kidding? I was only seventeen. And had I completely forgotten my resolve to protect Trent's heritage?

I groaned. The truth was, I wanted to have my own life. Why should I be denied love? There was a possibility that Hezekiah never married three hundred years ago. Maybe he wasn't Trent's ancestor. Maybe Trent came from Gyles's line. Maybe I *was* Hezekiah's destiny.

Hezekiah grinned. "Elizabeth, when the time comes, it will be perfect. That I do promise you."

Okay, I thought. I would wait and see if that was true.

Seventeen

Decisions

I laid awake that night in my room next to Martha's. She had left the door ajar, and her soft snoring comforted my frazzled nerves. I thought back to Hezekiah's words—strong, kind words from the best man I had ever known. He was so much like Trent. *Argh! Where did that come from? Get out of my head, Trent.* I wanted Trent out of my life—Trent, my very best friend years from now. Would there ever be any rest from that knowledge? I pushed his image away until sleep finally overtook me. By morning, I had all but forgotten my struggle with memories of Trent the night before. The golden rays of sunshine beating around the sides of the curtains made it easy to focus on the new day. I sat on the side of my bed and stretched.

Mrs. Fayette stepped into the room. "Good morning, Miss Elizabeth." She handed me a clean dress.

"Good morning."

She pursed her lips tight and I could tell something was up.

"What's wrong, Mrs. Fayette?" She motioned for me to stand and then helped me out of my bedclothes.

"It's the English woman, my lady."

"Arabella."

"Yes, miss."

Pulling the new dress over my shoulders, Mrs. Fayette continued, "She told me the most awful news."

"Really?"

"She says Hezekiah has asked her to be his wife."

"What?" *That little conniving . . .* I suppressed a growl. "When?" I pushed my feet into a pair of slippers.

"Just a moment ago."

I reached behind me and tried to help button and lace up the back of the dress. "Hurry!" I urged Mrs. Fayette. Her fingers flew over the buttons, and then I hurried to the door.

"Wait!" She rushed to me and ran a brush through my tangled hair, then quickly piled it on top of my head and secured it with a barrette. As soon as she had pinched my cheeks, I was off.

I had no idea what to do, but somehow I had to let everyone know Arabella was lying. *She is lying, right?* I shook my head. *Of course she is.* I headed toward the dining room, but stopped when I saw Victoria standing outside a room, listening through the slightly open door. She glanced over at me, held her finger to her lips, and motioned for me to join her.

As I came near, Arabella's shrill voice met my ears.

"You stupid girl! I will see that you are sent away for this." A few scrapes, a long moment of silence, and then—"I will be making a lot of changes around here, starting with the likes of you." Another pause. "And the dreadful colors on these drab walls."

Victoria looked my way and grimaced. She took up the hem of her skirt, threw her head back, and quickly walked away. Clearly, Draculette had not scored well with her. I watched as Victoria turned a corner farther down the hallway.

Arabella's barrage of cruel words went on. "You insignificant . . . ah, just—go!"

I pushed the door open. "Is everything all right in here? I heard yelling." I walked over to Arabella and asked in a concerned tone, "Are you all right?" She gave a curt nod toward the servant she had been berating—the brown-eyed girl from before.

I sighed. "Oh, I see. Would you like me to escort her from here?"

"That won't be necessary. Lucia can find her way out." Arabella glared at the girl, who picked up an overturned basket and left the room.

I curtsied and turned toward the door.

"Lady Elizabeth," Arabella said coolly. "Come here."

Oh, dang. Now she's giving me orders. I met her halfway. "Yes?"

"How long have you known my Hezi?"

I bit the sides of my mouth. "Not long—a few months, I guess."

"And you knew he was engaged to me?"

"No. He never mentioned you." It was cruel, I know, but true, and I enjoyed it. She looked perturbed. *Good.* I turned to leave.

"It is a shame you have fallen in love with him."

A short breath of air escaped my throat. I turned back to her. "What did you say?"

"It is sad that you think he would choose you over me."

"Hmm." I pursed my lips together in a straight line.

She lifted her chin. "He has asked me to be his wife, you know. We will announce it at breakfast."

"Hmm. When did he ask you?"

"Last night in the gardens."

"Hmm." *Hold your tongue, girl.* "Really."

"Yes. So you need to stay away from him."

"Well, that's not what I heard." I threw the palm of my hand over my forehead. "Oh, my Hezi, I will make you love me." I grimaced, but dropped my hand and continued in a lower range. "I do not want to commit to a marriage—unless we fall in love."

"You were in the gardens?" She clicked her tongue. "It matters not. We are in love."

"Hmm."

She made a face. "Will you stop that?"

Heck no. "Hmm." I said in a lower voice. "Well, you are wrong. You must not know what love is."

"And I suppose you can tell me?"

As a matter of fact, I could. I looked off to the side. "It's when you can think of no one else, but him—his smile, his laugh, the warmth of his touch. He takes your breath away and you think you might die if you could never see him again." I glanced over at Arabella and for a brief moment saw her countenance soften.

Suddenly, she jumped up. "It is a fairy tale," she said gruffly.

"No, it is not. Do not marry for money, Arabella, or you will miss out on the greatest feeling ever."

"I—I will come to love him, and he will come to love me."

"How can you be sure of that?"

"It has happened before."

She was probably right. Arranged marriages could lead to love, especially if the man and woman were compatible. But, I was sure she and Hezekiah were not. "I may have only met him a short while ago," I said, "but I know this. If you announce your marriage this morning, without his blessing, he will send you off to England on the next ship."

Arabella bit her fingernail. "You're probably right."

Hardly believing I had just helped Draculette stay on longer, I walked out the door. A few moments later, Gyles caught up to me. He placed his hand under my elbow and led me into the dining room. I was surprised when Hezekiah escorted Arabella into the room ten minutes later. His mother had warmly welcomed me, but barely looked at Arabella as she sat.

"Good morning Arabella," Abner chimed in, standing as he had for me. He sat and nodded toward the servants. Soon, the table overflowed with breads, cheeses, sausages and fruits.

I ate little, wondering if Arabella would make her announcement. She glanced my way more than once, and I couldn't help but notice the contempt in her eyes. She knew I had overheard her conversation with Hezekiah, and I wondered if she had guessed why he was in the gardens in the first place. I would have to watch my step around her now.

We had almost made it through the meal when she laid her napkin on her plate and tapped her goblet with her fork. *Oh dang. Here it comes.* Victoria looked as surprised as I was.

"My dearest Hezi." Arabella gazed lovingly into Hezekiah's eyes. "In consequence of the words we shared privately last night in the gardens" —she glanced my way and smiled sourly— "I wondered if we could spend more time together. Perhaps a trip into town or a long stroll by the water?"

"That is a splendid idea," Abner said.

I kicked Hezekiah in the leg. Hard enough to make him jump. *Oops.* He rubbed his leg. "Well, yes, I think that is a good idea, Arabella." His hand blocked my foot before I could land a second kick. "Would you mind if Lady Elizabeth and Gyles came along?"

Looking a little put out, she parted her lips to speak—to complain, probably—but was interrupted by Hezekiah's brother.

"Wonderful!" Gyles jumped up from the table. "I've been meaning to do some shopping." He turned to one of the servants. "Will you tell Charles to ready the coach?" He came around the table and took me by the arm. "Lady Elizabeth, may I?"

"Of course." He escorted me to the front door, where we chatted softly while waiting for Charles. Hezekiah and Arabella joined us, though she stepped in between Hezekiah and me, blocking my view with her perfectly contoured hair and massive ringlets.

Gyles helped me into the coach first, but when Arabella tried to sit across from me, he gently urged her down and sat beside her. I assumed it was the proper way to sit—across from one's love interest—and didn't mind at all when Hezekiah squeezed in beside me. Arabella, however, was shooting darts at me with her eyes.

She leaned over and took one of Hezekiah's hands—the one nearest me. "My Hezi." He patted her on the hand and then placed her hand back on her lap, brushing his hand against my leg as he withdrew it. I tried not to gloat.

His gesture did not go unnoticed by Gyles, who tapped his fingers together in a thoughtful mode. "My dear brother," he said, "what do you make of this arranged marriage you have?"

Arabella looked shocked at his boldness, but I was pleased and anxious to hear his answer.

Hezekiah smiled at Arabella. "She is beautiful."

My heart stopped beating.

Gyles nodded. "Indeed." He glanced at me. "She is quite beautiful." He leaned forward. "And she has come here from England to be with you as arranged by both sets of parents years ago."

"Yes. I know that."

"How long will it take for you to make your decision?"

Hezekiah drew his head back. "What do you mean, Gyles?"

"Come now, Hezekiah. Do you think no one has noticed your affection for Lady Elizabeth?"

Arabella glared at me as the heat rose up my face.

Hezekiah pressed his fists into his knees. "We've had this conversation, Gyles."

"Yes, I know, but it is not fair to Elizabeth or to Arabella. Make up your mind, Brother." Gyles looked over at me with longing in his eyes and my heart froze. *Me? He is interested in me?*

Hezekiah reached across my lap and grabbed him by his collar. "Stay out of this, Gyles." I jumped back. I hadn't seen that side of Hezekiah and it startled me. The coach halted in front of a shop. Hezekiah popped the door open, grabbed my hand, and pulled me out of the coach. Then he pulled me down the walk.

"Hezi!" Arabella called from behind us.

"Stop!" I grabbed a post and held on, bringing Hezekiah to a sudden halt. "What are you doing?"

His angry eyes met mine. "I cannot do this, Elizabeth. I do not even like her, let alone love her."

A sudden intake of air behind me told me that Arabella had caught up to us and heard his harsh words. Suddenly, painfully, I realized I was altering their future. I pulled my hand away from his. "Hezekiah . . ." My voice trailed off. "You have to at least try." I reached behind me and pulled Arabella forward. "What if I'm changing the course of history? What if Arabella was meant to be your wife?"

They were very hard words to say, and it was even harder for me to turn around and walk to Gyles's open arms, even though I knew he meant more than just to comfort me. But as I whirled to see why I'd heard nothing from Hezekiah—I was shocked beyond words to find his lips pressed tightly against hers.

I guess, I deserved that. I buried my face against Gyles's chest and wept. Out of kindness to me, he ordered a different coach to take us around town and then back to the mansion. Arabella finally had her alone time with Hezi, and I wondered if I hadn't just made the biggest mistake of my life.

Eighteen

Confessions

The next few days were a blur. I took my meals in my room and refused all visitors, telling Martha and Mrs. Fayette that I wasn't feeling well, though I knew they realized the truth. I had seen the stares when a rented coach brought Gyles and me home alone without Hezekiah and Arabella. Trying to imagine my life in England, I made plans to leave as soon as I got the courage to borrow the money from Hezekiah to make the trip.

There was a knock on the door. "Come in." I had expected to see Hezekiah, since he had come by a couple times a day for the last few days, but it was Arabella. The folds of her petticoat swished against her legs as she entered the room and closed the door behind her.

"Lady Elizabeth." Her arrogant attitude gone, she came near the chair where I sat. "May we talk?"

"Yes, Arabella, what is it?" I said through my shock.

She wrung her hands in front of her. "I have wanted to thank you for what you did."

Oh. That. "There's no need to thank me."

She swept her dress out behind her and sat in the chair beside me. "Oh, yes, there is."

Waiting for her to continue, I dreaded what she might say. Had they fallen in love that easily?

"Hezekiah is . . . attentive." She picked at a fingernail.

That hurt, but it was good that he was doing the right thing. "I'm happy for you." It was a bold-faced lie—I was miserable. "Have you picked a wedding date?"

She looked at me quickly. "What? Oh, no. He's sticking to his conviction of making sure we fall in love first."

"Oh. And?"

"And what?"

"Have you fallen in love with him?"

She hesitated, her face drawn up in deep thought. "Remember what you said about love?"

Not really. "Uh, yeah."

"About thinking of no one else but him?" Arabella paused. "And how you might die if you never saw him again?"

I held back a groan. "Yes." I hoped she wasn't going to elaborate about her newly discovered feelings for Hezekiah. I wasn't sure how I would take it.

She sighed. It was not the sigh of someone in love. It was profoundly sad. "What's wrong?" I asked her.

She wiped a glistening tear from the corner of her eye. "I have felt that before, and I can't seem to get him out of my mind."

I coughed. "What?"

She kept her head down. "His name is Nathaniel."

Whoa. Wait. Hold on. "Who is Nathaniel?"

She looked up at me through teary eyes. "He's the son of a wealthy merchant."

"You're in love with the son of a wealthy merchant and that's a problem for you?"

"Not for me, but for my father." Arabella buried her head in her hands. "My father expects me to marry into the Hanson family—to keep the money in the family."

I sat up straight. "What? You and Hezekiah are related?"

She looked at me funny, like everyone should have known that. "He's my cousin. Didn't he tell you?"

Eew. That was just gross, even though I knew it was a common practice back then. I shook my head. Cousins were like extended brothers where I came from.

Arabella tilted her head. "What's wrong with that?"

Oh, a possible increased risk of genetic disorders. "Nothing." The risk was at least a small one. I narrowed my eyes at her. "You're in love with Nathaniel."

She nodded and wiped her nose on a handkerchief she pulled from her pocket. "His smile, as you said, is always on my mind."

I leaned back. This was truly a problem. For me. I had resolved to stay out of it, to not get involved, but Arabella was in love with someone else! "You'll forget all about him after a while." *Where the heck had that come from?*

"I doubt that." She looked out the window between us and fingered a locket hanging from a chain around her neck. She held it up for me to see, then opened it. A lock of blond hair was stuffed inside.

"His?"

She nodded.

Great. She had Nathaniel's hair close to her heart and Hezekiah's money close to her pocket.

"What should I do?"

I agonized for a few seconds before answering and then decided to do the best thing—the right thing. "I can't tell you what to do. You must make your own choice."

Arabella grimaced. "You are a strange one, Elizabeth." She stood. "If I were you and you me, I would have pushed Nathaniel on you just to get rid of you." She frowned. "I can tell you love Hezekiah, but evidently not enough."

"I do love him enough!" *Oops.* "And the thought to tell you to follow your heart did cross my mind."

She seemed pleased. "I thought you might feel that way." She turned to leave. "Oh, and Hezi loves you too."

Really? My heart fluttered. "Wait! What are you going to do?"

A smile played at her lips. "Follow my heart." She opened the door and stepped into the hallway, then looked back at me. "And you should follow yours too."

Follow my heart? I wished I could, but I had to flee from my heart—as far away as I could get. Deciding to go down to dinner, I allowed Mrs. Fayette to help me get ready.

"You look lovely, Lady Elizabeth."

"Thank you." I waved her away when she offered to escort me downstairs. Knowing dinner was still another hour away, I thought a stroll in the gardens would be a good place to clear my head. Deep into the lush greenery, I heard voices—Hezekiah and someone with a thick French accent. I could not see them through the bushes and stood still.

"It has been done before. It is high magic, though, and comes with a price."

"How much then, de Nostredame?" Hezekiah grumbled. I could not see what they were doing but heard the rustle of paper exchanging hands. "Now, be gone with you!"

"Of course, but Hezekiah, I must warn you to take heed with what I have just given you. It could kill you just as well as not."

"Yes, yes," Hezekiah snapped.

I swallowed hard. What had he just bought from that Frenchman? I heard their footsteps and scurried down the path and around a corner. Peeking around the hedge, I watched them walk away, Hezekiah and a finely dressed, tall man with a cane—de Nostredame.

My stomach was in knots. Of course I would have to confront Hezekiah. I'd just have to make sure no one was around when I did.

I freshened up before going into the dining room and was greeted by a warm smile from Arabella. Hezekiah and Gyles stood and came toward me to escort me to my chair. "Thank you," I said graciously.

"It is wonderful to see you up and about," Abner said. Victoria gave a formal nod my way.

"Yes, quite so," said Gyles, returning to his seat across from me.

"How are you feeling?" Victoria asked, placing her napkin on her lap.

"I'm much better, thank you." I glanced over at Hezekiah. He would not look my way. Arabella tapped her goblet with a fork. I glanced at her. *What now?*

She stood. "I have something I would like to say."

"Proceed," Abner said after a quick look at Hezekiah, who shrugged.

"My father, your brother," she said, nodding to Abner, "expects me to marry Hezi."

"Of course, we do too," Abner replied with a smile.

She raised her glass to Hezekiah. "Hezi, you are a young man who is destined to go far—your success will be unparalleled. The woman who stands beside you in life will no doubt be fortunate indeed, but it will not be me."

Abner gasped, Victoria's eyes widened, and Hezekiah dropped his fork. I just grinned.

"I am sorry, my dear cousin, but I do not love you, not that way." She looked over at me. "My father is going to be very angry with me, but he loves me, and he'll get over it."

Abner stood, but Victoria was quick to hush him. He sat back down.

"I will stay here until the end of July, and then I will return to England."

Abner looked at his younger son. "Hezekiah?"

"It is best father. Arabella and I had a long talk this afternoon. She's in love with someone in England."

"Yes. He is a merchant, and his ship will be here in July. I will return with him." She looked my way and smiled.

Her face radiated happiness, and I'd never seen her look so beautiful. It's funny how love does that to a person. I found my gaze shift to Hezekiah, but he still would not look at me. It was better that way, and now it was my turn. I tapped my goblet.

"Oh my, another announcement," Gyles said, staring at me.

"Yes," I said slowly. "I'd like to be on that ship with you, Arabella." My words brought greater looks of surprise than hers, especially from Hezekiah, who was now looking at me with wide eyes.

"You are returning to England too?" Abner asked.

I nodded.

"So soon?" Gyles said with a frown.

"It's hardly soon—yet another six weeks," Arabella said slowly, studying my face. "Lady Elizabeth, of course you may go with Nathaniel and me, but maybe by then you will change your mind."

Hezekiah pushed away from the table and left the room.

Victoria cleared her throat and said, "Go after him."

"Mother?" Gyles's voice was gruff.

"Not you. Lady Elizabeth." She looked at me. "Something is bothering him and has been ever since you took ill. Whatever it is that has come between you two, you need to speak about it."

I sighed. This was going to be very hard. I would tell him it was over and that I did not love him. I would lie.

Nineteen

De Nostredame

I stepped out of the dining room, with no idea of where Hezekiah had gone. Lucia walked farther down the hall. "Lucia!" I called. She turned to me and I asked, "Did you see which way Hezekiah went?" She pointed timidly toward the doors that led to the deck.

I thanked her, then scurried out the door. Seeing him descending the steps toward the gardens, I slowed down and followed. I didn't want to get too far behind, otherwise I might not be able to find him. "Hezekiah!" I called to him as he disappeared into the hedges. *Darn.* I strolled into the gardens. "Hezekiah!"

"What do you want with me?" He stepped out from behind a hedge.

I wish I could tell you. "We need to talk."

"Speak then, but be quick about it." He folded his arms across his chest.

Speak. Right. "You're upset with me because of my announcement."

He stared at me, but said nothing.

"And you have a right to be. I should have told you first." I waited for him to say something—anything. "Uh, I need to start a new life." I wrung my hands anxiously. "I cannot stay anywhere in Massachusetts Bay—not in 1692." I waited, but still no response from him. "Okay, so here's the thing." I took to pacing between the two hedges on either side of us. "As you know, I am from the future—and you are not." I folded my hands in front of me. "You told me I couldn't save anybody from the Salem travesty that is unfolding, and though it hurts terribly, you are right. I cannot change history that has, in fact, already happened in the future." His countenance did not soften in the least bit. "But I cannot bear to be here either, and I especially" —my words caught in my throat— "I especially cannot alter your future and that of your already-born descendants from my time."

His eyebrows rose as he appeared to ponder that.

"So, you have to help me," I said quickly, "just for as long as it takes me to find a job as a governess, and then I will pay you back." *There. I said it.*

He cleared his throat. "You have been distant." He tilted his head. "Yet it has not been because you do not have feelings for me, but because you wish to protect my posterity?"

I looked down. "Um, I have, uh, no feelings for you."

"Yes." He chuckled. "Right. As you say." The twinkle in his eyes returned. "Well, I will not give you a shilling."

I huffed. "You won't? Then I will get it from Gyles."

"Go ahead and try. He wants you to stay almost as much as I do."

Frustrated and desperate, I slammed the palms of my hands into Hezekiah's chest. "I have to leave! Don't you see?"

He grasped my hands tight. "I agree."

"You do? Then you will loan me the money?"

He shook his head. "No." He dropped his hands to his sides.

I growled. "Then what? Where will I go and what will I do?"

"You will go home."

I drew my head back. "What?"

"To 2015."

I shook my head in a daze. "I can't go home. It's impossible!"

"As impossible as coming here?"

"Yes! No! I mean . . . oh, I don't know! Surely what ever happened to send me here cannot happen twice."

His calm expression of assurance surprised me. "And, my dear Elizabeth, why not?" He took my hand and pulled me along. "Come with me."

As if I had a choice. Hezekiah dragged me deeper into the gardens to an inner structure made of stone. If I had known it was there, I would have spent all of my time inside its open walls. Lined with thick vines on the sides and above, the entire enclosure was scattered with flowering plants and stone benches. I twirled around and took in its wonder. "What is this place?"

"My father had it built for my mother—it is much like the one she left in England."

"This must be where she disappears to so often."

"Yes, she brings her books and sewing out here on good days." Hezekiah led me to a stone table with its own benches. He reached in between a pocket in the wall and pulled out a box, then sat and patted the bench beside him.

I sat down across from him instead. He opened the box. Inside was a small book that looked super old, even for 1692. "Why do you hide it out here?" I asked.

He looked at me and grinned. "It is an ancient book of magic."

"Yikes! Are you kidding me?" I scooted back. Magic in 1692 was the last thing I wanted to be near.

He sighed. "Not all magic is evil, Bess."

I wrapped a loose strand of hair around my finger, and had to agree, being a huge fan of Harry Potter. I drew in a breath and asked, "Is this what you bought from de Nostredame—that Frenchman with a cane?"

Hezekiah's eyes widened. "How did you know that?"

Theresa Sneed

"I, um, was in the gardens and overheard you."

He grabbed my hands. "Was there anyone else in the gardens?"

"Not that I know of."

He relaxed. "That is good. De Nostredame does not have a favorable reputation—especially these days. He is a scholar in the ways of magic."

"Like a warlock?"

Hezekiah guffawed. "No. He's a learned man who obtained his doctoral degree from Montpellier. He travels the world over seeking answers to questions most people would never think to ask."

"Like Nostradamus?"

Hezekiah nodded and said, "You never cease to surprise me, Bess. Yes. He's quite like his great-uncle in his passion for astrology, and as a child, even bore Nostradamus' nickname, 'little astrologer.'"

"Whoa! Your friend is the great-nephew of *the* Nostradamus?" My hands flew to my chest. "I was just in the presence of Nostradamus' nephew?" *Oh. My. Goodness. Wow.* My eyes narrowed. "How is it that de Nostredame is here in Salem in 1692?"

Hezekiah shrugged. "I sent for him."

I glanced at the book. "Just so you could buy this?"

"Oh, this is not a purchase. De Nostredame would never part with something so valuable. He's staying at the tavern until I call for him and then he will return home with his book." He leaned across the table. "I sent for this months ago, because of a curiosity of mine, but now it is something I hope will help to get you home."

I gasped. "How?"

"I had heard about a theory recorded in this book years ago and found it most intriguing." Hezekiah's expression sobered.

218

"Time only exists on this planet. Everything else surrounds the earth—encapsulates it—causing time to be placed within eternity—with no end to eternity on either side. Interesting, isn't it?"

I looked at him blankly. "What do you mean?"

He grinned and continued, as if I got it. "Anyhow, the theory of stagnant time nestled within a flowing eternity is just the foundation of the theory. Being able to manipulate that motionless time—or move within its realm—is based on a catastrophic event that happened thousands of years ago." He leafed through the book. "I've been studying it ever since I obtained this from de Nostredame." He tapped the pages. "Here it is."

"Oh." I leaned over to take a look. "It's in Latin," I said, disappointed I would not be able to read it.

Hezekiah however, appeared to be proficient in the language, as he read aloud parts of several passages. One passage included hand drawn illustrations, and he pointed to them excitedly. He all but forgot me then and with him completely absorbed in a book, I got up and walked around the lush outdoor sanctuary. While I appreciated Hezekiah's intellect, I did not trust that he was on to anything. The whole thing was utterly ridiculous.

Strolling through the beautiful garden and admiring the stone columns and its two walls, I looped around until I made a full circle back to Hezekiah. The serious look on his face told me to not disturb him. What did he think he would find in that old book? And how could it possibly ever help me get back?

"Bess, come here, please." He gestured for me to sit, but did not take his eyes from the book. I sat down and he looked up. "You must tell me everything you remember about the day and night you time traveled."

"O-kay," I began slowly. "Well, Trent and my little brother Seth and I went fishing."

"On what day? What month?"

I thought back. It seemed like a lifetime ago. "It was a Saturday in October—no, November. Oh yeah, I remember now. It was the day after Halloween, the first day of November."

Hezekiah cocked his head to the side. "What is Halloween?"

"You know, All Hallows Eve?"

"Sounds like a pagan holiday."

"Well, yeah, it is."

"Go on," he said. "What was the weather like?"

I bit my lip. "Um, well, it was warm for that time of the year, in fact, unseasonably warm, but then it suddenly got really cold. Oh wait, that was after I was already here."

He nodded. "Anything else?"

"It was foggy—freaky foggy, and the sky had strange lights."

He leaned forward suddenly. "What kind of lights?"

I shrugged. "Swirly . . . I don't know. Like the aurora borealis, I guess."

Hezekiah appeared to be deep in thought. "Like the French astronomer Gassendi proposed." He muttered something, then sucked in a sharp breath. "That's it!" He jumped up and away from the table, nearly falling over the bench. Then he walked around in a small circle repeating something in Latin. *"Diu, fuit in rerum divisionem! Diu, fuit in rerum divisionem!"*

"Hezekiah—you're scaring me!" I said. "What is it?"

He dropped his hand and returned to the table, his finger pressed to the drawing. "This, Bess. This is how you came here, and this is how you will return to the future." He spoke in Latin again, so I reminded him I wasn't getting it. "Oh. Yes, of course, well, here it is." He pointed to the drawing again. "I will translate for you."

He cleared his throat. "Many years ago, there was a rift in the universe—a rip or tear that happened because of an astronomical event."

That got my attention. "What was the event?"

His face paled. "God was killed."

"God was killed?" I thought for a moment and then drew in a breath as realization hit. "You don't mean—Jesus Christ?"

Hezekiah nodded, then continued translating from the Latin. "At His unjust death, His creation—the earth—groaned and rent in twain, pushing up land that once was flat and leveling great mountains, sinking cities into the depths of the oceans, and creating deep fissures in the cosmos."

"Fissures—you mean like rips?"

"Exactly." Hezekiah patted the book. "These rips will remain until the end of time, when God Himself will repair them."

"End of time? Hmm." I paused until I got it. "Ohh. The *end* of time—with eternity still existing on either side of it. Kind of like a good movie that ends and then you go back to whatever you were doing before it?"

He laughed. "Great analogy."

"But the fissures are still open?"

"Yes. The one you came through was magnetically charged by conditions in the aurora borealis, so that anything within the rip passed through the fissure to another time."

I swallowed hard. That actually made sense—in a weird way. I had read that mountains were leveled and great cities sank beneath the ocean when Christ was crucified. A rip in the universe caused by the death of a perfect Being who had created the earth didn't seem too farfetched.

I shook my head—and modern man was worried about the ozone layer. "Okay, that might explain how I got here, but how does it explain how I'm going to get back?"

Hezekiah counted on his fingers as he replied, "The warm weather, the aurora borealis, and being in the right spot at the right time when they converge."

"That's impossible," I said, frowning. "No one knows when that might happen again, especially in 1692."

"It's not a precise calendar." Hezekiah pointed to the next few pages in the book. "But it does indicate that the rift you came through is prime. We know—well, you know—where one of the rips is, Bess. Now all we need is warm weather and the aurora borealis to activate it."

"So, what do we do—wait for it to be super warm and sprout an aurora?"

Hezekiah pursed his lips together and nodded, and I started to plan my trip to England to be a governess.

Twenty

What Will Be

The days went by swiftly. Hezekiah and I talked every day and spent all of our time together. Neither one of us pursued an active relationship again, but I sure felt something around him, something warm and wonderful. One afternoon, when I went looking for him, I stumbled upon a room I hadn't seen before— a schoolroom, right in the middle of the estate. No one was there, and I decided to take a look around. I was drawn to the corner of the small room near the windows, where an easel was tucked away. I stepped in front of it and was taken aback by the vibrant portrait in front of me. It was Isabella, and it was nearly finished. I heard voices coming toward the room.

"Come on, Bella. We are going to get this finished today. I've only got a few things left." Hezekiah stepped into the room with his younger sister and was surprised to find me there. "Elizabeth!"

"Hezekiah?" I gestured to the painting. "Did you do this?"

"Yes," Bella giggled. "He's almost as good as Gyles."

"Almost as good?" Hezekiah playfully ruffled her hair. "Now you've got to go get it combed again."

"No, I don't. You're done with my hair, remember?" Still, she took off out of the room, calling over her shoulder, "I'll be right back!"

Hezekiah grinned and stepped near me. "I've only a few details left and then, with your permission, I'd like to paint you."

"Oh! But why?"

His faced took on a somber look. "Why do you think?"

"Oh." He was trying to send me back to the future. I guessed he wanted something to remember me by. "All right." I looked down at my dress. "Is this good enough?"

"Yes. You're perfect."

And there was that look from him again that I was trying so hard not to sink into. "Um, okay." I sat back and watched him work on his sister's painting. After a while, I said, "How come you never told me you could paint?"

Hezekiah drew the brush across the canvas. "Have you told me everything that you can do?"

"Well, no." *Good point.* "But painting is kind of a big deal."

He shrugged. "It's just a painting, Bess."

"To you, maybe, but oil paintings are one of the few things that survive time."

He looked at me oddly, like maybe that was his intention. Soon, he placed the finished painting of his sister on a different easel away from the windows.

Bella rushed over to me and grabbed my hands. "Now it's your turn, Lady Elizabeth."

I bit my lower lip and sat down on the chair she had just vacated. How hard could it be to get your image painted? Pretty hard. Two hours passed and I wanted to scream. It was difficult to sit perfectly still. "How much longer?"

"Patience, Bess." He looked up at me. "And don't pucker your lips." He held the brush still and stared at me. "Or roll your eyes." He sighed when he saw my sour expression. "All right, that's it for the day."

"Yay!" I jumped up. "Let me see." He held his hands out and blocked me from coming around in front of the easel. "What? After all that time, you are not going to let me see it?"

"That's right. I'm not." He smirked and folded his arms across his chest.

I huffed. "Not fair, Hezekiah."

224

"You'll see it soon enough." He held his arm out and I looped mine through it. "It's time for dinner anyhow."

Pictures and I have never gotten along that great. It seemed I would always be cut off, blurry, blocked, have food in my teeth, or something else disgusting. That's why I loved selfies, especially the delete button, where I had complete control over whether or not I would save a photo or, most likely, trash it. I wondered if Hezekiah had captured my true likeness. There was no delete button with paintings. I grimaced.

We spent the next few days in that small room, but finally, Hezekiah set his brush down and grinned. "It is done."

"Yes!" Once again, I jumped up, and once again, he held his hand up to stop me.

"I have plans for this." He led me into the hallway toward the dining room. "Let me show you it in my way, please?"

"Do I have a choice?" I mumbled.

We stepped into the dining room. No one smiled or greeted us. Hezekiah's parents spoke softly and motioned for him to come near after he seated me. Whatever they told him made his countenance fall. Once everyone was seated, Abner revealed his news. "They hanged a woman in Salem Town today."

"Bridget Bishop." I gasped, then covered my mouth with trembling fingers.

Abner's eyebrows knit together. "Yes. How did you know?"

"I—I—"

"I just told her," Hezekiah said, covering my blunder. "Right when I sat down."

"It is a terrible thing," Victoria remarked. "A terrible, terrible thing."

I nodded. No longer hungry, I asked to be excused. My grandmother only had weeks to live. Her second examination was later this month, on June 29th. I wanted to support her but was not sure I had the emotional strength to endure it again. I berated myself, *Oh please—you're living in luxury getting your portrait painted, and she is in a filthy jail.*

That did it. I would be at her next trial, come heck or high water. And since heck was already in Salem, I prayed it wouldn't rain.

After dinner, he took me aside. "I'm sorry, Bess. That must have been difficult to hear."

"Yes." I searched his eyes. "Hezekiah, I know you will not approve, but I need to go to my grandmother's trial."

"No, you can't. It is too dangerous. We barely made it out the last time without being spotted."

I figured he would say that, and he was right, of course. He took me by the hand and led me outside. We walked toward the gardens. "I want to show you something." He released my hand and walked beside me.

He took me deep inside the gardens to the secret room—no surprise there. But then he led me to a set of stone steps going down into the ground, hidden by vines and bushes. The last time we were there, I had strolled throughout that outdoor room several times and had never seen the stairs.

Hidden in the darkening shadows and overgrown with vines and cobwebs, the ominous steps did not look inviting. Hezekiah went down first. He took something off the wall and held it up for me to see.

"Oh. A torch." I tried not to grimace. Did he really think I was going to follow him down into a dark hole lined with cobwebs? Apparently he did, as he struck a flint with a stone and ignited the torch, then gestured for me to follow.

He grinned. His dimples, illuminated by the dim light, are what did me in. "Sure," I said, then carefully descended the steps, trying to avoid the cobwebs. As I got closer, I could tell they had already been disturbed. Someone had been there just before us. The light from the torch made the thin threads look like spun silver. "Who cleared those away?" I asked nervously.

"I did," Hezekiah said, looking at me funny.

"Oh yeah." Of course he had been the one to clear cobwebs away from his secluded man cave. What was I thinking? I was way too jittery, but in all fairness, I was in 1692, and going down into a dark, creepy hole in the ground. Were girls even allowed in man caves?

The steps leveled out and we came to an iron door with a lock. Hezekiah reached above the door for the key. I smirked. We still did that in 2015. You'd think mankind would have gotten a little cleverer with their hiding places.

He unlocked the door and ushered me inside a room, then went from torch to torch, lighting them. "I used to use the lanterns," he said, gesturing to several beautiful lanterns on the table, "but on a trip to Egypt, I found these to give more light."

Wow. Wow. Wow. The room was as luxurious as any in the mansion. I drew my head back. "And you're just now showing me this?"

He grinned. "It's not really a place you take a woman you're not married to."

Good point. Deep in the ground like it is. "So, you're bringing me now because . . ."

"Because I want to show you where I put your things. I want to bring them with us to Salem Village." He opened a wooden box and pointed inside.

"Oh!" I was excited to see my belongings, but fearful of taking them to Salem Village—the very place where they shouldn't be seen. He must have seen the fear in my eyes.

"We have to hide them where you entered 1692—in the woods by Salem Village. I've been studying the book, Bess." Hezekiah picked up the ancient book from a nearby end table. "We need to hide these things right where you entered the rift."

"Why?"

"So when you get back, you can retrieve them."

If I go back, you mean. I stared at the book. I wondered why he had hidden it in the stone wall when he could've just hidden it down here. "Why did you hide the book up there?"

"I had been studying it and knew I was going to show it to you. I often stick things in the crack in the wall, especially when I'm in a hurry. It wasn't there long. Later that night, I came back and brought it down here."

"Oh." So, now we were going to hide my things in a box in the ground where they would remain forever. I wasn't going back to the future. It was simply impossible, ancient writings or not. But Hezekiah wanted to go to Salem Village, and maybe I could make the best of it. I chewed on a thumbnail. "Uh, could we could bury it the day before my grandmother's trial?"

"Not a chance, Bess." He gestured to the box. "We're going tonight—right now—but I'm taking one of the coaches. The stone box is too heavy to carry on a horse." He patted the wooden box and gestured to the larger stone one on the floor. "It fits perfectly inside."

The stone box would definitely protect the wooden box, kind of like a tomb. It would be hundreds of years before it would become common practice for anyone other than royalty to be buried thus. I looked into the box and saw my Indian bag with my phone resting on top. I loved that bag, far more than my phone, for sure. Still, I picked up my phone first. As expected, it had a black screen, but I rebooted it anyway. I was surprised to find Hezekiah had turned it off, so it had retained some of the battery life.

He gestured around the room. "This is built in a cave. Here, let me show you." He went to the far end of the room and opened a door. "Come see." He took a torch off the wall and stepped outside the door.

I swallowed hard. I have a touch of claustrophobia, so going into a dark cave is like driving in a roundabout in Boston traffic during rush hour—really terrifying for me.

I stuck my head through the doorway and was taken aback with what I saw from the light of the torch. The walls glistened with veins of shiny yellow. My heart skipped a beat. "You do know what this is, right?"

He laughed. "It's not real gold, Bess."

Oh. It must be fools' gold—iron pyrite—but still, it was very pretty. "Who built this room?" I asked, pulling my head back into it. He followed me inside.

"My father had it built for my mother, but it was too dark and cold for her.

"No fireplace?" I looked around.

"I thought about adding one, but then the chimney smoke would alert our neighbors of the room's existence." Hezekiah leaned against the door frame. "It gets locked up for the winter and opened after the snow melts and the ground thaws."

Getting the wooden box up the dark stairs was a lot easier than the stone box. Hezekiah used two bars as levers to walk it up the steps and onto a flat cart. He hefted it into the coach with Charles's assistance and then helped me in beside it. I wondered how he intended to get the stone box up the hill in Salem Village, especially in the dark of night. I supposed that was Hezekiah's intention—transporting my phone, the greatest technology unknown to his modern time, in the dark of night, when there was less of a chance of discovery.

I enjoyed the bumpy carriage ride a lot more than riding sidesaddle and was even able to sleep from time to time. Hezekiah buried his nose in the ancient book and read by lantern light the entire way there. At least that's what he was doing every time I woke up.

Once we reached Salem Village, I directed Charles to the spot I had stumbled down the hill months earlier. I used Zebulon's house to find the path, as his was much closer to the path than Martha's. We stayed out of sight, and then under cover of the predawn sky, we loaded the stone box and a shovel on the cart and pushed it up the hill. I carried the wooden box, which was about the size of a small suitcase. Once up the hill, Hezekiah dismissed Charles and told him to ride on into Salem Village, stay at the tavern, and then come back shortly after nightfall.

With great effort, we pushed and pulled the cart deeper into the woods, while I retraced the steps I had taken months earlier. It would take a miracle to find the exact spot I had entered 1692. How big was the rift anyway? Surely, it was not a teeny-tiny rip? I asked Hezekiah when we stopped to rest.

"I don't know. I don't think they're very big, otherwise things would time travel pretty regularly when the alignment was prime."

Warm, damp weather. Magnetic particles attaching to the rift fused by solar wind. It all seemed so hokey to me—me who had already experienced it. It looked like finding the rift would be more difficult than I had imagined. Even if we found the place that Seth and I had been, finding a tiny tear in the universe seemed an even more immense task.

At least the rising sun made travel easier. I remembered following the circle girls into Salem Village on a straight path—ironic, huh, beings it was even narrow. If I kept following this path far enough, we would eventually come to the spot where I had met with them that eerie night months ago. I had entered their path from the left, which of course means that on the way back, it would be on the right side. If my memory served correctly, the trek from the boulder I had tumbled down to the edge of the hill took about thirty minutes. Pulling a rock on a cart over roots and otherwise rough terrain would take three times that long.

The straight path was not too bad, but where it actually broke off and veered to the right was very difficult to find. I stopped several times wondering where we needed to turn.

"What's that?" Hezekiah pointed to something blue to his right. He worked his way to it and picked it up. It was a blue headband with a big letter D with the word Falcons embroidered across it. "What is this strange thing?" He made a face then rolled his eyes. "It's yours, isn't it?"

I took it from him. "Either that or someone else from Danvers High has traveled back to 1692." I smirked. Turning to the right, I pointed. "This way." The sun was directly above us now. Rather than pulling the stone box around, we pushed it inside a cluster of thick ferns, covered it with fallen branches and twigs, and then went looking for the rock. I kept the wooden box with me and waved Hezekiah off when he offered to carry it.

It was surreal, being back in an area I had been before I time traveled—kind of like coming a full circle. I glanced over at Hezekiah, a lump forming in my throat. Did I really want to go back? Of course! Yes! . . . Heck no. There it was, directly in front of us, the boulder and the small rock—the one Seth had sat on. "There." I pointed ahead of us.

Hezekiah turned back for the cart. Sitting down on the rock, I thought back to everything that had happened. For a brief second, I saw where the hunters had entered, and where Seth and they had faded away to nothing. The terrain was nearly identical. I realized the trees had come and gone, and come and gone again, and that the ones that stood before me would eventually give seed to the trees of the future. I brushed my hand over the small, flat rock and looked back at the boulder behind it. The rocks would stay the same throughout time—solid and immovable. The only thing that could happen to them in these woods would be to eventually be buried by decaying trees. I had seen this very rock and boulder 323 years from now, and they weren't that much different, maybe a little less covered with sediment, but not much.

Hezekiah pulled the cart up beside the rock. He laid down on a large patch of moss and looked up into the sky. "This is the place?"

"It is." I sat beside him, wrapped my arms around my knees, and tucked them under my chin. I pointed straight ahead. "That's where the hunters came in." I gestured with my chin. "And that's where they disappeared with my brother."

He sat up quick. "What did you say?"

I repeated, pointing to the left of the rock. "That's where they disappeared."

He leaned forward. "And you Bess—where were you when they disappeared?"

I stood up and brushed my dress off. "Hmm." I walked around the small clearing and then stopped. "Right here. I remember because Seth was on that small rock. He was a little to my left when the hunters bent down to pick him up. They vanished right then—I rushed to them, but they were already fading and quickly were gone."

Hezekiah jumped up and spun around in a circle looking up to the sky. He held his hands up high. "It's right here, Bess."

"Yes, I know—this is where I saw them fade, Hezekiah."

"No, Bess. It is not."

I rolled my eyes. I was here, he wasn't. I knew where my brother faded away from. "Yes, it is."

"No Bess. It's not where they faded, it's where you faded."

That took a moment to absorb. "I don't understand. How could I see them and they not see me? Hadn't I already time traveled?"

"You had begun to time travel. You were inside the rift, but hadn't passed all the way through it. It's kind of like a very thin gossamer layer, or veil that you could see through, because it was right at your face, but they could not see you, because they were outside of the fissure."

I cocked my head to the side. "Huh. So, when I passed deeper into the veil-like tunnel and then out on the other side, I entered a time that they were not in, but in a parallel universe, they were still right here and hadn't faded at all." I pointed to the ground where they had stood.

"Very good, Bess. You'd make a great scientist."

Yep. I guess I was born before my time. Actually, way before my time, sent to an era where few women merited any kind of scientific genius. Though plenty of women had sought to understand the laws of the universe and live by those laws, they were branded a witch. The irony was too painful to consider.

Hezekiah removed the shovel from the cart and began digging around the small rock.

"Wait, if you move that rock, how will I know where I am, if I get back to 2015?"

"Have a little faith, Bess. I'm going to put it right back in the same spot." He grunted, as he stuck a broken tree limb under it and tried to lift.

"Oh wait, I know how to do this." I searched for a smaller rock and found one nearby. "Here, put this under the pole to act as a lever."

He sat back and watched, seemingly amused.

"What?"

He smirked. "Give me the place to stand, and I shall move the earth."

I grinned. "Archimedes." I loved a smart man.

"Yes." He took over and easily pried the flat rock from the ground. I was amazed how small the flat rock really was. Very little of it had been buried in the ground and even if time buried more of it, by 2015, it would still be relatively easy to dig up.

I watched as he continued to dig a hole under the rock for the stone box. "Hezekiah. I appreciate all that you are doing, but what if it doesn't work? What if the cosmos—" I gestured to the heavens. "What if there is never a prime time again? What if it was just a fluke of the universe?"

He tilted his head. "Well, it was a fluke of the universe." He leaned on the shovel. "And what's the worst that could happen if it doesn't work? You'd be stuck here with me."

The heat rose on my cheeks, and I wished that that could be true. "Hezekiah, you know that can't be. I can't alter your future and the future of your ancestors. You said so yourself."

"Well, I've been meaning to talk to you about that." He sat on the overturned rock. "What if I never married? Maybe I will die in the war—you know I have to go to war, right?"

My eyes widened. "No you don't. It's perfectly legal to pay someone else to go for you." Sad, but true. Rebecca Nurse's youngest son, Benjamin got out of military duty because his father paid someone else to go in his place. That probably ticked off more than one person who couldn't afford that luxury.

Hezekiah shook his head. "I know that, but neither my dad, nor I agree with it."

My face reddened. I couldn't believe I had said that, let alone thought it. "Sorry."

"It's alright, Bess." He grinned. "It shows you care."

Well of course I cared, and yet, he had a good point. What if he really did die in the war and never fathered any children? Gyles could be Trent's ancestor just as well as he could. Of course, if Hezekiah had died in the war, he would then be dead.

"Wait." I pressed my fingers into his chest. "Will you listen to yourself with the, "I might die in the war" scenario—isn't that kind of a lose-lose situation?"

"Lose-lose?"

"Yeah, where no one wins." I flipped my right hand in the air. "You could die." I flipped my left hand in the air. "I could die." I dropped both hands. "It's not like you or I would be able to change any of that, Hezekiah." All this talk about what might happen was moot. I would go to England, and he might die in war. Yikes. Over-thinking was never productive. Couldn't we just live our lives and take whatever comes our way? I hated knowing my grandmother's future and several others in the surrounding communities, but I did not know my future, or Hezekiah's. Maybe it was best to stop trying to second guess it and just live.

"You're right Bess." He turned back to digging the hole.

I was right about what? I had been so deep into my thoughts, I forgot the last thing I actually said out loud.

"We don't know the future, and we can't change anything, but the present."

"Yep."

He leaned on his shovel again. "Which means that we can't play God, even if we try. That should make you happy." He stuck the shovel into the earth.

"Why?"

"Do you really think God will not allow relationships that have already transpired to stay intact because of a rift in His universe?" He looked off to the side, deep in thought. "There is a small paragraph in the book that until recently I didn't quite understand." His eyes softened. "It says that all souls are meant to live regardless of any circumstance—everyone gets a chance at life."

My heart fluttered. "Does that mean what I think it does?"

He looked up at me with his gorgeous green eyes. "It means, that whatever will be, will be, Bess." He grinned wide. "Which further means that we can be together for as long as we'd like, because this is all meant to be." He wiped the sweat off his forehead. "There are no accidents, Bess."

Oh, my. I had always thought that. "You think I was supposed to slip through that rift?"

"Yes."

"To meet you?" I liked that idea.

A half grin drew up on the side of Hezekiah's mouth. "Yep."

I held my hands up in the air and stepped back. I would need to process all of these new ideas. Hezekiah returned to his shoveling. After a while, he stopped and laid the shovel down. He removed the stone lid from the box and laid it on the ground by the hole. Pushing the cart close to the hole, he eased the stone box in. I brought the wooden box to him and set it at his feet.

"Let me look one last time." I reached in and took the Indian bag out, removing each item one by one. I held on to Nashota's feathers the longest, before gently placing them back into the bag. My phone was still on. I took a picture of the stone box, the bag, and then Hezekiah, though he grimaced. Finally, I stepped beside him and took a selfie of the both of us.

"What do you think?" I asked him, showing him each picture.

"I think you are a witch," he said with a grin. He stopped grinning when he saw I didn't think that it was funny in the least. "Sorry, Bess."

I rolled my eyes and stared down at the picture of us together. With this new-found theory of it being okay for me to stay here and for us to be together, would he still want me to return to 2015? I bit my lip.

As if he could read my mind, Hezekiah took my phone and turned it off, then placed it in the wooden box. He lowered the box into its tomb. "What will be, will be." He set the stone lid on top and then shoveled dirt over it. Using his homemade lever, he positioned the flat rock on top of the dirt, covering everything materially important to me in 1692.

Even though we were way out in the woods, I brushed the loose dirt around and tried to make it look as if it had never been touched. I doubted anyone passing by this rock for generations to come would ever know the secret buried beneath it.

I looked over at Hezekiah, hoping I never had to be the one to dig it up.

Twenty-One

Accusations

Charles was waiting when we descended the hill. Hezekiah slept all the way back to Boston. I figured he was tired from staying awake reading the night before and from hauling that heavy stone box up the hill. I thought I might take a look at the ancient book—the pictures, at least—but I couldn't find it.

Later, when we pulled into his estate, I told Hezekiah, "I looked for the book last night."

He seemed a little off. "Yes, well, it is right here." He patted his shirt pocket and then pulled the book out.

I held it for a few seconds and then gave it back. "Maybe another time." I was too tired to read.

He helped me out of the coach. It was still dark out, though the sun was cresting the horizon. He led me into the house, and soon he sweetly wished me good night at my bedroom door.

Hoping to sleep a bit, I tried to be super quiet when I entered the room. But I heard Martha's voice seconds later. "Ah, there ye are, me wane. I was worried about ye."

"I'm sorry, Aunt Martha. Hezekiah and I had a long and tiring day." I let her pull my dress over my head and replace it with nightclothes.

"All is right wi' the two of ye?"

I bit my lower lip. "Yes, I think it is."

She let out a long sigh. "'Tis grand." She helped me into bed and pulled the covers up to my chin. "Sleep well. I will see ta it that no one disturbs ye in the mornin'."

"Thank you," I said with a sigh. *It's going to be a good day.*

Those peaceful thoughts must have been delirium brought on by lack of sleep, because the morning came with a fury. And though I told myself to go back to sleep, too many jumbled emotions prevented it. Trent invaded my brain, making me want to scream. Hadn't we resolved that? The book had explained that all souls were meant to live regardless of any circumstance. Still, I wasn't completely buying into it. I couldn't bear the idea of Trent not existing as Trent.

I met Arabella in the hall on our way down to breakfast. I hadn't seen much of her lately, as she spent most of her time at the docks or browsing through Boston's finest stores. She'd be bringing more than four suitcases back to England for sure.

"Good morning, Arabella."

"Good morning!" She grabbed my hand. "I'm so excited that I get to take you home with me!" She kissed me on the cheek. "I got a letter back from Papa and he says we've plenty of room." She smoothed a strand of loose hair from my face. "So, now you won't have to take a nasty governess position you were telling me about. You can just stay in London with me."

I was surprised and now a little conflicted. "Thank you, Arabella." I thought it best to not tell her of the new development between Hezekiah and me until there actually was one—*if* there was one. We were met by Hezekiah and Gyles at the bottom of the stairs.

"Oh, Hezi! Isn't it great?" she exclaimed. He took her by the elbow and led her toward the dining room.

Gyles escorted me close behind. He leaned into me. "What is she talking about? I thought they broke it off."

"They did. I think she's talking about her plans to kidnap me." I nudged Gyles playfully. "She wrote to her father and got permission for me to stay with them for a while."

"Why is that? Won't you be returning to your own home?"

"No. I have no home, Gyles—well, no home from my youth."

He was quiet. "I'm sorry, Elizabeth."

Before he could ask a ton of questions I couldn't answer, I said, "Thanks for not asking me about it. It really is too painful to talk about."

"Oh. The war."

I left it at that and changed the subject. "What about you? What plans do you have?" That worked. Gyles droned on about his political aspirations well into the morning meal. Abner joined in and so did Hezekiah. Again, a subject I could not get involved in—a history I did not want to influence. It was nothing short of a true miracle that our nation was born in 1776—less than a hundred years after 1692. There was no way I was going to mess with a single strand of the history that laid the foundation for it to come to pass. Their political rhetoric was fascinating to listen to, but because they were Royalists, predecessors to Tories or Loyalists, I had to bite my tongue several times.

At one point, Abner laid his napkin on his plate and announced, "I received word today that Sibley is selling his acreage. He's given me the chance to make an offer before it goes public."

Gyles seemed surprised. "That is wonderful news, Father."

"Yes, it is." He looked hard at Hezekiah and then Gyles. "I cannot see him until next week."

"Father, you know Sibley," Gyles said. "He is too impatient to wait around for an answer."

"Exactly."

"It is a long trip, but Hezekiah and I can do it," Gyles said, then looked to his younger brother for approval.

"Yes, of course. How soon do you want to leave?" Hezekiah took a drink.

"I can be ready in an hour. How about you, Hezekiah?"

"I can be ready then."

"But I thought we were going into town today," Arabella said, pouting. She turned to me. "We will still go."

I shrugged. With Hezekiah on a business trip, I wouldn't be doing much. "All right, Arabella. Let's go shopping."

I thought I would enjoy myself, but that was an understatement. Arabella knew how to shop. I don't think we left a single store unvisited. Hezekiah had given me a few shillings to spend, but I didn't see anything that jumped out and said, "Buy me." In fact, I still had the shillings in my pocket when I stood with her as she stuffed her latest purchases into the coach.

"Doesn't anything interest you, Elizabeth?" Arabella asked.

I shrugged. "I did like that brooch in the last store we were at."

He eyes widened and she grabbed my hand. "Then, you shall have it!" She pulled me toward the store.

"No, Arabella. That is not necessary—I would have bought it if I really wanted to."

She stopped pulling and dropped my hand. "Nonsense." She lifted her petticoats and crossed the dusty road. "Come along, Elizabeth!"

"Really—I don't need it!" I called after her.

She turned back. "Of course you need it. Every woman needs a proper brooch." Arabella tilted her head. "You best come with me. I'm buying a brooch for you whether you like it or not, so you might as well show me the one you were admiring, or you will be stuck with the one I pick."

I followed her reluctantly into the shop. It was always hard for me to accept the charity of others, but of course this was more of a gift than charity. Arabella picked up a gaudy brooch with a large blue stone, and I shook my head. She gestured to a brooch lined with emeralds and pearls. "Oh, no! Way too expensive." I waved it away.

She held it in front of me. "Well, I'm going to buy this one, unless you—"

Her cunning trick worked. A puff of exasperated air left my throat. "There. That one." I pointed to a far less extravagant one—a small, silver brooch inlaid with purple stones shaped like a flower.

"It is very beautiful, indeed, Elizabeth."

I laid my hand on her arm. "It is too much, Arabella. Please don't spend your money on me."

"It's not my money, Elizabeth." She turned and smiled at me. "It's Papa's."

I sighed as she pinned it on my dress. There were plenty of privileged families where I came from. I went to school with a few students whose parents adorned them with the most expensive cars and clothes. Though I wasn't one of them, I didn't need to wonder what that was like—I had a wealthy grandfather. The year my father died, his dad, my grandpa Martin, showed up at our door loaded with gifts. I mean, too many gifts, stacked all over the place, like he had robbed a shopping mall, backed up a truck, and loaded everything imaginable into it.

It was really cool at first, but then I realized I didn't like them as much as the things I had bought with my own money. Weird, huh. I can't explain the feeling, but the items I worked for just meant more to me. I fingered the brooch. Of course, I could make an exception with this—I loved bling.

Arabella and I went shopping two or three times a week while Hezekiah and Gyles were gone. She bought me more 17th Century jewelry pieces than I'd ever be able to wear. Once I figured out how to stop her by purchasing things myself, I started buying far less substantial things like maple sugar candies, and yes, dark chocolate imported from Europe. I needed chocolate, but not even that could calm my racing heart. My grandmother's trial was fast approaching.

Finally, the day came when Hezekiah walked back into my life. He seemed a little edgy.

"I need to go to Salem Village tomorrow."

I drew in a quick breath. "Me too! How did you know?" I had been thinking of little else.

He looked at me funny. "What are you talking about?"

"My grandmother's trial is tomorrow."

He scuffed his shoe against the wooden floor. "If I hadn't returned—" He ran his finger across his chin. "You were going to go without me, weren't you?"

Eeks. Was I that transparent? "Um, yeah, about that." I bit my thumbnail and gave a slight nod.

His lips pursed. "Elizabeth. That is foolhardy and dangerous." He nearly growled as he paced the floor. "You leave me no other recourse." He grimaced, "other than tying you up until the trials are over or locking you in the room." He pointed down.

My eyes widened. Even though the underground room was beautiful, being locked in it would make it a prison.

He drew in a long breath and stared at me. "How soon can you be ready?"

He didn't laugh, when I said, "Now."

I hurried upstairs and grabbed my bag. Tomorrow morning, I would be at the trials when they began. This time, it would be different. I would be quiet, stay completely hidden in the back, and slip out before it was over. That was my plan. Whether or not it happened that way, we would see.

Just before nightfall, we arrived at Zebulon's and dismounted. He was working in his garden but stood when we approached. "Oh, hello!" he said, then embraced us both. "What a splendid surprise."

"I'm sorry we come unannounced," Hezekiah replied.

"Not to worry." Zebulon turned to me. "And how are you?"

"I am fine, thank you."

"Wonderful. Why don't we go inside, and I'll tell Sarah to put two more plates out for supper."

As soon as we entered the house, Sarah threw her arms around me. "How are you, Elizabeth?"

"I'm good," I said, returning her hug. "And you?"

She patted her round belly and grinned wide.

"Oh!" I hugged her again. "Congratulations!"

"That's wonderful, Zeb." Hezekiah grabbed his cousin's shoulders and gave him an affectionate shake.

Zebulon grinned and pointed at us. "So, when are you two going to get married, Hezekiah?"

The heat rose on my cheeks. "Um . . ."

"I'm hoping for a November wedding." Hezekiah put his arm around my shoulders.

I slapped his arm away. "You haven't even asked me, Hezekiah." I mean, after all, he could have at least done that.

Zebulon laughed. "Well, November is a good time for a wedding—very popular, too."

I turned to Sarah. "So, have you picked out any baby names?" The men sidestepped the baby talk and began a heated discussion about the ongoing war.

"Yes," she said timidly. "We've decided to name the child after Zebulon, if it's a boy, and . . . well . . . you, if it's a girl."

"Me?" I drew my head back. "Sweet!"

She tilted her head. "Sweet?"

"It's very nice, thank you."

"You're welcome."

She went to pick up the heavy, cast-iron pot of soup, but I stopped her and carried it to the table. "You shouldn't lift really heavy things when you are pregnant."

"Truly? I did not know that."

Immediately, I realized that piece of information might save the life of more than just her child if she passed it around. Maybe I should go back to the future before I totally changed the fabric of the past. I held so very little hope that would ever happen. Besides, Hezekiah and I might have been meant to be together, according to his theory and his little book of magic. I thought about Trent and cringed.

Maybe I could join a monastery and become a nun. Did nuns take an oath of silence like some monks? If so, I'd last for about an hour and then be on the street again. Nope. Governess was the best position for me. I would wear my hair in a tight bun and practice being straight-lipped. Perfect. I could do that.

Sarah made a face. "What are you doing?"

"Oh!" I laughed. "I was deep in thought, I guess."

"About what?"

I sighed. I needed a friend to talk to, but even as nice as Sarah was, she would toss me to the curb if I told her where I came from. But I could tell her some of the truth. "I'm not sure about getting married."

Her eyes widened. "Why not? Is it Hezekiah?"

"Oh, heavens, no."

"Then what?"

I didn't know what to say. "Oh, I guess it's just the wedding jitters—nervous about being a wife and all."

She nodded. "Yes, I know what you mean, but don't worry. Being with Zebulon is the most natural thing in the world to me."

"Oh, that's so sweet—uh . . . nice." I studied her face. "Do you think certain couples are meant to be together?"

"You mean predestination?"

Predestination—I ran that word through my memory bank. That was the belief that no matter what you did, it didn't matter. Things were already set in place—God had already assigned you to go to heaven or hell when you died, before you had a chance to do anything to merit one or the other. I didn't believe in that at all. "No, not that. I mean, do you think there's only one man for one woman?"

She drew her head back. "Certainly not. Men go off to war and never come back. A woman has got to marry again when that happens."

"Yes, of course." I could see I was getting nowhere with this. "Why did you choose Zebulon to be your husband over all the other men out there?"

She looked at me funny. "He was the only one that asked."

"Oh." *Never mind. New subject.* "How did you make your soup?"

Later that night, while I lay awake wondering if Hezekiah made it to the tavern okay, I thought about Sarah's simplistic approach to life. She seemed happy, which made me wonder if I thought too much or tried to analyze everything too deeply. I shook my head. I was in so much trouble being a 2015 girl stuck in the past. I couldn't even voice my strong opinion in 1692 without people deciding I was totally weird.

Tomorrow was going to be difficult, and the circle girls would be there again in all their theatrical hysteria. Trying not to think about it, I eventually fell into a restless sleep.

The delicious aroma of bacon sizzling over a fire woke me. I sat up and rubbed my eyes. The sun was just beginning to rise over the horizon.

"Good morning, Elizabeth. Hezekiah is already here. He's tying his horse up."

"Good morning." I stretched and then stood.

Zebulon sat at the table. "Elizabeth, may I talk to you?"

"Of course." I pulled a chair out across from him.

"I'll get right to the point. Sarah tells me you're afraid of getting married."

I saw her squirm off to the side while turning the bacon over. "It's okay, Sarah," I told her. "I don't mind talking about it."

"It's true then?" He looked at me solemnly.

I nodded.

"Well, before he comes in here, let me tell you that our Hezekiah is deeply in love with you. I've never seen him happier."

Mmm. Nice. "Um, yes, but he's only what, seventeen?"

Zebulon shook his head. "No, ma'am. Hezekiah is eighteen."

I shrugged. I was close. Puritans often married older, well, the women at least. Oh, wait. Hezekiah was not a Puritan, but as an English Royalist, he was definitely at a marriageable age at eighteen.

"Do you love him enough to be his wife?" Zebulon leaned across the table.

I sighed. "Yes. I love Hezekiah very much. I want nothing more than to be his wife. To be by his side forever would be like heaven." My voice trailed off to nothing. Zebulon looked past me and smirked. I swallowed hard. "He's behind me, isn't he?" Zebulon nodded as if he just played the best joke. I wanted to strangle him. I turned around.

"Back door." Hezekiah timidly pointed to the door behind him.

I noted a glimmer of hope and a trace of amusement in his eyes. *Dang.* Weeks of carefully laid groundwork destroyed in one fleeting moment of truth. Oh well—if he was right about the souls God creates, it didn't matter. Anyway, he knew about that theory and still planned to send me back to the future. I wondered what Zebulon and Sarah would say to that. It is true love to sacrifice one's own wants for another. Hezekiah was trying to do for me what I was trying to do for him. We were perfect for each other, so why did God have us born so far apart?

After breakfast dishes, I excused myself and joined Hezekiah and Zebulon at the front door.

"You aren't really going to that atrocious display of misguided justice?" Zebulon said, his hand on Hezekiah's shoulder.

"I'm afraid we are, but I need to pick up a document in Beverly for my father first," Hezekiah replied.

I waited patiently, trying not to show my anxiety. I had no idea why I was in such a hurry to get to a place that I would be visually, mentally, and spiritually accosted.

Hezekiah took my hand. "Are you ready?"

I hugged Zebulon and Sarah and followed Hezekiah out the door. After picking up the document, we proceeded toward Salem Town. It was a lovely day. We couldn't have asked for better weather. In front of the courthouse, Hezekiah took my hand in his. "Are you sure about this?"

No. "Yes," I said. "Just stay close to me."

"You can count on that."

We stepped through the door into a madhouse. Court was already in session.

"How do you plead, Goody Martin?"

My aged grandmother stood on a square platform raised a foot from the floor. "I have no hand in witchcraft."

The afflicted writhed on the floor, some gagging and choking and screaming, like they would die.

The judges seemed distressed and unable to control the situation. I recognized Reverend Deodat Lawson, whom I had met when I first arrived in Salem Village.

"Sirs, sirs!" Reverend Lawson banged his hand on the desk. "I must point out that the judges need patience to garner their testimonies between these spectral attacks!" He gestured to the girls. "Look how some are twisting grotesquely as if every joint was dislocated! And there—some vomit!" He gasped. "Why I think it is blood, is it not?"

A woman close to the front bent down, stuck her finger in it, and brought it to her nose. She nearly fainted but finally managed to say, "Yes, it is indeed blood!" The entire room erupted in a riotous uproar. I thought I would get crushed by some of the spectators in their frantic hurry to leave.

Reverend Lawson banged the desk repeatedly, until finally, the scene settled somewhat. I held my fingers to my stomach. Some of the girls had blood still seeping from their mouths. It was like *The Zombies Meet Salem,* only with real blood and authentic makeup. Trembling, I turned my head into Hezekiah. *What am I doing here?*

"We can leave anytime, Bess. Just say the word." He tugged gently on me.

"No, I'm all right." I sat up and listened numbly as the Court of Oyer and Terminer read the transcript from my grandmother's first examination. She did not react to it, but stood straight, her hands folded in front of her. It had been nearly two months since I had last seen her, and she looked thin and weak.

I felt sick to my stomach as I realized most of the people sitting directly behind the girls at the front of the room must have been my grandmother's neighbors, there to testify against her. I recognized John Atkinson, the man Hezekiah and I had seen arguing with my uncle outside of Salem Village a few months back. John seemed eager to retell his lies.

Sure enough, neighbor after neighbor stood before the court and made accusations against my grandmother—none of which had any substance at all. Ghost stories. Spectral evidence. Not a single piece of solid proof. *Are you kidding me?* I bit my finger hard to keep from calling out.

"Goody Atkins of Newbury," Judge Hathorne addressed a woman who had taken the stand.

"Yes, I am Sarah Atkins."

The magistrate sat back in his chair, looking bored with the proceedings. "What is your grievance against Goody Martin?"

"A few years back, it had been raining and the roads were a terrible mess." She pointed outside.

"Yes, yes, get on with it," the judge urged.

She wound a kerchief around in her hands. "I wasn't expecting any company that day—foot traffic seemed hardly likely."

Reverend Parris dipped his quill into the inkwell and continued recording the trial.

"But Goody Martin appeared at my door." Sarah's eyebrows rose. "I shooed my children away from the hearth so that she could dry her petticoats, but she told me that she was quite dry and didn't need to sit by the fire."

"And?" Hathorne said impatiently.

Sarah's eyes widened as she recalled the incident. "Her petticoats didn't have a trace of mud, and even the soles of her shoes looked dry." The loud murmur that arose from the spectators seemed to fuel Sarah's indignance, and she continued, "Such weather would have had me wet to the knee!" Several women in the crowd nodded.

"What do you conclude from this, Goody Atkins?" Hathorne asked gruffly. "Did she take a coach or ride a horse?"

"Oh no, no. She told me she had walked the whole way from Amesbury."

Hathorne's lips twitched. "Really?" He turned to my grandmother and lowered his eyes. "What do you have to say to that, Goody Martin?"

She grimaced. "I scorn to have a dragged tail," my grandmother replied sharply.

Yeah, well who wouldn't? I didn't like to soil the hem of my jeans, either, and rolled them up or stuffed them in my boots if I had to walk down a muddy road. She probably hefted her petticoat high to keep it from getting muddy, but I knew Sarah would go down in history as claiming my grandmother had flown to Newbury on a broom instead of walking.

"Is that all you have to say for yourself?"

My grandmother's frail hands formed into fists at her sides. "I have no hand in witchcraft," she snapped. "I have led a most virtuous and holy life."

"Well, it seems like your neighbors think otherwise," said Hathorne haughtily. He looked out over the crowd. "Is there any here that would speak for Goody Martin?" He challenged.

"She's innocent," I mumbled, under my breath. Hezekiah pulled me closer. The woman in front of us turned and looked at me.

"The court finds you guilty." Hathorne shooed my grandmother away like she was a naughty child that annoyed him.

I tensed and bit down on my tongue.

Hezekiah whispered in my ear. "We've stayed too long." He started to turn me around.

Suddenly, the woman in front of us cried out. "She thinks Goody Martin is innocent!" She pointed at me.

"Come, Elizabeth," Hezekiah said sternly and moved me quickly toward the door.

Just as we stepped through it, I looked back. Betty Hubbard caught my eye. Her hands flew above her head and she twisted like a pretzel as she pointed at me and screamed.

"WITCH!"

Twenty-Two
The Warrant

A few people rushed out the door after us, but mostly just to stare. Hezekiah steadied my horse and helped me on, then mounted his own. I was numb with grief, and now fear as well. We rode quickly out of town and did not stop for several minutes. Finally, when it appeared no one was following us, Hezekiah slowed his horse to a trot.

"We should not have gone to the trial."

My heart raced. I had wanted to support my grandmother and help if I could, but now I really might share her fate. She and four other women would be hanged in twenty days. *What was I thinking showing up there?* Meda had warned me to keep my tongue, and I had tried, but obviously not hard enough.

We rode on silently while I imagined my trial in front of Judge Hathorne. If he thought my grandmother had a sharp tongue, wait until he heard me. At least I'd have the pleasure of telling him how I felt, and I wondered if my grandmother had thought the same.

We arrived back to the estate late that night. I was dead tired and fell onto my bed. Early in the morning, I awoke to the sound of angry voices downstairs. Mrs. Fayette and Martha rushed into my room and pulled me from my bed. Lucia hurried in after them and began to straighten the bed I had lain on.

"Come, Lady Elizabeth," Mrs. Fayette whispered urgently.

Martha stuck her head out the doorway and then ushered us into the hall. "This way!" She gestured for us to follow. The yelling continued downstairs. Mrs. Fayette and Martha pulled me along until we got to the servants' doors at the end of the hall.

"What's wrong?" I asked, fearing their answer.

"Hurry, me wane! They have come for ye!" Martha's hands shook as she pulled me onto the narrow, steep steps that led down to the servants' area.

"They have a warrant for your arrest, but we won't let them find you!" Mrs. Fayette led us quickly to a room. Charles was already there and had opened a trap door in the floor. "They will never find you down there. Quick!"

Argh. Another underground room. I was sure this one was not going to be nearly as pleasant as Hezekiah's. As I hurried down the wooden ladder, I missed most of the rungs and nearly fell more than once. Mrs. Fayette followed me. Halfway down, Charles handed her a lantern and a basket. Martha looked at me from above.

"I'm comin', lass—give me a minute."

Lowering herself slowly, she slipped like I did but regained her footing. Charles came partway down and handed us another lantern. "I'll bang the floor three times when they are coming. Don't make a sound." He pulled himself back up and closed the trap door, leaving us with only the light from the two lanterns.

"How long will we have to stay down here?" I asked, my voice quivering.

"Shh!" Martha whispered. "We mustn't make a sound."

The shadows cast on Mrs. Fayette's and Martha's faces gave them an eerie, almost spectral look. Martha shone her lantern around the room. Its walls were large stones piled on top of each other like the cellar in my mother's house back in Danvers. Interesting how some things survived time. As I recalled, though, those stone walls could let in a host of unwanted visitors. Still, I was too freaked out about getting a warrant for my arrest in 1692 Salem to worry about a few rats.

It would take a long while for them to search the house, as big as it was, and then they would no doubt search the barns and gardens as well. It could be hours before we were able to go back upstairs.

Pacing the small room, I wondered how I was going to get out of this. I imagined Hezekiah would send me off to England as quickly as possible. I opened my mouth to ask the women about it, then closed it. With no idea how close the officers were to the trap door, I could not risk making a sound.

I found two small crates and quietly brought them over for Martha and Mrs. Fayette to sit on. Then I resumed pacing. It was hard to tell how much time passed, but after what seemed like at least a couple of hours, my gaze fell upon the basket. Mrs. Fayette quietly lifted the lid to reveal bread, cheese, and fruit. She sat it down between us, then removed a napkin and laid it on top of the basket. I nibbled on a piece of cheese but otherwise couldn't eat.

Suddenly, a rat scampered across my foot and dashed toward the cheese, knocking it to the ground. "Eeks!" I screamed, jumped back, and fell into Martha. She grabbed me and covered my mouth with her trembling hand, but it was too late.

THUMP THUMP THUMP

Fear swept through me as the loud knocks echoed above. I grabbed at the folds of my dress. They must have heard my scream—I was doomed. I glanced at Mrs. Fayette and Martha, whose faces reflected my fear. I swallowed hard. "Stay back in the shadows," I whispered. When the officers opened the door, they would see only me, so only I would be apprehended.

Footsteps scratched the floor above us. We waited. After a few minutes, I began to have hope that they hadn't heard me, and after thirty minutes, I was sure they hadn't. At first, I felt irrepressible joy, and then I plummeted into a tapestry of conflicted feelings, from rage and panic to gratitude and love.

I broke into tears and fought back the sobs teetering at the edge of my throat, ready to burst out. Martha put her arm around me. That was meant to help, but I only wanted to cry louder. I wanted to scream. I wanted to hit something. I wanted to shake some sense into Betty Hubbard. I wanted to laugh, and to love, and to live, and not to die.

Much later, the trap door scraped against its frame and popped up. Hezekiah looked down into our hole with a solemn expression like I'd never seen before. He gestured for me to come up first, but I shook my head. "They will go before me."

After we emerged out of the dungeon, he showed us the warrant.

You are in their Majesties' Names hereby Required to Apprehend & bring before us (upon Friday next being the Eighth day of July by Ten of the Clock afore noon at the house of Nathaniel Ingersoll in Salem Village) the body of Elizabeth Bowley of Salem Village, who standeth charged in behalf of their Majesties with high Suspicion of Sundry Acts of Witchcraft done upon the Body of Elizabeth Hubbard ae. Betty Hubbard & others in Salem Village, whereby great hurt hath been done them: And hereof you are not to fail.

Salem dated July 1, 1692
John Hathorne
Jonathan Corwin

Uncontrollable spasms rushed down my spine like water off a cliff and my knees gave way. Hezekiah grabbed me from behind and helped me sit. "Oh no! Oh no! Oh no!" I gasped. The world closed in around me, spinning. My lungs constricted, pressing out precious air that I could no longer breathe in. I sobbed hysterically.

Hezekiah shooed everyone away and drew me near. "I won't let them take you."

His body trembled beside me. I felt his fear and it fueled mine. I desperately wanted to believe him, but would he be able to? And what if he was caught aiding and abetting a suspected witch? Surely, they would be watching him closely now. I knew what they would do next. I had read the transcripts and knew them well. The men that delivered the warrant would return to the court of Oyer and Terminer, which would issue a second warrant. "They will be back, Hezekiah."

"Yes, I know, but you will not be here." He caressed my hair. "I sent Charles to follow them to make sure they aren't watching the place. We will wait to see what he says."

I nodded and turned my face into his chest. "Where will I go?"

"I will not let them hurt you, Elizabeth."

I looked up and saw Hezekiah's lips moving, but for a second, it was my father's reassuring voice I heard. I suppose that should have given me great comfort, but instead it made me long for my father more than ever. I shook my head and wiped tears from my face.

All of a sudden it hit me that there was no sense in getting all worked up. If I died, I died. My grandmother's last words were "I have lived a good and virtuous life." I believed in God and that life continued on after death. I was my grandmother's granddaughter. It was time for me to act like it. I breathed in deep. "All right, what can I do?"

He cocked his head to the side. "What do you mean?"

"I'm not going to go into hiding, Hezekiah. I am innocent, and I will not act guilty."

"Elizabeth. They will arrest you and you will be tried for acts of witchcraft." He grabbed my shoulders. "You cannot fight them. You will not win."

"Then I will die trying."

He dropped his hands. "You are so stubborn!"

"Yep." I had been told that all of my life, and now I knew why. "It's in my blood." My body tingled with fright and my heart raced, but a peaceful, sweet calm settled over me. I took a deep breath and let it roll out slowly. I would not live in fear—I would simply live. "Let's have a party to celebrate our engagement."

"What?" He looked at me like I was crazy.

I drew my head back and grinned. "You do want to marry me, right?"

"Well, yes, of course, but—"

"I'll take that as an offer. We'll put Arabella in charge of it. She likes parties."

"Elizabeth, this is no time for a party."

"Sure it is. We can announce our engagement and invite everyone—even Judge Hathorne."

His eyes widened. "That is ridiculous!"

"We will have it right here at the estate. And while everyone is looking for me here . . ."

His eyebrows rose. "Oh, I get it. You won't be here. It's a decoy." He tilted his head. "Isn't that kind of like hiding?"

"Hiding in broad daylight? No. Not really. They will not expect me to run if we've announced an engagement party. They just won't be able to find me until then, because I will be so busy getting ready for it."

"And then what, Bess? What happens when they do not find you here?"

"Hopefully, I'll already be on a ship out of here with Arabella. Remember? She leaves next week."

"Yes, but what about me?"

"You." I paused. You will do your best acting ever. You will be the grieving fiancé, who can't find his love anywhere."

"But what will I tell them?"

"You will tell them . . . I was abducted by Indians along the trail."

"Hmm, that's not bad."

"Yeah, I know. It's a talent I have." I could make up a story. It used to get me in trouble. Now, I hoped it would get me out of it.

Twenty-Three
Decoy

Charles returned with a good report. He had followed the officers from a distance several miles out of town. They were headed back toward Salem. That would give us time to put our plan in place. It was supper time, and Hezekiah led me into the dining room.

Abner jumped up. "Oh, Lady Elizabeth!" He looked like he was in shock. "I am so very sorry."

Victoria came over and wrapped her arms around my shoulders. "Oh, my dear, Gyles has told us everything. It's just incredible that in this day and age, something as barbaric as this still happens." She made a small exasperated sound. "And to think we left England to get away from this type of small mindedness."

Arabella slapped the table. "Well, my papa will never hear of it." She turned to me. "My ship sets sail in three days, but we must leave for England at once."

Hezekiah spoke up. "You cannot leave any earlier. There is an embargo on all vessels departing the harbor, but Phips is working to get that lifted and expects it any day."

Touched by their concern, I ran my fingers across the carved wood on the top of the chair I stood behind. "Hopefully the embargo will be lifted in time, because we have a plan."

"You have a plan?" Abner leaned forward.

"Yes, and it's a pretty good one, Father," said Gyles slyly.

Hezekiah cleared his throat. "Elizabeth is going to be attacked by Indians."

"Again," Gyles said drolly. "Only this time, she is going to die."

Arabella gasped. "No! You can't let that happen!"

"It won't really happen," Gyles replied. "She's just going to pretend."

"Whatever for?"

"They'll stop looking for her if they think she is dead, and then she can board the ship with you to England."

"Oh, but, that's three days from now," Arabella said slowly. "What if they find her before then?" She wrung her hands nervously.

"Well, that's where you come in." I took her hand in mine. "I want you to help me throw a party." I sat down across from her.

She made a face. "What? At a time like this?"

"Especially at a time like this, Arabella," Hezekiah said quietly. He stood, picked up his goblet, and tapped it with his fork. "If she says yes, then Lady Elizabeth will be my wife."

Victoria's hands flew to her face. "That is wonderful!"

Abner frowned. "I don't understand. Elizabeth has a warrant for her arrest and you are announcing your engagement?"

Hezekiah's eyes twinkled. "If she says, yes."

Gyles stood up beside his brother and explained, "We will throw an engagement party, and on the day of that party," Giles began.

"If she says yes," Hezekiah repeated.

Giles continued, "During the engagement party, Charles will come back with the news of Elizabeth's abduction." He looked at me. "That will explain her absence from her own party, but she will really be on the ship set sail for England."

Arabella cocked her head to the side. "Does that mean you're really not engaged?"

Wondering about that too, I gazed questioningly at Hezekiah.

He looked down at me with those green eyes. "Well, actually . . ." He got down on one knee.

My heart stopped beating. *What is he doing? OMHeck. He is not going to—.* My eyes widened. He held a beautiful topaz-and-diamond ring in his fingers. It had to be a family heirloom. I glanced quickly at his mother and saw the merriment in her eyes.

Hezekiah cleared his throat. "Elizabeth Bowley, will you be my wife?"

Arabella clasped her hands together and squealed—really, a real squeal.

I stared at the ring and then at his eyes. Was this part of the ruse? He had used my fake surname of Bowley, so I assumed it was and played along. Placing my hand on my hip, I flipped my other hand in the air. "Why yes, Hezekiah Hanson. Of course I will." He slipped the ring on my finger, and I closed my eyes and waited. It was a sweet howbeit quick kiss. Hoping for a second one, I closed my eyes, but after a few empty seconds, I opened them to find him talking quietly to Gyles.

Gyles sat down next to Arabella. "Do you want to help us save Elizabeth?"

She brought her hands to her neck. "Of course I do!"

"All right, then this is what we need you to do—shop, shop, shop."

She looked confused. "You want me to go shopping?"

"It's what you do best, Arabella." Gyles grinned. "We will stay two steps ahead of them—take them on a wild goose chase."

"We?"

"Yes, Charles and I will accompany you, along with Mrs. Fayette and Martha. They will think we are in one town, when we will really be in another."

Arabella's eyes widened. "Ohh." She nodded. "I like that plan."

Hezekiah looked at Arabella. "I want you and Elizabeth to make a list of all the stores and shops in Boston and the surrounding areas. Make another list from the first—but reverse the order of the stores. That is the list we will leave on the desk in the study for the men serving the second warrant to find."

Mrs. Fayette entered the room and handed Abner a sealed envelope. She gave me a formal nod, her face fraught with worry. I wanted to jump up and hug her, to reassure her that everything would be all right, but I wasn't sure it would be. And I knew it wouldn't be for my grandmother and many others.

Abner opened the envelope, read the paper inside, and then waved it in the air. "Good news. The embargo will be lifted tomorrow."

"That is good news," Hezekiah said.

"Indeed!" Gyles turned to his mother. "Will you create the guest invitations for the engagement party and send them off today?"

"For what day?"

"July 19th."

My eyes widened. "But that's the day of the hangings."

"Exactly. Everyone will be headed to Salem, making it fairly easy for the staged Indian attack to be seen and then relayed to the court." Gyles sighed. "We have to stage the attack near Salem. The court needs to believe you are dead, Elizabeth."

That made sense, as long as no one tried to rescue me. Suddenly, all I could think about was my grandmother. Hezekiah and Gyles were going all out so I could escape with my life to England, but my grandmother . . . I groaned.

Arabella was the only one who noticed. "What's wrong, Elizabeth?"

I pushed a loose strand of hair behind my ear and stuffed my emotions away. "It's just so soon." Too soon for my grandmother to die and too soon to be separated from Hezekiah. I glanced over at him.

Arabella came around the table and rubbed my back. "He'll join us later, Elizabeth."

It was so kind of her. I was ashamed of my initial judgment of her as Draculette, but isn't that the way it always is? Once you get to know someone, you really do love them. Although, I might still call her Draculette in a purely endearing way. "Thanks, Arabella. You really think he will join us soon?"

She nodded. "Oh yes, very much so." Hezekiah looked my way and smiled and then returned to his conversation with his father and older brother.

The double doors opened and the servants came in bearing trays of food. I had only eaten a few bites of cheese that day, and I was famished. When we finished eating, Hezekiah escorted Arabella and me to the study. He pulled out an inkwell and quill and opened a drawer with parchment paper stored in it. "If you need anything else, I'll be in the parlor."

I pulled up a chair alongside Arabella's. "Well, let's make that shopping list." I didn't have to say it twice. She dipped the quill into the inkwell, and soon a long list of every existing shop in Boston and the surrounding areas lay before us. She placed one to three stars beside each one according to her preference. Then she looked at the list and said, "It looks good, doesn't it?"

I nodded. "Yes, and now it's time to make the decoy list." That took a little more time and a lot more strategy, but finally, we placed both lists side by side and checked to make sure we were always far away from the locations on the decoy list.

Theresa Sneed

"My turn." I took out a clean sheet of parchment paper and meticulously recopied the faux list. What a mess. I missed the simple things in life, like the pencil. By the time I was done with the copy, my fingers were covered in ink. Arabella checked on me throughout, shaking her head at my poor penmanship. *Yeah, I'd like to see her handle a tablet.* I fanned the wet ink with my blotchy fingers.

After a while, Hezekiah and Gyles returned. All three lists lay on the desk. Gyles leaned over them. "Very well done." He picked up one of the decoy lists. "Why did you make two of these?"

"I thought it would be good to remember where we had sent them."

He nodded. "Good thinking, Elizabeth." He picked up the quill. "One more thing—we need to make sure you are on the road to Salem Town on the morning of the nineteenth and have plenty of time to get on that ship before it sails." He dipped the quill in the inkwell, then wrote on the bottom of the list.

I swallowed hard. The nineteenth was the day I dreaded the most, the day my grandmother would be hanged in Salem Town. I would be so close to the hangings—one last chance to save her. I bit my lower lip.

Gyles continued. "We will position servants to signal us when a passerby is coming."

"After we receive the signal, I start screaming?"

"Yes. Dressed as an Indian, Charles is going to let himself be briefly seen before pulling you kicking and screaming into the trees. Once in the dense woods, he will change out of the Indian clothes and work his way with you farther down the road, where I will be waiting, ready to whisk you away to the ship."

Charles had dark hair and a deep tan—he might be able to pull it off, if no one got close enough to see his blue eyes. But I worried he'd get shot. "What if someone tries to follow us?"

268

"The servants will choose unlikely people to witness the attack—those who would flee from a conflict rather than face it."

I smirked. *Well, that covers pretty much everyone around here.* In all fairness, they were scared to death to say what was really on their minds, for fear they would be accused, tried, and hanged too. Not many would go after an Indian into the woods and risk their own lives. Equally so, not many would step forward to save the lives of five innocent women who would be cruelly executed that day.

"Where will you be?" I asked Hezekiah.

He cleared his throat. "I will be close, but not involved. We don't want to arouse any suspicion."

He didn't tell me where he would be that morning, but I suspected he'd be near the port, and maybe even at the hangings. Suddenly, I realized something. I could sneak by the hangings on my way to the port too. I just couldn't let anyone see me, especially after our hopefully successful enactment of my death. I knew it wasn't a good idea, but it wouldn't leave my head.

Gyles tapped the top of the desk. "I'm going to place this decoy list right here." He carefully laid it on the desk. "Take these other two and put them in your bags." He handed one to Arabella—the master mind and list navigator—and the other to me. "You must follow this list perfectly, Arabella."

She nodded. "I will do my best."

We didn't expect the court to show up that night. They would need another full day of travel to get back from Salem Town after acquiring a second warrant. We took that time to check and recheck our plan. Victoria had finished the invitations and sent them off, hand delivered to their various locations— mostly family friends and associates in the Boston area. We were going to have a quite an engagement party in a couple of days, and I wasn't even going to be there to enjoy it.

Victoria entered the room. "The cooks are preparing a feast like none other for the party."

I frowned. "It's such an extravagance—I hate to see your time and money wasted." I turned to Hezekiah. "Why do we need to have a party—isn't the Indian attack enough?"

"Having you and Arabella out on a shopping spree for the party is the perfect cover and will keep the men busy who are serving the second warrant. It will also keep you safe for the time being. When Hathorne reads his invitation, he might even call the pursuit off and just plan to have his men show up at the party to arrest you. In fact, I'm fairly sure he will do just that."

Gyles nodded. "That's when Charles will show up without you and tell everyone what happened. You will already be on the ship, as it leaves right around the time the party will start."

"Why would they believe that I was dead?"

Hezekiah smoothed his hands on his shirt. "Well, now work with us on this, Elizabeth." I didn't like the look in his eye. "Charles is going to drag you into the woods, and, uh . . . Martha is going to cut your hair off."

My eyes popped open. "What?"

"Martha and Mrs. Fayette will be waiting in the woods to help you change your dress and stab holes in it. Then, they will splash a pint of cow's blood on your chopped-off hair and your dress. That's what Charles will show everyone at the party."

"Don't you think they'll need more proof than that?" I asked.

Gyles said two words: "Spectral evidence."

True that. In the bizarre world of the court of Oyer and Terminer, finding a bloody dress and my hair would be stone-solid proof.

Charles entered the room. He held a large box.

"Oh good. You found them." Victoria opened the box and pulled out a traditional Indian outfit. She held it up to Charles's body.

I didn't want to know where she got the clothes, or why she had them. I bit down on my tongue, reminding myself that she wanted to help me.

The plan was in place. We would leave early in the morning and head to Boston to go shopping. Once our pursuers arrived, the decoy list would send them straight back to Salem. That should take care of day one. We would not come back to the mansion again, so I needed to say goodbye and bring all of my belongings with me. Arabella had her things boxed up and sent to the docks. I knew that after this was all over, many more boxes filled with items from her shopping spree would be aboard the ship heading for England.

The next morning, I awoke with a start. Today, I would say goodbye to Hezekiah. Today, I would in effect, be running harder than I ever ran before.

I pulled myself out of bed and dressed. Martha knocked lightly on the door and stuck her head inside. "Ye are up early." She came over to me. I nodded and let her lace up the back of my dress. "'Tis gonna be a grand day."

I hoped so. I looked out the window at a breathtaking sunrise. "Yes," I said numbly, trying hard not to think about Hezekiah.

After a quick breakfast, we loaded up. Hezekiah helped me into the coach beside Martha, Mrs. Fayette, and Arabella. Gyles would ride shotgun, with Charles driving the coach.

Hezekiah seemed preoccupied. He held my hand a little longer than usual. "I will see you soon," he said, stumbling over his words. He stepped away and closed the door, and before I could say a word, Charles whipped the horses and we were off. I turned all the way around in the coach and watched Hezekiah until he was nothing more than a speck, and I was nothing more than a compete and hopeless wreck.

Twenty-Four
Change of Plans

It didn't take long for me to realize I loathed shopping, though I did enjoy the company. And despite how worried we were that somehow the officers would find me, I managed to learn new things about all three of my female traveling companions. With each stop, the men watched outside while we shopped away. Even Martha and Mrs. Fayette enjoyed themselves and bought a few things as well.

Both nights we stayed in the taverns scheduled on our list. The second night was the worst for me. I didn't know how well everyone else slept, but I was nervous for the following day—the day of my staged death, and the day of my grandmother's real one. She was going to the gallows, and I couldn't do anything about it. The thought made me physically ill.

Suddenly Martha was next to me, wrapping her arm around my shoulders. "Are ye all right, me wane?"

I almost told her everything—my relation to Susannah Martin, my knowledge of the travesty happening in Salem Town, and my great need to stop it from happening. "It's—it's . . ." I sighed heavily. "I guess I'm just afraid, Aunt Martha."

"There, there me love," she said softly, stroking my hair. "Everythin' will go all right."

I wanted to believe her, but fear gripped my heart. We were about to stage an Indian attack, and if it was discovered to be a ruse, we would all be arrested. How could I put them at risk? I should leave right now—do this on my own. Hezekiah had given me a good amount of money. I could buy my own horse and just go—ride hard, far away. I loved Maine. I could go there, live up north. *Whew.* A puff of air escaped my throat. Martha held me tighter. I pulled away. "I can't do this to you. I just can't."

She studied my eyes, as if she knew my thoughts, and maybe she had guessed them. "Ah, me dear wane. Ye would help me if it was me in trouble. Wouldn't ye?"

I turned into her chest and wept. Yes. Without a doubt, I would spend my last breath helping my aunt Martha. A calmness settled over me. Why hadn't I thought of that before? *I will spend my last breath helping my grandmother.* It was the struggle I had kept buried deep down. How could I ever live with myself if I didn't try to stop the hangings?

Mrs. Fayette came into the room with a new dress. I grimaced, knowing it would be ruined soon—stabbed and stained with cow's blood. I ran my fingers through my hair. The next time I did that, it would be short.

Gyles helped us into the coach. He set a leather jug on the floor beside me and said with a grimace, "Fresh cow blood."

Ugh. Too much information. Time passed. I hardly spoke at all, but listened to my friends talk and even laugh from time to time. I was happy for the diversion, yet my mind kept returning to the new plan brewing inside it.

We would travel north from Boston—the opposite direction from Hezekiah's home in Dorchester. Gyles had arranged for three servants to meet us on the outskirts of Boston and join our entourage with a second coach. I had hoped Hezekiah would be there, but when he wasn't, I realized he had probably left much earlier. With Arabella's packages stowed on the other coach, the travel was much easier. I was exhausted. Even with the heightened anxiety and bumpy road, I slept and dreamed I was home with Seth and Trent and his twin brother, Hezekiah.

A particularly harsh bump woke me with a start. The lingering dream was still fresh, and I grinned, but only briefly. The coach had stopped, and we were at our destination. From the height of the morning sun, I figured it to be around 7:00, one hour before the hangings were to begin.

A servant got off the second coach and stood in the middle of the road. He held a red cloth in front of him. He was to wave it once for a walker, twice for a coach, and then quickly hide it in his pocket. Both coaches moved farther down the road. Gyles hopped off ours and opened the door, then helped us out and told us to hurry to the trees and conceal ourselves.

From the trees, we watched the servants and Gyles remove one of our wheels and then lay it down to feign a disabled coach. He pointed a little way off. "We'll be waiting there for you." They quickly climbed into the other coach and went down the road and stopped. Gyles moved to the center of the road, holding a red cloth just like the servant on the other end.

Charles led us into the woods and changed into the Indian clothes, but we stayed close enough to the road to see both red cloths. We hadn't been there too long when the servant to our right waved his flag once in front of him. He stuffed it in his pocket and darted our way. "Someone is coming!" After relaying his message, he stopped short, threw his hands in the air, and sprinted back toward the oncoming people in a panic. "Indians! Indians!"

I didn't have time to think. Charles grabbed my hand and pulled me into the middle of the road, his feathers tousling in the morning breeze. They must have been a quarter mile down the road, but a small group of people walked toward us—most likely a young family. It looked to be a man and a woman and three small children. The man carried a long musket at his side. Great.

Charles gripped my arm firmly. "We passed them a while back and expected we'd see them first, unless a coach overtook them." He paused and then looked at me. "It's time to start screaming, my lady."

Tears welled up in my eyes as I realized I was about to frighten those young children, making them watch a terrible scene that could haunt them for the rest of their lives. But I knew what I had to do, for my life and the lives of my conspirators. I jerked my bonnet off and pulled long strands of hair from the neat bun Mrs. Fayette had just formed, and let out a shrill, piercing scream. I did not let up and filled the silent road with the horrifying sound while struggling against my faux attacker. The approaching man hustled his wife and children to the other side of the road near the servant.

"Sorry," Charles said just before he yanked me by the hair of my head, pulling me into the woods. Now my screams were no longer fake—my scalp was on fire. At the edge of the woods, Charles paused long enough for us to assess the situation. My hands flew to my chest. The man with the musket was actually running toward us! Charles released me. "Run, Lady Elizabeth! Run!"

I ran harder than I had ever run before. I did not hear the musket fire. Maybe the servant had detained him. Still, Charles and I hurried without stopping, stumbling over roots and bushes, until we got to where we'd left Mrs. Fayette and Martha.

With no time to talk, Charles peeled his clothing off, dressed in regular clothes, and stuffed the Indian garb into a sack on his back. Martha nearly tore my dress off and while she mercilessly stabbed at it, Mrs. Fayette furiously pulled another dress over my head. After lacing it, she took out a knife. "Sorry, my lady," she whispered coarsely and then sawed through my hair, close to my head. I had thought it would be traumatic, but my worry that the man would find us made the adrenaline rush through my veins. I reached up and held my hair taut for Mrs. Fayette to cut through, and soon my head was free from its long ringlets.

Charles splattered the blood on the dress and then dragged my cut hair through it. He rubbed some of the blood on himself and then handed the sack and the leather jug to Martha, motioning for her to go. He turned and rushed back toward the broken-down coach, and hopefully, more witnesses.

"Aye. We will go!" Martha grabbed my hand and tugged me through the woods behind Mrs. Fayette.

"Let go, Aunt Martha, I can hurry better on my own." I pulled my hand away.

"T'be sure, me wane." She fell back behind me, keeping me between herself and Mrs. Fayette. Soon, we spied a servant who waved us forward and then followed after us. We broke through the trees and dashed toward the coach. I was pulled into the back with the packages and boxes.

"We came up with this idea just now, Elizabeth." Gyles gestured to a large wooden box previously packed with a small but very nice table that Arabella had fallen in love with. The table was now tied on top of one of the other boxes. I gulped. I was claustrophobic, but there was no time to argue, as the sound of running hooves drew near.

I stepped into the box, and Gyles stuffed my long dress in after me. I drew in a deep breath as the lid came down. Loud scraping told me that he had pulled another box on top of the one I was in. How long did they intend to keep me there? *Surely, not all the way to the docks!*

Gaps between some of the boards that made up the box allowed me to breathe. I could also see a rather nice-looking coach draw near and stop. The side door opened, and a man exited the coach, followed by another. I gasped as Judges

Hathorne and Corwin approached Gyles. Hathorne waved a piece of paper in his hand.

"Mr. Hanson, what a pleasant surprise," Hathorne said haughtily. He eyed the boxes and packages. "How convenient for us to run into you here." He stood next to the box I was crammed into.

If he had looked closely, he would have seen my frightened eyes and the shocked look on my face, as I stared at the paper in his hands. It was the decoy list, and at the bottom was written in Gyles's handwriting, "Salem Road." All at once it hit me. *Gyles wrote our location on the wrong list!*

Hathorne stepped to the coach. "Elizabeth Bowley, come with me."

I could not turn to see what he was doing, but I could hear Arabella's response. "Elizabeth is in the carriage behind us."

"What? The broken-down one we just past?"

"Broken down?" she exclaimed. "Oh my! We must turn back!"

Corwin spoke. "You don't want to do that, my lady."

"And why not?" she said indignantly.

"We slowed down just enough to hear of an Indian attack. The servant held a bloodied dress and bloodied hair torn right off the woman."

Hathorne grunted. "What was she wearing?"

"Excuse me?" Arabella said in a quivering voice.

"Elizabeth Bowley—what was she wearing?"

"Why, a blue dress," she said breathlessly.

"Yes. The dress the servant held was blue," Hathorne said with about as much emotion as a dead fish. "Come along, Corwin. We must get to the court. Sorry for your loss. Mr. Hanson, please relay our condolences to your brother."

He stopped right in front of me. "Well, at least we've one less trial to endure," he said smugly. "But if it turns out not to be Elizabeth, we will find her, and she will face charges of witchcraft."

Gyles waited until they pulled ahead of us and then came back for me. "Are you all right?" he asked, gently helping me from my wooden tomb.

I nodded numbly, Hathorne's words echoing through my mind. He really would not rest until he knew for sure. Hopefully, Charles's proof would convince him, because I was sure Hathorne would still show up at my engagement party. I swallowed hard. What did it matter? He'd see me soon enough anyway—long before the party.

Our coach approached the edge of town. "Are we going straight to the docks?"

"Yes, that is my understanding," Arabella said, studying my eyes. "Why?"

I bit my lower lip. "I have to relieve myself."

"Oh, of course. Me too." She gave a slight grin, then leaned out the small window and called to Gyles, "We need to stop, please."

The coach came to a stop in front of a tavern. Gyles opened the door. "You must be careful, Elizabeth."

I fastened my bonnet securely over my short hair and nodded. He led us to the door of the tavern.

"I will buy some food here, while you take care of yourselves."

I kept my head low, for fear of recognition, and overheard a couple guests as I passed by.

"They are lining them up right now."

"Are you going to watch?"

"Heavens no. I will not support such a thing."

"I do not want to either, but if we are not there, won't they think us guilty too?"

"Perhaps you are right. I will go, but I will stand behind the largest man I can find so I do not have to see the hangings."

I kept walking to the back of the tavern where a door exited to a smaller outhouse. It was now or never. I could flee with Arabella to England, or I could make one last attempt to stop the horrid hangings. I wondered what the world would be like if I succeeded, leaving only the one hanging of Bridget Bishop, instead of the nineteen hangings and one man pressed to death. I assumed Bridgett's hanging would be treated as Goody Glover's had been four years prior—recorded, but not made epic.

I motioned for Arabella to go into the outhouse first. Then I blended into the gathering crowd and walked silently beside them.

Twenty-Five

Gallows Hill

The road merged with another. On either side, spectators jeered and called out names. I lifted my eyes toward the ruckus. My knees buckled beneath me as a wooden cart bearing five women moved slowly into view, with Judge Corwin himself walking ahead of it.

Rebecca Nurse, Elizabeth How, Sarah Good, Sarah Wildes, and my grandmother, Susannah Martin, leaned against the rails to which they were chained, fervently praying aloud, their eyes to the heavens. "Spare us, dear Lord! Prove our innocence!"

It was like a scene from a distasteful movie—five innocent women going to their untimely deaths, on display, and at the mercy of the taunting and heckling crowd. My heart raced as I pushed through the crowd toward them. Soon, I reached their side and managed to grab hold of the cart. I held on and worked my way up to my grandmother, then wrapped my fingers around her frail hands chained to the rail.

She looked down at me, but said nothing. I wanted to tell her how much I loved her and how proud I was of her for standing true to her word. I wanted her to know how much I was like her—sharp tongue and all. "I . . . I . . ."

"Step back!" A man angrily pushed my hand down.

My eyes narrowed. "Leave me alone."

He grabbed me by the waist and held me as the cart continued on. "Stay back away from the wagon," he snarled.

He turned around, and I defiantly picked up the hem of my petticoat and rushed toward the cart, which was now turning a corner in the road. Rounding the bend, I gasped—two men had finished digging a long shallow grave and leaned on shovels waiting for the cart to approach. My breath caught in my throat. Gallows Hill stood before us in all its horror.

Rays of morning light filtered through the trees atop its rocky ledge, revealing three giant oaks melded together as one. Hanging from its massive limbs, five nooses were silhouetted against the blue sky. I froze into place, letting the crowd weave around me. This wasn't real—this couldn't be happening. And yet it was. Violent tremors overtook me, sweeping up the sides of my body.

Unable to move, I stared at the cart as it continued on. As the five women were carried to an unjust and cruel death, unfathomable fear etched their faces, and yet they still prayed. The cart approached the hill and began its slow ascent. Numbly, I watched from below.

Soon, the cart stopped under the first noose. Corwin and two other men helped one of the women up onto a tall wooden box built into the end of the cart and then slipped the noose around her neck.

Corwin stood before her. "What say ye, Rebecca Nurse? Will you not save your soul?" He turned to a man standing beside him holding a Bible. "Reverend Noyes, will you speak to her?"

The reverend looked a little unnerved, perhaps because of Rebecca's impeccable reputation and the reverent hush that fell over the crowd. He cleared his throat and would not look up at her. "Will you not confess, Goody Nurse?"

"I am innocent."

In three words, Rebecca had stated the truth. Three words that would be ignored five times that day. My body tingled. This was my chance—to support those words, to refute the courts' intended punishment for a crime not committed. She is innocent! I would say just that. I opened my mouth and punctuated each word while slamming my fists to my sides. "SHE . . . IS . . ."

A man grabbed my shoulder and swiftly covered my mouth with his hand. My eyes widened. It was the finely dressed, tall man with the cane—de Nostredame, the man from France who had loaned the ancient book to Hezekiah. A few people turned to see who had dared to interrupt the proceedings, but then returned their gazes to the hanging. The man put his finger to his lips as I pulled away from his firm grasp.

Suddenly, a scream erupted from one of Rebecca's family members. The cart moved ahead, faster than I'd seen it move all morning. It tossed the four remaining women around like ragdolls, then pulled away from Rebecca with a sudden snap. Her body swayed violently to and fro like a cockeyed pendulum, until it slowed down to a stop, still and lifeless. A unanimous groan burst forth from the crowd, low and muffled, as if everyone was afraid to express their horror and disbelief. Rebecca's family stood nearby the tree, clinging to each other and sobbing, while a few of their menfolk pulled them aside.

Noyes reluctantly turned to the next. "Sarah Good, I urge you to confess."

I was not surprised to see her reaction. I had read about it. She spat on the ground.

Noyes seemed irritated. "The courts have already proven your acts of witchcraft. Confess, and at least not die a liar!"

She looked him directly in the eye. "I will not confess. You are the liar!"

Noyes drew his head back. "I knew you were a witch."

"I am no more a witch than you are a wizard," she snapped, "and if you take away my life, God will give you blood to drink."

I shivered. History had recorded that later on, he died bleeding at the mouth when a blood vessel burst in his head.

I was drawn back to Rebecca's unmoving body. At least it would not remain in the shallow graves dug beside the tree, but would be exhumed and secretly whisked away in the middle of the night for a proper burial on her family's land.

A sudden movement returned my eyes to Sarah. The cart sped forward once more, and she joined Rebecca in the land of the dead, soon to be followed by Elizabeth How and Sarah Wildes, both ardently proclaiming their innocence to their dying breaths.

"Let's go," the man whispered urgently in my ear. He tugged on my arm and led me to a horse standing nearby. I wanted to fight. I wanted to climb the hill to my grandmother's side, but instead, I got on the horse. My heart pounded in my chest and broken sobs escaped my throat as Corwin helped my grandmother to the box, while two men tied her dress to her legs, as they had the others. He gave Noyes a nod.

"Goody Martin," Noyes said, "will you not confess?"

My grandmother held her head high. "I am innocent." Her voice quivered. "I have not hurt man, woman, or child, but have led a most virtuous and holy life."

I could bear it no longer. "YAH!" I cracked the whip and galloped the horse up the rocky hill, shouting, "Leave her alone!"

I'm not sure why, but when catastrophe strikes at the heart, it moves in slow motion. My world stopped spinning, and it became completely silent, all but the loud creaking of the cart's dastardly wooden wheels, which rolled forward. I could not breathe as my grandmother's body jerked sideways and then finally came to a stop.

I was too late. I buried my face in my hands and wept, while the horse pranced sideways.

Judge Corwin wagged his finger at me. "I could have you arrested for this! Who are you? Are you family?"

Yes. I am family, and I failed her. I looked at him through teary eyes. "Can you not see what you've done?" I wiped at the tears and pointed to her silent body swaying back and forth. "One day, you will pay for this, for it is you who have committed a grievous crime in the eyes of God, and not them!"

Suddenly, Betty Hubbard broke through to the front of the crowd. "It is she! Elizabeth Bowley! She is a witch come to rescue the devil's followers!"

"She's a little late," mused one spectator.

I threw an angry look at him, and then I whirled the horse around so I faced Betty. "You are lucky I am not a witch," I snarled, "because if I were, you'd be getting more than bites and pinches from me!"

She screamed and fell to the ground in a frenzied fit.

I spun the mare around and dug my heels into her sides. "Go!"

From behind me, I heard Corwin yell, "You there—go after her! Do not let her escape!"

With my death cover blown, I suspected the docks would be the first place they would check. Besides, I had no idea where the docks were. I knew of only one place to go, one road to take—the road to Salem Village, to the place Hezekiah would know to find me.

I had a head start, but I knew many people would flock after me in an attempt to rid their village of one so defiant. I jumped off the horse, whacked it hard, and sent it down the road without me. Just as quickly, I scrambled for the thick trees—and none too soon, as a small posse of would-be jailors galloped by.

I kept to the edge of the trees and hurried as fast as I could on foot through the thick undergrowth. They would comb these woods, as soon as they caught up to the rider-less horse. I shivered. Images of my grandmother's dead body swinging from the tree alongside the other four women haunted my every thought.

The sun began its slow descent, casting hazy rays of filtering light, filling the sky with an odd, gyrating sunset. The darkening sky would make for easier travel. I could now keep to just outside the edge of the trees. Arabella's ship would soon set sail without me. Charles would show up at my engagement party with the bloodied dress. How would he be received? I shuddered, wondering if word of my escapade had made it to Hezekiah's home yet. Were they continuing the ruse? Probably not. I had to believe de Nostredame would somehow warn them.

I recognized the bend I was nearing. The hill where I had entered this bizarre world months ago was on the other side. The hill that led to the rock where we had buried my things, the hill where I hoped Hezekiah would think to go to look for me.

As I rounded the bend, I ran smack into Betty Hubbard. I should have remembered it was also the hill the circle girls climbed for their secret rendezvous.

She gasped for breath and pointed at me with a shaky hand, then let out a piercing scream. Nearby, a group of men dropped what they were doing and dashed toward us. I had no time to react to Betty, no time to give her the tongue lashing I wanted to, and definitely no time to smack her like she deserved. I turned and sprinted up the hill, stumbling over rocks and tuffs of grass and tall golden rod. If I could just get to the trees, I could lose them. I barely made it to the edge of the forest, when one of the men grabbed my arm, but instead of pulling me back, he pushed me forward. My heart leaped within me. Hezekiah!

"There she is! Up there!" Betty's shrill voice carried up the hill. Through the evening's dusk, I looked down. No less than a half dozen men wielding axes and shovels scrambled after us.

Long streaks of muted colors softly lit the sky, barely illuminating the rough path. We hurried down it toward the entrance to our secret hideaway. Suddenly, my foot caught hold of a root, twisting my ankle violently. "Ahh!" Hezekiah tugged on my trapped foot, and upon releasing it, scooped me up in his arms. I clung to him, digging my fingernails into his arm, holding back the screams in my throat.

Angry voices neared. "This way! Follow me!"

Hezekiah had rolled a log across the path as a marker months ago, inadvertently blocking the direction we now needed to turn. There was no time to move it out of the way. He balanced me on it and climbed over.

"I see her!"

Oh, no! I scooted forward on the log. Hezekiah snatched me up.

"There she is!"

They were nearly on us. Hezekiah could not possibly run faster than them while he carried me.

"Put me down," I said. At least one of us could get away— at least one of us might live.

"No." He tightened his grip. "Don't try to make me. I will not leave your side."

I knew he meant it, but I could see the men getting closer, could hear their exasperated breaths and the clanking of their axes and shovels. "At least let me fight! They will be on us in seconds!"

Hezekiah stopped and sat me down. We were there. Our rock—at least, I was fairly sure it was in the gathering fog. We turned to face scowls and jeers.

Suddenly, the closest man dropped his axe and jumped back. "Did you see that, Albert?" He grabbed the man next to him, his eyes wide with fear.

Albert threw his shovel down and stumbled backward. He raised a trembling finger at me as the other men caught up and stared into the mist.

"What is it, John?"

"I saw her! She was standing right there!" He swept his hand near me, and I jumped back away from him. I turned quickly to Hezekiah. What was going on? Why couldn't he see me? Was the fog that thick? No, I could see him clearly—I could see all of them.

"I'm getting out of here," James said. He bent down and grabbed his ax near my feet like he was picking up a hot coal or was afraid of what might lay near it. "She's a specter," he said with a quiver in his voice.

"I knew it!" John exclaimed.

"We've been chasing a ghost." James's face went white.

The fear on their faces was almost comical, especially because I was hidden in plain view, protected by the dense fog.

"Aw, come on. She's not a specter," one of the other men said. "I saw her running away from us as clear as day."

"I saw her too." John pointed directly at me. "And then she faded right before my eyes."

I gasped and turned to Hezekiah as realization sank in. I pointed to the strange lights gathering above us, shimmering and twisting in the night sky—the aurora borealis!

John cautiously poked his leg into the mist and used his toe to move the handle of the shovel toward him. "She's dead all right, and come to pay them other witches a visit. I heard an Indian killed her early today."

I do not know what came over me, possibly insanity, but I stuck just my head out of the fog. I waited until they saw my head floating in the mist. "Boo!" I yelled, then quickly pulled my head back.

The men threw their hands in the air and ran helter-skelter, crashing into each other like chickens trapped in a pen with a fox, their pitiful screams filling the night air. I laughed and fell back on my sore foot, which served me right for scaring them almost to death.

Hezekiah was not amused. He grabbed my hand and hurried deeper into the dissipating fog. "Quick! It's closing!"

In an instant, my life in 1692 passed before me—my existence with the one man I loved, Hezekiah. He was forcing me into the decreasing rift. If it worked, we would be separated by 323 years, but if it didn't work, I might be able to board another ship to England. The fog was so thick I could not see him, but could only feel his strong tug, his warm fingers woven through mine. I couldn't bear to be without him. I couldn't leave 1692! My fingers separated from his, as I let go of his hand and heard his anguished cry.

"BESS!"

Twenty-Six

Hezekiah

I hit the ground hard and rolled, slamming into the rock. The strange misty lights were gone, the thick fog dissipated, and the night had turned to day. I scrambled to my feet, frantically looking for her. Had she not followed me through? "Bess! Bess!" I cried, turning in a full circle. Maybe she had landed nearby, but no. From studying that blasted book night after night, I knew she should have come out right beside me. She had broken the connection when she released my hand, and now only God knew where she was.

My heart felt as if it had been ripped from my chest as I realized Bess must have fallen back into 1692. I anguished over her fate and wept bitterly. If I was indeed in 2015 like I had planned, my Bess was trapped back in time and had been dead for hundreds of years.

I fell to the earth and lay there for hours, not wanting to move, not wanting to think, and not wanting to go on. Finally, when there was nothing left for me to do, I pulled myself up. I wondered what I would find on the other side of these woods, here in Bess's time.

I broke through the trees and fell back with what met my eyes. Without a doubt, I was in the future. Nothing, none of Bess's pictures could have prepared me for what I saw. Houses crammed together so tight a coach couldn't fit between them. And so tall! How could a house have that many levels? I slumped to the ground and watched the queer coaches without horses roar by, in all sizes and shapes. What had she called them? Oh, yes, cars and trucks, I remembered.

I walked down the hill toward the city, which looked bigger than ten Bostons put together. Unsure of where to go, I stood on the road at the bottom of the hill and watched. People walking by gave me strange looks, some pointing to me. To them, my clothing must have been completely outdated. And even though I had seen some attire like theirs in Bess's pictures, I still found it to be very odd indeed. I fingered the coins in my pocket. *At least I have enough money to buy myself adequate clothing.*

I walked down the street, shocked at the strange variety and the sheer amount of shops on the street.

"Excuse me," I said to a passerby, who literally turned his nose up at me. "I wonder if you might help me," I said to another, who quickly passed me by.

"I can help you," a young girl said, looking up at me under thick eyelashes.

I bowed to her. "Thank you." She giggled, and I forged ahead. "I need to purchase an outfit—pants and a shirt, but I'm new to . . . where am I?"

Her eyes went wide. "Danvers."

"Oh."

"Oh," she repeated with a nod. "Wait right here, mister." She scurried into the shop and came out dragging a young woman beside her. I was shocked to see her wearing pants, but recalled Bess saying that hardly anyone wore dresses in 2015.

"May I help you?" the young woman said after giving the girl a wary look.

"Why yes." I pulled out some coins. "Will I be able to use these here?"

Her eyes widened. "Oh my, where did you get these?"

I licked my lips. "They've been in my family for years." *Three hundred and twenty-three, at least,* I mused.

"My grandfather collects old coins. May I?" She reached for the coins and turned them over in her fingers. "Hold on." She pulled a phone from her pocket, similar to Bess's, pushed a button, and spoke into it. "Hi, Grandpa. Hey, there's a guy here with some pretty old coins."

I was taken aback with her conversation—not the gist of it, but that she could actually talk to her grandfather through a small, rectangular box.

She put her phone back into her pocket. "He says not to let you go anywhere. Buy him anything he wants, he said, but just don't let him leave." She smirked. "He'll be right here." She pointed inside the building behind her. "In the meantime, let's go shopping."

She assured me that I had plenty of money to buy anything I wanted in the store—probably even the whole store—and suggested a more appropriate attire for me to wear while I visited Danvers.

"Where are you from?" she asked.

"Boston."

She nodded. "Figures, although we have our share of interesting people here too." She pointed to a woman with pink hair and I had to agree.

"What's your name?" I asked politely.

"Oh, I'm Samantha. What's yours?"

"My name is Hezekiah."

"That is a very odd name," she said, twirling her hair around her finger.

"Really? Are there not many Hezekiahs here?"

"I've never heard of one before." She paid for my clothing and then led me to a room with a sign that read MEN. Gesturing for me to enter, she said, "The changing rooms are being remodeled. You can change in there."

I didn't want her to think I didn't know what I was doing, so I nodded and walked inside. It was by far the oddest place I had ever seen. I was shocked and amazed at the same time. The ceilings had bright lights coming from round glass, yet I couldn't see the flames that kept them lit. I shrugged and looked around. Narrow rooms nestled side by side inside the larger room, each with a water-filled stone bowl sitting on the floor—very peculiar indeed.

Grateful there was no one in the large room but me, I started to strip my clothes off, when a man and his son came into the room. The man gave me a pointed look and quickly pulled his son out of the room. Another man entered the room. He put his hands on his hips. "Excuse me, but you cannot change out in the open, sir."

"Oh," I said. That made sense. "Where do I change?"

He rolled his eyes and pointed to the narrow rooms with the stone bowls on the floor. "In there."

I grumbled. There was hardly enough room to stand inside one of them. He glared at me and continued to point to the narrow room. "All right," I said, hopping on one foot with half my pant leg pulled up. I'd never done anything so ridiculous in my life. I could hardly turn around and stubbed my toe on the dastardly bowl three times. Once dressed, I stepped out of the smaller room and stared back at the bowl. It was obviously a modern toilet, but I had never seen such clean water. A young boy stepped past me and over to a row of bowls attached to the wall. He stuck his hand inside and water appeared.

My eyes widened. "How did you do that?"

He smiled. "Here, let me show you. I had to have my brother show me."

He waved his hand under a shiny metal pipe. Instantly, clean water ran from it.

"That is amazing."

"Yeah, it's kind of like magic, huh?" The young boy grinned and did it again. Then he reached up and ran his hand under a small box, whereupon a bit of white foam came out of it. I gasped.

"It's soap," the boy explained. "Kind of like more magic, huh?"

I nodded, completely in awe. "How does it work?"

"I dunno, mister. Some kind of sensor."

"Sensor?"

"Yeah, well, I gotta go."

"Yes, of course," I said. Once he was gone, I ran my hand several times under the water and the soap. My hands were dripping wet and the sink was full of white foam when another man came into the room. I was amused by the look he gave me—like I was a lunatic. I had to grin. I wiped my hands on my pants and left the room.

Samantha sat in a bench attached to a table. She patted the top of it and gestured for me to sit across from her. "Grandpa is here. He's coming inside." She leaned over and pulled a small white piece of paper off my shirt. "You forgot to remove the tag."

Oh. I had wondered about that. I'd never seen a tag attached to a shirt with anything but a pin.

"Ah, there's my girl!" An older man spouting a bushy, white moustache hugged Samantha and eyed me suspiciously. He offered his hand. "Name's Kenneth."

Samantha unfolded her hand and showed him my coins. His eyes widened. He reached forward, cautiously took them, and studied them closely. Then he looked over at me. "What's your name, son?"

"Hezekiah Hanson."

His face dropped. "You don't say." He fell back in his seat. "You don't say," he repeated. "I wondered, when my

Theresa Sneed

granddaughter said you had coins dating back to the seventeenth century." He nodded slowly. "And now you claim to be Hezekiah Hanson." He leaned forward and scowled. "What's your price, son?"

I drew my head back. "Price? For the coins, you mean?"

"You know what I mean." He stood and glared at me. "Coming in here and claiming to be Hezekiah Hanson." He gave me a stern look. "Who told you about him? Where'd you get these coins?" His eyes fell to the bundle of clothes I had just changed out of. He drew in a sharp breath. "What are those?"

Samantha fidgeted as if she was as uncomfortable with her grandfather's rude interrogation as I was. "Ah, Grandpa, he was looking for new clothes to wear. He can't wear those." She made a face and pointed to the clothing resting on top of the table. "Not unless he's going to a costume party."

Kenneth reached over and picked up the clothes, then turned them over in his hands. He brought them to his nose and sniffed. His eyes widened, and he stared at me. "It can't be."

He knows. But how? "Pardon me?"

"It's true. The legend." Kenneth jumped up and gestured for me to follow. Outside, he walked swiftly to a car and opened the door. "Did you just get here today?" he asked excitedly. Samantha crawled into the back.

"Yes," I said, unsure of what to do.

"Oh, yes, of course, this will have been the first time you've ever been in a car." He patted the top of it. "Well, come on." He slipped inside and gestured for me to do the same.

Easier said than done. I pulled on the handle but couldn't open it. Samantha seemed to understand my dilemma and got out. "Like this," she said, reaching her fingers under the handle and pulling it up. "Now, you do it."

After the third try, I could open it just fine, but for the love of everything, I could not, as hard as I tried, get the belt strapped around me like Kenneth had. Samantha leaned over the seat, pulled the belt around my waist, and slipped the metal tongue into a metal crevice. "What is this for?" I asked.

"Safety. Oh, and government regulations." She smirked.

I wondered if England treated them any better than back in 1692, but thought better of inquiring at the present. As a Royalist, I wasn't sure where I'd stand in the modern- day world.

Kenneth put his hands on a round circle in front of his chest and turned it. The car turned with his hands like a horse with a bit, sort of. I was okay for the initial start, but held my stomach as the car sped up faster than any horse I'd ever ridden. I closed my eyes tight and thought about other things.

"Are you okay?" Kenneth said with a chuckle.

I groaned but kept my eyes squeezed shut. Anytime I ventured to open them, the trees and buildings speeding by was worse than the motion of the car. I clenched my eyes tighter, resolving to not open them again.

After a while, the car slowed down. "We are here."

It was none too soon for me. When the car came to a stop, I struggled with the handle, forced it open, and then vomited all over the ground.

"Eew!" Samantha made a face and rushed past me toward the house adjacent to where the car had stopped.

I wiped my hand across my mouth and looked up. I nearly fell over and had to lean back against the car. I knew this place. Although it was vastly different, it was without a doubt, my house from a few hundred years ago. But why was he here and who exactly was he? Tingles went up my back. "You're a Hanson?"

Kenneth laughed aloud. "Yes, yes, I am." He grinned and pointed to the now enormous mansion. "I thought you might recognize the place."

I studied his face. "This is incredible." He gestured for me to follow him. Many additions had been added to the original structure, making the estate wider and deeper. The barn had been replaced with several long buildings. On the other side of the estate, a blue bath like the ancient pools of Rome sparkled in the sun. Samantha and another girl, dressed rather scantily, stood on the edge and jumped in. What a strange place my home had become indeed!

Inside, Kenneth led me to the study. At least, that hadn't changed much and was nearly identical to my day, except for the addition of a wider and higher wall of books. Kenneth closed the door to the study and locked it. "Follow me." Near the wall of books, he pushed on a section that opened into a smaller, dimly lit room. I hadn't seen that before, but realized it could have been added at any time during the last three hundred years.

"Your father had this built for you."

I drew my head back. "What?"

"Sit down." Kenneth pulled out a chair. He opened a drawer and removed a discolored piece of parchment paper worn on the edges, and then he handed it to me. My hands shook as I read my father's last words to me. I had just left him a day ago, now 323 years in the past.

My dearest Hezekiah,

Nostredame informed me about your fascination with time travel. He has shown me the book. I must admit for these many years, I would not entertain the notion, but as I near my death, I now hope it to be true and prepare for it for your sake. My dear son, all of our descendants will know your name and hear your story. The book and many other treasures

*are secured in your secret room, though none
but you will ever know of its existence. God be
with you, Hezekiah. I pray that this letter finds
you well . . .*

Kenneth handed me an old rusty key. "We never have found the secret room. Perhaps you could enlighten us?"

I turned the key over in my hands, having recognized it immediately. "Yes, of course." I looked up, giving him an inquisitive look.

He seemed to read my mind. "I am the ninth-great-grandson of Abner Gyles Hanson II."

I fell back against my chair. "My brother goes by Gyles. Just Gyles," I said breathlessly. My lip twitched. "He got married?"

"Yes, to a woman only known as Arabella."

A laugh caught in my throat as I wondered how that had happened. "She is his . . . uh . . . our cousin." I looked at Kenneth sadly, realizing both she and my brother had been dead for three hundred years. Not only had I lost Bess, but also everyone I had ever loved.

Kenneth seemed to understand my sudden sadness. He placed his hand on my shoulder. "It's time travel, son." He shrugged. "You had to expect this. Still, I'm very sorry for your loss, and apparently theirs too." He tapped the letter.

I had forced myself not to think about leaving my family behind. I was plenty happy with leaving everything except them, and now I was really here—in Bess's world, only without her.

"You'll stay here, of course. We've plenty of rooms, but you already know that." Kenneth gestured for me to follow him. "School just started, and we'll get you in the best. I imagine you must be a clever student to have figured out time travel."

I nodded. I had been attending Harvard College, but guessed that place was long gone now. "Yes, that would be fine."

"We may have to hire a private tutor for a while—just to get you up to speed with the past three hundred years."

I sighed. He was right. Ask me about anything from 1692 or before, but with three hundred years passing in a second, I had a lot to learn. I didn't even understand how the men's room worked, and I figured that was pretty basic information. We stopped in front of my old room—at least, I thought it was mine. Kenneth opened the door and ushered me in.

I was taken aback with how much it looked like my original room from the past, with very few alterations. The walls had been smoothed over and painted, and the bed coverings were quite different, but the high bed posts and bureaus were exactly the same.

"The Hanson clan has kept this up for you all these years. Legend had it that you were trying for 2015, and here you are." Kenneth beamed.

Nostredame must have revealed that to my father, or maybe Bess, if she survived. A sudden pang gripped my heart.

"Now, the big question. Who will you be?" Kenneth scratched his chin. "I guess you'll be my grandson." He grinned. "It'll go over much better than my ninth-great-uncle."

"Yes, it will." I stepped to the window at the now massive estate.

"Would you like to take a look around?"

"Yes, I would."

"Well, alrighty. Take your time." He looked at what appeared to be a clock or maybe a pocket watch strapped to his wrist. He saw my curiosity and removed it from his wrist. Grinning, he said, "Here—take my time!"

I turned it around in my hands. "How do you wind it?"

Kenneth let out a chuckle. "You don't, son. It rewinds on its own."

"Fascinating."

"Yep." He slapped me on the back and left my room.

I walked slowly through the room, opening and closing the bureau drawers. Most of them were empty. I imagined 323-year-old clothing probably didn't weather well. But in some of the drawers, I found things just the way I had left them—a few papers, a quill, and a dried-up ink well. They held little interest to me. I had kept the things that mattered the most in my room under the gardens—my books, all of my time-travel notes, and my oil painting of Bess. It had been my best work, and now I wished I had let her see it. Suddenly, I wanted nothing more than that picture. I pressed the key to my lips, stuffed it back into my pocket, and hurried out of the room.

Twenty-Seven
Trent

What if the gardens weren't there anymore? With great apprehension, I opened the door on the side of the mansion. Relief washed over me as the tall hedges met my view. From where I stood, the gardens seemed to about the same size as they had been in my day. I hurried down the steps toward them.

As it turned out, the hedges were the only thing that looked remotely the same as in 1692. I got lost in them trying to find my mother's inner garden. If it hadn't been for the stone columns, I never would have found it. The flowers and shrubbery were different, yet the columns, tables, and benches were the same. I eagerly approached the area where the bushes had been, but found only short green grass. I searched the entire garden several times and did not find a sign that steps had been there those many years ago. *What happened?*

Sitting down where the steps had once been, I remembered the words in my father's letter: "The book and many other treasures are secured in your secret room, though none but you will ever know of its existence." I knew my father well. He was a man of his word. He would have made sure that no one after him could know where the room had been. The only way to keep an underground room hidden would be to fill in the steps that led down to it. I patted the solid ground, knowing I was probably sitting right on top of it.

I did not want to act too hastily. After I left the gardens, I scanned the surrounding area and realized my old neighborhood now had many more houses in it than it had the last time I was here. I did not want anyone else to know about my hidden room, except for Kenneth, and felt confident he would keep my secret.

He was overly exuberant to the point of gushing. "Kenneth, I really want this kept quiet," I reminded him.

"Yes, yes, of course!" He paced the room, slapping his forehead. "The gardens—why didn't I think of that? We were given specific instructions not to disturb the gardens, especially the hidden one, but to keep it intact and only add new flowers and plants as needed." He grinned. "Brilliant."

"But how do we unearth it without anyone knowing?"

"Why, that's the easy part," Kenneth beamed. "We'll build ourselves an extravagant folly over it." He stuck his hands in his pockets. "I've always wanted one of those."

I had no idea what he was talking about.

"Well, we'll center the structure on the buried steps, dig them up, and no one will be the wiser. I'll get my architects on it right away."

"That's fine and all, but how are we going to find where to center the folly?"

He grinned. "No, I guess you wouldn't know about that, but nowadays, we can see into the ground, son."

"What?"

"It's called GPR—ground-penetrating radar, and I know just the person who can do it. My, er, our cousin Reggie. He's a retired archeologist with connections."

"He can see in the ground, through the soil?"

"Well, no, just reflected signals bouncing back from whatever is down there." Kenneth took a cell phone out of his pocket. I was particularly interested to see how it worked. He pressed the buttons, just as Bess had explained, and then commenced in having a conversation through the phone. He saw my curiosity and pushed another button. I jumped back with the voice that came from the box.

"Well, hello there, Kenny! How've you been?"

I found myself drawn to the phone.

"I'm fine, Reggie. Hey, you remember that family sworn-to-secrecy thing?"

It was silent. "Well, of course I do—ridiculous, but fascinating, nonetheless."

"Well, it's not ridiculous anymore, but you're right about the fascinating part."

"What?"

"How soon can you get here?"

"Twenty or thirty minutes."

"Any chance you could rustle up a portable GPR?"

"I guess so. You want to try that again? What did you find now? Not another false lead on that secret room, I hope."

"Just get here as soon as you can, Reg."

"All right."

An hour later, a man who had to be Reggie walked into the room and asked, "What's this all about, Kenny?"

Kenneth picked up my old clothing and tossed it to him.

His face went ashen white as he studied them. "Where'd you get these?"

Kenneth pointed to me. "From him."

Reggie turned to me. "Where'd you get them?"

"They are mine," I said matter-of-factly. "Let me introduce myself." I extended my hand. "My name is Hezekiah Hanson."

A small cough left his throat. He growled at me and glared at Kenneth. "Not funny, Kenny."

"I'm not laughing." Kenneth grinned wide.

Reggie threw the clothes on a chair. "Next time, play your little jokes on someone who isn't so busy." He stormed toward the door.

Kenneth grabbed his arm. "I'm not joking, Reggie, and since when are you too busy for anything these days?" He folded his arms across his chest.

Reggie faced me. "So, he's the real Hezekiah, huh? Right." He pointed his finger at me. "Prove it."

I'd never been challenged to prove my identity before. I shrugged. "My name is Hezekiah Hanson. Birthdate, July 11, 1675. Birthplace, Boston, Massachusetts Bay Colony. Parents, Abner and Victoria Hanson—my mother was a Davenport."

Reggie huffed. "Anyone could have looked that up."

"I was set to graduate from Harvard next year and studied abroad in my earlier years." He didn't seem impressed. "And I know where the secret room is, because I was just in it yesterday." That got his attention.

He raised his eyebrows. "All right. I'll play along. Show us."

"Did you bring the ground penetrating thing?"

He rolled his eyes. "Yes."

"Well, let's go." I strode out of the room without another word and didn't stop until I was standing over where I thought the room to be. It took a few minutes for them to catch up with Reggie's contraption.

He patted it. "Kind of looks like a lawn mower, doesn't it?"

I didn't have a clue what he was talking about. Kenneth tapped him on the shoulder. "He's never seen a lawnmower."

"How does this work?" I bent down, examining the GPR closer. Reggie was happy to explain, and I equally as thrilled to learn. The best part was when he demonstrated it. We were without doubt, directly above the steps leading down into my room. Reggie's mouth dropped open and he fell back, staring at me like I was a ghost, which for his time, technically, I should have been.

"Amazing, simply amazing," he mumbled, eyes wide, and then he poked me with his finger.

I jumped back. "Pardon me?" After all, I was not a display at a market.

"Oh, I'm terribly sorry, it's just that, well, It's amazing—you're amazing."

Kenneth chuckled and then took his phone out again. "We'll get you one of these today." He gestured to his phone.

"Oh." My own phone. *Wait.* I drew in a breath as Reggie proceeded to ask me a hundred questions. I already had a phone—well, it belonged to Bess and was buried outside of Salem Village. I guess my face must have reflected my sadness.

"What's wrong, Hezekiah?"

I shook it off. I knew at some point I would track her mother and little brother down, if for no other reason than to see them in person. As far as the stone box with Bess's treasures—I didn't know what I would do. Part of me wanted to locate the rock, but the other part of me wanted to let her things rest in peace, undisturbed. I wasn't sure I could really do that, though—anything of Bess's was extremely important to me. It didn't take long for me to decide. Once my hidden room was unearthed, I would retrieve her things and bring them down there—the final resting place of everything that had been Bess. Reggie was already taking wooden stakes and pounding them into the perimeter of the stone steps, and Kenneth was talking excitedly into his phone.

"Yes. You can expect a hefty bonus if you are here in less than one hour, and an even heftier bonus if you have my folly built to my specifications within the week."

"Is that even possible?" I asked, unsure of how fast things could be built in 2015.

He nodded. "Possible and quite probable, Hezekiah, given the right motivation."

He sounded like my father now. I mused at the fact that he was Gyles' great-grandson and wondered how Gyles had finally fared in life. Glancing around, I had little doubt that he and Arabella had anything but success, and that comforted me somewhat in my loss of them.

Kenneth pointed to the stakes. "I have a rough idea on how the folly should be built. I'm thinking an ancient Roman ruin look, with massive columns, there and there, and an arch or two on either side. There will, of course, be an enclosed room in the center directly over the steps. What do you think?"

I could have cared less about his folly and how it would look. I was way more interested in excavating the steps to my room, hidden for over three hundred years.

Kenneth's architect and builder did exactly what he paid them well to do. In one week to the day, the impressive Roman folly rose above that part of the garden.

The harder part was about to begin. Everyone agreed that no one would dig up the steps but the three of us. We spent the next several days unearthing the steps, loading the dirt into what they called a wheelbarrow, and then later, dumping it into a large canvas bag, which was hoisted up and down the deepening hole by a pulley system. The long descent was lined with battery-operated lamps—another fascinating invention that I understood once it was explained to me, and completely marveled at. Every evening, the mound of dirt outside the folly was hefted into a cart and taken away. My muscles were sorer than ever before, but I went to bed each night with a wide grin on my face, knowing I was that much closer to the painting of Bess.

Suddenly, early the next morning, my shovel broke through to nothing but air, and I knew I was at the bottom of the steps within feet of the door. I pushed a preset button on my new phone to alert Kenneth, then worked furiously, ditching the dirt behind me into the bag. Finally, I pushed through to the last few steps into a small vestibule in front of the iron door. Kenneth and Reggie eagerly joined me. I stuck the key into the lock and turned.

To me, it was like coming home after a long, hard day, but to them, I imagined it was much more. They had known about my secret room for all of their lives, yet had been unable to find it. Today they would finally get to see what treasures had always lain beneath their feet.

A terrible stench met our noses. I guess it shouldn't have surprised me, with the room closed up for hundreds of years. The light attached to the hard helmet I wore shone throughout the small room. Kenneth and Reggie both held long sticks with light coming out of the end—flashlights, they called them. Reggie tossed me one, but I had already made it to the first torch.

"Wait!" Reggie grabbed my arm. "We don't know what gases may have accumulated down here all these years—they could be flammable."

I shrugged. "All right." We used our flashlights to survey the room. My mouth fell open. My father had stowed more than just my belongings down there. The room was cluttered with crates with who knew what inside.

"The first thing we need to do after this place airs out is move a generator down here."

"A what?"

Reggie patted my shoulder. "Electromagnetic induction, my boy, fueled by gas." He chuckled at my confused look. "Like a car." He sighed. "You have much to learn, Hezekiah."

"Yes." That was an understatement. I wondered what he meant by "fueled by gas" and couldn't wait to see how it worked in both the generator and the car.

"We'll need a source of oxygen, too."

I could help with that. "We use to have two tubes that broke the surface into the gardens."

"They probably got blocked over the years."

"Maybe even covered up," added Reggie.

"If you did nothing to my mother's gardens, they should be all right. The tubes came up through the stone columns we connected the folly to. The other ends of the tubes are right here." I tapped two small, iron-latticed windows with my foot.

"Alrighty then, let's go take a look." Kenneth pointed toward the door with his flashlight. "Reggie and I will go retrieve a generator. I've got some in the barn."

I nodded. Not knowing how a generator worked, I was anxious to see it. "Yes, I'd like to get more light down here. I wonder what's in those." I gestured to the many crates.

"You don't know?"

I shook my head. "They weren't here yester . . . er, I mean, the last time I was here."

"Really?" Kenneth lingered while Reggie and I went toward the door. "Very intriguing!" He hurriedly followed us up the steps.

I had no problem climbing the columns, as I had regularly done so back in my day. Once on top, I discovered it was just as I had suspected. The iron grate nestled inside the end of the tube was packed with leaves, twigs, and dirt. In no time, they both were cleared of debris and able to let the precious air flow once more.

Reggie and Kenneth returned with an odd-looking machine—the generator. We used the bag still attached to the pulley to lower it down into the hole.

Reggie looked at me with a twinkle in his eye. "Ready?"

I jumped back when the thing fired to life, but was even more amazed when Kenneth took a metal pipe with glass boxes on it and attached it to the generator. He pushed a red square, and immediately, bright light flowed from the glass boxes. I stumbled backwards over a crate. I stared at the light. "I love 2015," I mumbled. I had a new respect for what Bess must have experienced going back to a time before such things as brilliant as lights, cars, fast-food, and flushing toilets. I felt sorry for her. Frowning, I shook my head. Every time I thought of her, I was moved to profound sadness.

Kenneth helped me up. Reggie and he stood side by side, respectfully awaiting my instructions. I appreciated that, but really wanted to be alone. I stepped past them to the wall where I had hung the painting of Bess. Her painting was not there, but I was pleasantly surprised to see a row of pictures of my family—my mother and father, Gyles and Arabella, Isabella and someone else—probably her husband, and then the rest of my siblings, with their spouses and children. Still, my heart fell as I looked from wall to wall for Bess. Kenneth must have noticed my anguish.

He took Reggie by the arm. "We're going to go. Take your time, look around, and when you're ready, give us a holler." He led Reggie to the steps. "We'll wait up top."

"Eagerly wait!" Reggie added over his shoulder, as they ascended the steps.

I took to pacing the room and reading the labels attached to the crates, hoping I would find one with Bess's painting. Some of the crates were significantly taller than the others and could have her painting stored in them. Faded with time, the labels were hard to decipher, but it became quickly apparent that my father had purchased some fairly expensive items, and just as apparent that none of the crates held her painting. They were all from Egypt.

I pushed the alert button on my phone and within seconds, Kenneth and Reggie were back. I introduced them to my family. Kenneth and Gyles were excited to see a new painting of their ninth-great grandfather, my brother Gyles as a younger man. Apparently the ones in the estate were of him quite older.

"They are pretty amazing, Hezekiah." Kenneth turned to me. "Will you allow them to be placed in the mansion with the others?"

"Yes, of course."

Reggie ran his fingers deftly over the frame holding Isabella's painting. I didn't know her at that age. My Isabella was only twelve, and the painting I had done of her just weeks ago hung nearby. I pointed it out to Reggie. "That is the way I remember her. I'll be keeping that one myself, but the rest may go to the mansion."

Kenneth clapped his hands. "I'm so excited to hear you say that! What a find!"

Reggie gasped. "Ah, fellas—um, I love my family and all," he said breathlessly, "but I think we've got an even greater find here." He pointed to the crates. His mouth dropped open and his eyes widened. "They're from ancient Egypt!"

We pried the first lid off. "Incredible—just incredible!" Reaching in, I carefully removed a large gold statue of a cat. Reggie withdrew a gold bracelet with blue accents, and Kenneth removed a bowl with ancient pictures carved into it. We moved from box to box, prying the lids off, astounded with their contents—a variety of gem-studded bracelets, necklaces, bowls, statues, and figurines all made from gold. "What do you suppose the value is on these?"

Reggie drew in a breath. "Each one is priceless." His eyes widened. "They belong in a museum."

"I agree," I said. "Will you see to that?"

"Hold on," Kenneth said cautiously. "There will be questions—lots of them."

"All right. For now, let's keep them down here."

"Billions of dollars' worth of gold and you want to keep them buried down here?" Kenneth said incredulously. "Might I suggest we introduce them into the mansion a few at a time? We can tell the others we've come upon a stack of crates hidden between the walls of the older part of the estate, or something like that."

Reggie nodded. "I like that idea and then perhaps after time we can—"

I interrupted, "I do not care what you do—sell them, if you'd like."

Kenneth pressed his lips together. "I might just do that. The proceeds will be yours." He stared at me. "That's probably why your father put them down here in the first place."

"Spoken like a true Hanson," said Reggie, perusing an old piece of parchment paper. He handed it to me.

My dear Hezekiah,

These Egyptian artifacts are for you to do with what you may. They are priceless today, and I am sure will remain priceless forever. This assures me that you will be well taken care of in the future.

As always, your father

"Hezekiah, you will have unlimited funds made available to you."

I wasn't sure why I would ever need the funds, but I was grateful. "Thank you," I said, staring down at the letter from my father.

We put the artifacts back into their crates. Kenneth and Reggie moved toward the door. I waved them off. "I'll be up in a minute."

I looked around the room. My books were exactly where I put them, lined up on several bookshelves—and quite a collection of books they were. The notes I had painstakingly taken on time travel lay neatly in a small wooden box on top of my desk, but I hadn't had the chance to look inside the desk. I opened the drawer and to my astonishment, there was de Nostredame's book—the book I had hoped I would see again. Father's first letter had explained that Nostredame had shown him the book. I don't know how, but somehow my father had acquired the ancient book that had led me to 2015. But, it didn't make sense. Nostredame would never part with that book.

Suddenly, it came to me—the only reason Nostredame would have ever let his book slip away. He expected I would use it to come back. They wanted me to use the ancient book and come back to 1692—to them, and to Bess!

I raced to the estate to tell Kenneth and Reggie my theory. I would need their support in helping me return to one of the most horrific times in the history of North America. But if it meant rescuing Bess, I was going to do it.

Kenneth met me in the hall. "Follow me," he said motioning with his hand. "I've got something to show you."

We went into the library, which had been remodeled—too large, from my perspective. How could anyone ever read that many books? "What did you want to show me?"

He pointed to a painting on the wall. "Can you identify her?" He tapped the bottom of the oil painting. "Those are your initials, I presume."

I drew in a sharp breath. The image before me was breathtaking—so accurate, right down to the stubborn curl of hair that was always out of place. I fought to hold back tears. "That's her," I barely breathed out. "That's my Bess."

"Bess?" His eyes widened.

"Yes, well, Elizabeth."

"Interesting. We have an employee who has a daughter named Bess. She is the spitting image of your Bess—only a younger version, but with each passing year, she takes on more of this young ladies' attributes." He pointed to the painting.

I fell back with his words. "What?"

"Your Bess—she looks just like our Bess." He gestured to the window. "She's outside with Sam right now—at the stables. She's a fairly decent rider, too." He patted me on the back. "Go on, take a look." He grinned. "But close your mouth first."

I took the steps two at a time and sprinted out the door to the back, slowing down as I neared the barn. I rushed through the door and stopped in my tracks. Farther down, stood Samantha and her friend—her back to me.

Samantha looked my way. "Oh, hi! It's you!" She turned to her friend. "My cute cousin I was telling you about."

Kenneth must have informed her of my family status.

I took long strides and was quickly by her side. My heart raced as Samantha's friend turned to face me.

"Oh, hello, Trent."

My breath froze within me. It was her eyes, her nose, and her hair, but it was not the Bess I knew, yet it was her! I wanted to grab her and kiss her, but she didn't know me. And why of all the names in the world did she call me Trent? "What did you say?" I had forgotten all about him, but it seemed like this distant relative of mine had already stolen her heart.

Samantha's face reddened. "Oh, sorry. My bad. I told her your name was Trent, because your other name is so—you know, weird."

Bess drew her head back. "Your name is not Trent? What is it?"

"I, uh, well . . ."

"It's Trent." Samantha's eyebrows rose as she emphasized the name.

"Whatever. It doesn't matter to me." Bess turned toward the front of the barn, where a younger boy and his mother waited. "I'll be right there, Mom!" She turned back to me. "It was nice meeting you, Trent. I'll see you later."

I watched her walk toward her mother and little brother. "I—I don't understand."

"Clearly," Samantha said.

I turned to Samantha. "Why did you name me Trent? Won't that get confusing?"

"Why would that be confusing? It's not like using Hezekiah for your name."

"Of course not, beings it is my name," I said gruffly. I rolled my eyes. "I mean, won't having two cousins named Trent be a little baffling?"

She stared at me like I didn't have a brain. "I don't have two cousins named Trent—only you."

Bess waved to us from the end of the barn. I was amazed. She must have come through the rift with me. "She's so young looking—"

Samantha threw her hands on her hips. "Hey, you got something against fourteen-year-olds?"

"Fourteen? Bess is seventeen!"

"What world are you from? She just had her fourteenth birthday. I should know, because I threw her an awesome birthday party." She smirked. "It's 2012 now." She held up her fingers and counted. "So, she'll be seventeen in . . . 2013 . . . 2014 . . . in 2015."

"What?" *Whoa. What?* Numbly, I turned from her. I had to get away to think. Suddenly, every joint in my body froze as realization struck hard. *It's not 2015, but it's only 2012, and that means ... I am TRENT.* Somehow, when I came through the rift, I ended up coming three years too early. Bess had known *me* first as Trent.

Twenty-Eight

In Theory

I knew the exact day Bess had time-traveled to 1692, because she had told me. November 1, 2015—the day after Halloween. I had called it a pagan holiday, and was it ever, although the free candy thing was epic. I had waited patiently—three birthdays, and now, three Halloweens. I spent every moment I could with Bess, which was torture at times. Not so much because of her immaturity, though that was trying, but mostly, it was pure agony not being able to kiss her. Even when she turned "sweet sixteen," it was clear she had no interest in me. And to think I had actually worried about her true feelings for Trent back in 1692.

Samantha had just wowed us with her latest Salem witch play. I was wide awake, waiting for the early morning when I would pick up Bess and her little brother, Seth, and take them to our rock.

In the past three years, I had read and reread the ancient book, looking for a way to understand what had happened. All I knew was that Bess would have to time-travel, or otherwise I would cease to exist in 2015, having never met her, and likewise never have time-traveled myself. I was careful not to force things, trying to let them progress naturally and happen the way they had the first time around. Yet in reality, nothing had happened yet—Bess and I hadn't fallen in love, because she hadn't gone back in time!

Theresa Sneed

I held within my hands the ability to change history. I could prevent her from going at all, but was I willing then to completely forget her? No way.

The morning sun crested the horizon as I pulled into her driveway. She was already at the door. I rushed up to help her carry her sleeping brother. I loved the warmth of her touch and didn't pull Seth from her arms right away. I grinned, though inside I was a mess. I didn't like knowing Bess would soon be thrust back into 1692.

Before I knew it, the storm came, the rain fell, and the mist enveloped us. For the past three years I had wondered why Trent hadn't followed Bess into the rift—and now I knew. I screamed in agony as the iron claws of a bear trap snapped tight around my ankle, ripping into my flesh and crushing the bones. "ARGH!" My mind was in a whirl. *You couldn't have told me about this part, Bess?* I moaned loudly, beads of sweat gathering on my brow. It hurt like crazy.

Bess appeared through the mist and dropped down by my side. Soon, the dastardly trap was removed from my mangled ankle. I had her tear up my shirt and wrap it around the bloody mess. Suddenly, the mist lifted, and Seth was nowhere to be seen.

Bess's mouth dropped open. "Seth! Show yourself!" The wild look in her eyes frightened and saddened me. I knew the time was near.

I grabbed her hand, then pushed her forward. "I'm okay, go find him!" Her fingers lingered in mine, and then she turned to chase a brother she would never find ... well, I wasn't really sure about that. I didn't know how this would all end.

In a matter of seconds, I could simply cease to exist from the present. I knew this from the book. When time has already happened, as in my case, the present time takes precedence. The former time has already passed and cannot be lived again. A soul cannot exist beside itself in the same realm—there is only one soul per mortal, and according to the book, two of the same cannot coexist in one time period or in parallel times simultaneously. That is why Bess could not appear with me in 2012, a time she had already lived, because her soul was presently there. My hope, my dream—my everything—rested on that theory. If she could not come to 2012, because she was already there, surely, she could come to November 1, 2015, seconds after she had left, because it was a time she had not yet lived. I had waited three years to test my theory.

"Keep a bearing on yourself!" I called after her, pointing to the setting sun. But I had not planned on being weakened from the cold rain, the excruciating pain, and the loss of blood from the bear trap. I slipped in and out of consciousness, waiting for Bess to return from the past in the strangely lit sky.

Twenty-Nine

Onida

Did it work? Did it work? Strange, misty lights swirled around me, as I gyrated through them, suffocating and squeezing the air out of my lungs. I had purposely let go of Hezekiah's hand. I had made the decision to remain in 1692 with him and not return to 2015. I couldn't breathe. It felt as if the very mist was strangling me—punishing me for playing God. I had no right.

Suddenly, the mist spit me out and I smashed into the boulder—my boulder, my destiny, and probably my death.

My eyes were closed, but I could see light through my eyelids, sense motion, and hear sounds. And there was that awful stench. Where did I remember that from? *Ah, yes. The dentist. So, I'm in Hades.* I groaned.

"Bess?"

No. I must be in heaven. That was my mother's voice!

"Bess?"

I groaned again and then felt the warmth of her touch and the salty taste of her tears on my lips. My eyes fluttered open. Could it be? I gasped as my mother's face came into view. "Mom?"

"Oh, Bess! You had us so worried!"

My head felt like a truck had rammed into it. I tried to pull myself up on my elbows, but fell back into the pillow. "Mom? Where am I?"

Her eyebrows furrowed. "You're in the hospital, dear."

I looked around. "Ohh." It indeed was a hospital, but why was I there? Suddenly, I remembered everything. I must have come through the rift after all! "Hezekiah! Where is he?" I asked urgently, clinging to the sheets.

My mother gave me a strange look. "Who's Hezekiah?"

I sat up, still a little dizzy. "He's the man I'm going to marry, Mother."

She looked mortified. "What are you talking about? You were with Trent, fishing in the woods. Seth was with—"

"Seth!" I sucked in a breath. "Where's Seth?" I grabbed her hand. "Did they find him?"

"He is at home sleeping. Aunt Beth is with him."

"Oh!" I breathed out hard. "Oh, I'm so glad!"

"Sweetheart, you've had a nasty fall."

Yes. I remembered grazing my head, but that was months ago. I looked at her funny. "How did you know about that?"

"Two hunters found you beside Seth. You were unconscious." She pointed to my head. "You have quite a gash."

I brought my fingers gingerly to the gauze wrapped loose around my head. Confused, I glanced at the date on the nurses' whiteboard. November 2, 2015. That couldn't be. I was gone for months—months! I moaned and fell back against the bed. Had everything been a wild dream? It couldn't have been! I loved Hezekiah. I had felt his lips against mine, held him tight in my arms. It couldn't have been a dream, and yet, here I was in a hospital bed on November 2.

I looked at the clock. It was a little past seven in the morning—not even twenty-four hours had passed since Trent and I had gone fishing. The incessant throbbing in my skull, the bandages around my head, and the fact that only a few hours had passed were too much for me. I sobbed uncontrollably.

"Bess! It's okay, I'm here." My mother tenderly stroked my arm and whispered into my ear. I turned my face into the pillow and wept. After a while, I squeezed my eyes shut and pretended to be asleep.

Dr. Smith would have nothing of it. "Elizabeth." He gently nudged me. I pulled my eyes open to find my mother gone. I glanced up at the clock—I had slept most of the day. The doctor sat on the chair across from me. "Elizabeth. What do you remember about yesterday?"

There was no way I was going to tell him about 1692 Salem. I would have to deal with my own lunacy. "We went fishing."

"Who?"

"Trent, Seth, and I."

"What happened?"

I wet my lips. I wouldn't need to mention anything about time travel–just the normal things, minus the fading brother episode. "Well, it started to storm. Trent stepped in a bear trap, and Seth came up missing."

"Hmm." Dr. Smith tapped his stylus against his tablet. "You say that so calmly."

I opened my mouth to protest. After all, I had witnessed my grandmother's hanging—that was a little more traumatic than Trent's leg getting caught in a bear trap, or even Seth coming up missing. Of course, I could say that now, because Seth was safe, but what about Trent? I guess, I had assumed the same. "Is he okay? Trent, I mean?" I tried to show a little emotion by grimacing at the appropriate time—I think.

Dr. Smith was not impressed. He tapped something out with his stylus. "Trent is recovering from minor surgery."

Okay. Now I felt genuinely bad. "He is?" I sat up on my elbows.

"Yes. He's lucky he didn't permanently damage his leg."

I gasped. I truly did care for him—we had been so close those many months ago. *Wait. That was just yesterday.* I was so confused. Was my imagination that active? Evidently so.

"It looks like he probably won't play football for the rest of this season."

Football? Ah, yes—football. Big game. Big deal. "The ability for him to walk is far more important than football."

The doctor looked at me over his glasses. "Of course it is, Bess, but playing football is really important to him too. This is devastating for him."

I knew that, but now I knew so much more. In 1692, the lives of many were truly devastated. How could anything else appear more so to me for the rest of my life?

And yet it hadn't happened, so why did I care? It seemed so real. I guess that's why. I wiped at a tear coursing down my cheek. Why did life have to be so cruel? I was in love with an illusion—someone who never even existed. I had made him up, patterned him after my best friend Trent. I was so pathetic. I would need years of therapy, but then again, not, because I would never breathe a word of it to anyone. No one would ever know just how crazy I was. Cringing at that thought, I looked down and chewed on a fingernail.

"Hmm." Dr. Smith tapped a few more words into his tablet. "So, tell me what really happened."

I drew in a breath and looked up. "What do you mean? We went fishing—"

He nodded. "Yes, I know that. I mean, tell me about that—" He pointed to my shoulder and then to my back. "The scars, Bess. Where did they come from?" He cleared his throat. "And the hair—obviously hacked off with a blunt knife." His eyes narrowed. "Who did that to you?"

Scars? A tingle shot up my spine. I quickly reached behind me to touch the scars across my back. I couldn't breathe. I grabbed at my hair, or lack thereof. *Oh my goodness! Oh, my goodness! Oh, my goodness!* I twisted my neck sharply toward my shoulder where the flaming arrow had seared my skin, and nearly tumbled out of the narrow bed from the sudden movement. A series of wild, uncontrollable sobs burst out of me. I imagine I looked insane, hysterically but happily crying. *I didn't imagine Hezekiah!* "Yes!" I called out. Dr. Smith looked horrified and called for a nurse.

Then it hit me, and my euphoria plummeted to despair. Hezekiah was not here. They had not found him beside me, but my brother, Seth. Hezekiah had not made it through the rift. I had lost him forever. I groaned inside, holding in my anguish. After Dr. Smith and the nurse left, I let the pain burst forth and cried myself to sleep.

They kept me overnight at the hospital just to make sure I was done talking crazy. I was. I would keep my secret forever and never speak of it again, but in the middle of the night, I remembered. Our rock.

My mother slept on a recliner in the corner of the room. Her purse was on the floor beside her, the car keys hanging out of the side pocket. She had brought clothes for me to wear home tomorrow. I quietly slipped them on, pulled my hoodie over my face, took her keys, and made my escape.

I stopped at my house and stole a camp lantern and a shovel from my mother's gardening shed, then hit the road. I had to dig up my things—especially my phone with the selfie of Hezekiah and me. I pulled way down the woods road, concealing the car off to the side behind a large bush.

Now, for the long walk. It was not quite dawn, more dark than light. I held the lantern in front of me and took off. Having done this multiple times with Trent, I knew the way well enough. It was only the last leg of it that threw me. I kept the rising sun in front of me, just as I had seen Trent do.

An hour into the walk, I remembered that the storm had disoriented Trent. I slumped against a tree trunk, despair settling over me. I couldn't find the rock. I turned back toward the car. Maybe I could locate the rock from the hill outside of

Danvers—the one that had led to Zebulon's house. I walked quicker. Surely, a hill wouldn't change that much.

Inside the car, I yawned as an overwhelming tiredness settling over me. I pressed my head back against the seat, my thoughts turning to Hezekiah. I had not meant to doze off and awoke with a start. "W–What time is it?" I pressed the button on the clock on the dashboard and groaned. By now every police officer in Danvers would be looking for my mother's car. I could not risk heading back there.

I glanced up at the afternoon sky, determined to try again. Two hours in, two hours out, one hour to dig. I got out of the car. This time I went deeper into the woods.

I stumbled along the path, wondering how Trent was doing. I replayed his words from our last trek in my mind. When I finally broke through the dense trees and saw our fishing spot, I was elated. I hurried over, sat on the bank, and brought my knees to my chest. I gazed out over the water. *Where did we go from here?* I tried to remember every turn.

I stood and faced the path going home and then reran the storm in my mind. I remembered grabbing Seth's hand and heading back the way we had come, but then the beating rain threw us off the path. I looked up at the sky. "Any chance you could replicate that storm again?" No answer. Nothing.

I closed my eyes and took a step forward.

"That is the wrong way."

My eyes flew open. *Hezekiah?* I frowned. *No, it's Trent. Trent?* He hobbled toward me with a crutch under one arm.

"I thought . . . surgery . . . *minor* surgery . . ." I stood, staring at him.

"Yes. Yes. And yes."

"And they let you out?"

"That would be a no." He lowered his eyes. "Your mother came looking for you in my hospital room. I figured you'd be here."

"Oh." He looked so much like an older Hezekiah that it was hard to concentrate. I drew in a breath. "Wait. Oh, so you snuck out?" I waggled my finger at him. "Trent Hanson—that was a foolish thing to do."

"Really?" he said with a smirk.

I rolled my eyes. "But you need to be in a hospital bed, not hiking in the woods."

"You've got me there." He shifted his weight over the crutch and grimaced in pain.

I moved toward him and instinctively placed my hand on his arm. "Are you okay?"

"I haven't been better," he said with a wide grin. He touched the bottom of my hacked-off hair, and his grin faded.

I didn't want to talk about it. "Come on, let's get you back." I wrapped my arm around his waist, turning him back toward the path.

"Not yet, Elizabeth," he said. "I need to sit for a bit."

I dropped my hand. "Okay."

"There's a nice rock around that bend on the other side of the fishing hole." He pointed past us and began hobbling toward it.

"Is it far? We've got to get you home." I resolved to come back another time—by myself. "Plus, I've caused my mother enough anguish to last a lifetime."

"You've caused us all enough anguish to last ten lifetimes."

I grimaced. Again, anguish was reserved for the truly tried, not for minor happenings. We rounded the bend, and I stopped short in my tracks. "W–What?" My heart rose to my throat. Sitting before us was a large boulder and a smaller rock. I rushed over to the rock and fell to my knees, patting it vigorously. It was the rock Seth had sat on, and the rock Hezekiah had buried the stone box under!

Trent hobbled over to the rock and lowered himself to it. He looked at me with tender, green eyes—so much like Hezekiah's, they took my breath away. *Focus, girl.* I was not that fickle.

Gripping the handle of my shovel, I eyed the rock he sat on. How was I going to dig under it without telling him I'd gone back to 1692? Then I realized it would be the greatest thing ever to be able to tell my best friend what I had gone through. I drew in a deep breath and closed my eyes.

"I need to dig under that rock." I opened my eyes slowly.

His lips pressed together. He had a look of uncertainty in his eyes, like maybe he thought I was going crazy.

"No, Trent, I really do."

He slid off the rock and sat beside it, then wedged it up with a nearby stick, using the shovel as a lever. Soon, the rock slipped off to the side. A layer of dirt lay under it. I bent down and brushed at it with my fingers, and there, under an inch or two of dirt, was the stone box. Eagerly, I lifted the lid. Trent helped me push it aside.

The box was empty.

"No!" That was it. I could take no more. I buried my face in my hands and wept. Trent wrapped his arms around my shoulders. "Bess," he said softly. I could see the agony on his face and knew he wanted to comfort me, but no one could, not even my best friend. One day, I would tell him everything. I waved him off and pulled myself up.

It took a while, but we eventually made it back to where his chauffeur waited with a quad. *Ah, so that was how he made it in.* I refused to ride on it, but walked beside it, as Trent maneuvered slowly down the path.

His truck was parked beside my mother's. The chauffeur drove Trent's truck with the quad in the back, and Trent came with me, but we didn't go back to the hospital. He asked me to drive him to his grandfather's estate in Boston.

I pulled into one of the garages and parked his car. I loved this place, both in 1692 and in 2015, but being here brought a pang of sorrow.

Trent motioned for me to follow him into the gardens. He walked slowly with his crutch, and I wondered where he was taking me. I had been in the gardens several times with him, but not in the past few months. My recent memories of the gardens were all with Hezekiah.

I was a little surprised when Trent brought me to the inner garden. "What is that?" My mouth fell open when I saw an incredible Roman building connected to the old columns.

"My grandfather had it built."

"It's beautiful." I wondered if I should tell him about the underground room. Of course, that was over three hundred years ago. It was probably way gone by now.

Trent took me by the hand and maneuvered the steps like a pro, hopping up one at a time on his good foot. Holding my hand must have balanced him somehow, and strangely, I enjoyed it. At the top of the steps, he led me to the center of the building. "This is going to be the hard part," he said, caressing my hand with his thumb.

I looked down at his thumb resting on my hand. I swallowed. Um. The thrill that went through me both surprised and dismayed me. Was I really that fickle? Had I already forgotten about Hezekiah? I inwardly groaned and fought back the tears.

He pushed a button and the floor started to sink into the ground. Coming back to the present, I squeezed his hand so hard it must have hurt. I could barely breathe. We were going into the ground above Hezekiah's hidden room, but how would Trent have known about it? And why was he just now showing me? I had a lot of questions, but the look on Trent's face told me to wait.

My heart raced. Suddenly, I realized what probably had happened. They must have discovered Hezekiah's room while excavating for the Roman building they had built above it. I couldn't wait to see it again, even though I had just been in it a few days ago—well, 323 years ago. Weird.

The floor came to a stop, and Trent helped me into the ancient vestibule. He stood in front of the iron door. "Before I show this to you, I want you to know . . . I have always loved you, Bess."

I drew in a quick breath. It was as if Hezekiah was saying those words—as if it was he who stood before me, and not Trent. I felt weak at the knees as Trent pushed the door open with his crutch. "After you, my lady."

I turned my head sharply toward him. "Why did you call me that?" No one in 2015 ever addressed me like that. My mouth dropped open as my eyes slowly took in the room.

On every wall there was at least one large portrait, surrounded by several smaller ones. On the wall facing north hung a nice portrait of Trent and me at the Danvers High prom. I figured why go with anyone else but your best friend. On the west wall was a large picture of me riding sidesaddle in the last competition I had entered.

I turned to take in the next portrait on the southern wall. My eyes widened. Two paintings hung side by side. I remembered Hezekiah painting both—one of me, and one of his younger sister, Isabella, but I had never seen the one he had painted of me. My eyes narrowed. Yes, I had seen it. It used to hang in the library. I squeezed my eyes shut and opened them again. How could that be?

Trent stepped behind me, and with one hand on the crutch and the other in the small of my back, he turned me to the last wall. My knees buckled beneath me, but I caught myself, holding onto the side of his crutch.

"H–How did you get those pictures?" I pulled myself up and pointed to large, framed versions of the selfies I had taken of Hezekiah and myself. One showed his initial shock and fear of the camera phone, and in the other one, he was tolerating me wanting another photo of us together.

My body trembled. *Could it be? No, of course not! It is impossible!*

Trent turned me to face him. He held my arms firmly. "Haven't you figured it out yet?"

I bit my lower lip, tears streaming down my face. "It's impossible."

"What? That you can come through the rift, and I can't?"

I pulled away. "But you're Trent!"

He nodded. "Yep. I am."

"And Trent didn't go back to 1692!"

"Nope. He didn't."

My head was spinning. "But you just said you came through the rift!"

He grinned. "Yep."

"Stop it! Tell me the truth!" I pounded my fists into his chest, and he nearly fell over with his crutch.

He took a step back and sank into a leather couch—a nice addition to the once-antiquated room. In fact, as I looked around, I was impressed with how modern and comfortable the old room looked. Trent patted the couch beside him. "I think it might be safer for me to sit," he said with a smirk.

True that. Right at the moment, I couldn't promise complete civility. "Oh, wait. I get it. You found the rock—somehow." I twisted my lips. "And then you dug up my phone and printed the pictures off it." My eyes narrowed. "That's pretty lame, Trent."

He rolled his eyes. I wanted to smack him—he was Trent for sure.

"No, yes, and no."

"What?"

"No, I did not find your rock. You led me to it and we buried your things."

My eyes widened.

"Yes. I dug them up shortly after I got here."

"But . . . but—"

"And no, I did not print them off, but had my grandfather do it."

"B–but you're Trent," I said slowly, wanting so desperately to believe differently. "And Trent definitely didn't go back to 1692—I would have recognized him immediately."

"You'd think, huh, but that's because Trent didn't exist until 2012—a few days before you first met him."

Confused, I squeezed my eyes shut.

"Don't be afraid, Bess."

He sounded like Hezekiah. He took my quivering hands in his. His warm hands felt like Hezekiah's.

"I am Trent, and I did not go back to 1692."

"Yes, yes, of course you are Trent." I sighed. He was not Hezekiah. He just said so.

"Lady Elizabeth," he said softly.

I licked my lips but did not open my eyes. The illusion was better that way.

"Bess. Open your eyes." He waited.

Okay, illusion over—time now for the whole truth. My eyes fluttered open.

He reached up and cupped my face in his strong hands. "My sweet Bess." He studied my trembling lips with his fantastically green eyes—so much like Hezekiah's, so much like Trent's. He grinned. "I did not go back in time to 1692, because I came forward in time. Bess, I've been here since I came through the rift in 2012, waiting for you to grow up."

Oh. My. Heck. My hands flew to my face, and I could barely get his name out. "H–Hezekiah?"

A slow grin spread across his face. "Yes. It's me." He ran his hand down the side of my face, wiping at the tears that flowed freely. "I have something for you." He reached into the console on the side of the couch and brought out my leather bag. He removed Nashota's feathers and slipped them into my hair. "You can wear these proudly now."

I ran my fingers through the feathers. Hezekiah had left the door open, showing proper propriety as always. Outside—it must have been coming from the gardener's radio—a distant drumming wafted through the air, and then I heard the words of Meda. "You are Onida—the one searched for." I drew in a deep breath and gently pressed my lips to his.

Now, I was the one found.

Epilogue

Though most knew him as Trent, I decided early on to call him by his real name, Hezekiah. It made Samantha insane, but she finally got over it. Hezekiah came up behind me and kissed me on the top of my head. He was careful to maintain a respectable distance, now that we were in 2015—an inconvenient year, when compared to 1692, for two young people in love to act as such. I sighed. I had always thought that marriage right out of high school was not for me, but now, I couldn't wait. We were going to do the young-starving-couple-college-thing, except without the starving part. Hezekiah was undoubtedly the richest teenager in the world. However, few knew of it, and he intended to keep it that way.

I had taken it upon myself to create a scrapbook of sorts—not really a scrapbooking thing, but more of a collection of anything that I could find about his ancestry and our incredible story. Today, I was googling newspapers from October and November 2012. I wanted to find weather reports that mentioned the aurora borealis to add to my burgeoning collection. Hezekiah was making it everlastingly hard to concentrate. I felt his breath on the back of my neck as he leaned over me.

Suddenly, he drew in a quick breath.

"What? What's the matter?" Having believed he was kidding around, I grinned, and looked up at him. He was not smiling and his face was ashen white. Now, he was scaring me. "Hezekiah! What's wrong?"

At first, he would not answer me but took to pacing the floor behind me. Finally, he stopped. His lips pressed together in a tight line. My heart raced as I waited for an explanation of his weird behavior.

He stepped near me and pressed his finger against the computer screen, opening an article from November 2012—three years ago. The title read, "Young, Non-English Speaking, and Disoriented Indian Found Wandering Woods."

Meanings of Native American Names

In order of appearance in Salem Witch Haunt -

Awenita - fawn
Nashota - twin
Magena - moon
Ayiana – eternal blossom
Honovi - strong
Anevay - superior
Elan - friendly
Igasho – wanders
Meda - prophetess
Onida – the one searched for

Author Theresa Sneed's Ancestral Line

Susannah North **Martin**, b. 1621 (71 years old when hanged)

Abigail Martin **Hadlock**, b. 1659 (33 years old when her mother was hanged)

Hannah Hadlock **Bowley**, b. 1695 (born three years after her grandmother was hanged)

Oliver **Bowley**, b. 1726

Gideon **Bowley**, b. 1748

Oliver **Bowley** II, b. 1780 (a 17-year-old father to John)

John **Bowley**, b. 1797

Hiram **Bowley**, b. 1838

Clarence Lester **Bowley**, b. 1864

Lucy Mabel Bowley **Harris**, b. 1894

Judith Harris **Small**, b. 1930

Theresa Small **Sneed**, b. 1957

Author Bio

Author Theresa Sneed graduated cum laude with a BA in education, and loves teaching her 2nd grade students, especially about writing!

Her books are unique; each story taking you places you've never imagined before. She writes across five genres: mystery and suspense, fantasy, historical fiction/time travel, realistic paranormal, and nonfiction motivational. All of Theresa's fiction books have elements of sweet romance, and while none of her books have profanity or sexually explicit scenes, each book is intriguing and white-knuckle intense—the kind you can't put down.

Her nonfiction books are *So You Want to Write: A Guide to Writing Your First Book* where Theresa has pulled together her fifteen steps to writing success; and *Facing Mortality: Dreams & Other Significant Things* a compilation of Theresa's paranormal experiences that drove her to write her *No Angel* series and many scenes in her other works.

The *No Angel* series is the story about a guardian angel with an attitude, and the ever present, but misunderstood spirit world. There are four published books in the series with many more to come. Book one, formerly called *No Angel*, is now called *Angel with an Attitude;* book two, formerly called Earthbound, is now called *Earthbound Angel;* book three is called *Destiny's Angel;* and book four is called *Earth Angel.*

The *Sons of Elderberry* series has two books out called *Elias of Elderberry* and *The Wood Fairies of Estraelia.* Harry-Potterish—with wizards, fairies, elves, pixies, yōkai shapeshifters, and dragons, this story has it all! Theresa anticipates another three to five books to finish that series.

Escape is the story of a fifteen-year-old girl abducted by a corrupt sheriff in the 70's. He keeps her captive in his cellar for five years, until she escapes with his truck and his young daughter. *Escape* is book one in a two book series.

Salem Witch Haunt was intended to be a standalone book, until the shocking ending made it apparent that the characters were not finished telling their story. Hence, *Return to Salem*, where the second set of trials and hangings in Salem, 1692, are masterfully woven into the story. *Salem Bewitched* completes this series with the last of the trials and hangings and the peine forte et dure of Giles Corey.

As the ninth great-granddaughter of one of the women hanged as a witch in Salem, Theresa has a vested interest in this epic time travel. Thoroughly researched, all interactions with real people from that era are based on primary sources. In book one, the trial scene with Theresa's great-grandmother, Susannah Martin, is taken from Reverend Samuel Parris's handwritten transcript verbatim. An additional book, *Stranger than Fiction*, is being compiled on the primary sources Theresa used in her Salem Witch Haunt series.

All of Theresa Sneed's books may be purchased through Amazon or from links on her website at www.theresasneed.com. She loves hearing from her readers and may be contacted through her website or through her email at tmsneed.author@yahoo.com.

Stay connected with new releases and free e book offers by signing up at her website or from her Facebook author page at www.facebook.com/TheresaMSneed/